Trimming the tree is more fun with three.

Twin Cities developer Dale Davidson has come to Logan, Minnesota, to turn it into Christmas Town, not to give in to Arthur Anderson's offer to join him and his fiancé, Gabriel Higgins, for a Christmas Eve threesome. Dale is polyamorous, but it's clear Arthur is offering a night of fun and nothing more. Maybe one night with the couple he admires so much won't hurt…

Together the three of them light a fire hot enough to boil Lake Superior in January, and one night of fun becomes an extended engagement as Dale puts down some tentative roots in his new hometown. Everyone loves Dale, Logan's own Santa Claus, and somehow no one knows what wild times are happening right underneath their noses. No one knows, either, the complicated ways they're falling in love with one another.

But a shadow from Dale's past emerges, an abuser threatening him with violence and shame. Ronny doesn't want a happy ever after for Dale, only to draw him back into a consuming darkness. It will take the love of not only Gabriel and Arthur but all of Logan to convince their Santa he has nothing to be ashamed of—and that he will always have a home in their hearts.

Heidi Cullinan, POB 425, Ames, Iowa 50010
Copyright © 2016 by Heidi Cullinan
Print ISBN: 978-0-9961203-8-8
Print Edition
Edited by Sasha Knight
Cover by Kanaxa
Proofing by Lillie's Literary Services
Formatting by BB eBooks

First publication 2016
www.heidicullinan.com

Santa Baby

Heidi Cullinan

For Jess

Many thanks to

Christa Desir for the invaluable, generous beta read and revision advice

Sasha Knight for working me into her schedule and giving me the gift I didn't know I needed: a tight deadline

Dan Cullinan for beta reading and Dan, Vonnie, and Anna for surviving without Mom while I wrote this book in the maddest rush ever

Avon Gale for putting up with my insane texts, emails, and chats while I processed this story, and for heroic beta reading when she didn't really have the time

Twitter for going on the GIF journey with me during drafting and for the cute emergency rescue you'll never know how much I needed

My Patreon group, especially Erin Sharpe, Sarah M., Sarah Plunkett, Ashley Dugan, Rosie M., Karin Wollina, Pamela Bartual, and Susan Lee, but also the $30+ patrons who helped me nurture this idea in the first place and gave me the courage to give it a try. I love you guys so much and don't ever want to write without you at my side. I would be lost without your love and support.

Chapter One

December 19, 2015

LOGAN, MINNESOTA, BELONGED on the front of a Christmas card.

A set of cards, actually, and as the thought expanded in Dale Davidson's mind, he stepped away from the Winter Wonderland festivities to make a voice note on his phone. He took a few photos as well, examples to put in his ever-growing portfolio of ideas for how to turn sleepy Logan into a tourist destination.

He'd come to the small northern Minnesota town both as a favor to his longtime friend Marcus Gardner and as a straight-up business opportunity. Tiny hamlets like this, dressed up and spun the right way, could mean big tourist traffic for local businesses and investment money for the developers that helped the municipalities get those coveted visitor dollars. He saw a lot of potential profit in Logan.

Of course, because it was a small town, there'd already been trouble, chiefly at the informal city council meeting the other night, when a group calling themselves the Concerned Citizens for Logan had burst in and accused Dale of pushing a "homosexual agenda." As irony would have it, this *was* in fact a bit of why he was here. If Logan was LGBT friendly, it'd be more attractive to Twin City tourists. Marcus and his friends had managed to make this sleepy village unusually gay-friendly—or so Dale had thought until the Concerned Citizens had appeared. The city leaders had worked overtime ever since then to convince Dale the naysayers were nothing but an aberration, that Logan was ready for this project and the vast majority of its citizens were fully onboard.

No one had worked harder, though, than Gabriel Higgins, Logan's librarian. He had pulled Dale aside the day after the meeting and launched into a long speech about his own experience moving to Logan from Minneapolis. He'd explained the difference between Logan and his hometown of Roseau, Minnesota, making it clear Dale wasn't to paint all small towns with the same brush. All this was impressive enough. But then he'd pulled out a binder of research and grants on LGBTQIA youth and adults in rural areas, statistics on how little development was being done in those places, and projections on how much good attention and effort was believed to do for that population. This was presented in a *fat* three-ring binder, which he'd given Dale a forty-five minute tour of before sending him home with the same. Gabriel had made it clear he could fill three more volumes with as many bits of data Dale required to be convinced of Logan's worthiness.

Everyone on the city council and chamber of commerce had come up to Dale all day during the Winter Wonderland festival to make sure he hadn't been too put off by the Concerned Citizens' theatrics. They seemed sure Kyle Parks's clever snow sculptures or Gabriel's carefully delivered opening speech, or possibly Mrs. Jessup's delicious, state-fair-winning *Lussekatter* had been what convinced Dale to continue the Christmas Town project and not back away slowly from the potential headache the Concerned Citizens had shown him. The truth was none of these things had swayed him. Thirty percent had been the mayor's promise he'd pass local legislation if he had to in order to keep the riffraff at bay, which had kept Dale's hand in. Seventy percent, however, had been Gabriel Higgins. His binder full of data. His passion.

And the fact that Dale found him incredibly attractive.

All of Marcus's gay friends were a buffet of handsome and cleverness, but Gabriel in particular drew Dale. His wittiness, his devotion to causes he believed in, even his occasional awkwardness was endearing to Dale. Unfortunately Dale had missed his chance with the man by a year and some change, because Gabriel was also engaged, as were all the gay men in Logan, apparently. Normally when Dale felt an attraction this strong, he would push a bit, hoping perhaps the object of his affection was also polyamorous or at least open to hearing a pitch about joining his ranks. However, he wasn't in Logan to complicate his friend's life with his unconventional concept of relationships. He was here to develop the town's tourist interests. End scene.

This didn't mean he stopped pining for Gabriel, especially as he took his photos during the festival and discovered Arthur and Gabriel in one of his frames. They were thirty feet away from him: a tall male figure with glasses and a mop of curly hair smiling and holding a bag of something as he bent to kiss a shorter man with red hair and a full beard beneath a tall, wide-limbed tree draped with snow. Dale quickly snapped a photo, smiling to himself. He lowered the phone and pulled up the image, cropping it and editing the brightness and sharpness and adding a filter to make it the sort of image the two of them could use in their engagement announcements, if they wanted.

He had it pretty much perfect and was about to save it when a text-notification bubble drifted over the screen, and he hit it instead of the DONE button. The text, Dale noted with a riot of emotions, mostly negative, a few slightly anticipatory, was from Ronny.

Ronny Morgan: When are you done with Mayberry?

Dale rubbed his thumb along the side of his phone case, arguing with himself about how to respond and whether or not he should at all.

He'd gone six months without this relationship, except for the aberration at the company Christmas party last weekend. He couldn't even call Ronny his ex. They had…hooked up. Kinky, intense, power-play hooking up, which initially had been fun. But it had gotten weird, uncomfortable, borderline seriously not okay, especially after last Christmas, so he'd ended it. Or rather, he'd tried to end it, an effort which had become so much easier once he'd broken away from Kivino Enterprises to form Davidson Incorporated. He was still a subsidiary, still worked for the same CEO, but he and Ronny were in different office complexes now, on different sides of the metro area. All he had to do was ignore any of the man's texts that weren't about work. Which he had done without issue.

Until he'd had too many glasses of champagne and let Ronny put his hands on him in the hallway while he waited for an elevator at the Christmas party. Until he'd sent a mixed signal instead of a firm *not interested*. And now here he was, unable to know if Ronny was texting him about work or trying to start something up again.

And how like him to not let me know which direction in the opening text.

The only way to find out was to engage, so Dale tapped a reply. *Not sure. Why?*

His heart thudded as he waited for the answer, and it sank, twisted and confused, when it came.

Need to make sure I give you your Christmas present.

Dale put his phone in his pocket without replying and did his best to erase thoughts of Ronny from his mind. He'd made a mistake to engage. The odds of

Ronny having anything work related to say to him were low, and nothing would have been to do with the Logan project. It was Dale's sole focus at the moment. It needed to remain that way.

Think about Logan, he reminded himself. *Logan is why you're here.*

He mentally indexed the notes he'd made last night, the ones he'd put right on top of Gabriel's. But his mind was jumbled, thrown by Ronny's interjection into this safe, idyllic space. His phone buzzed against his thigh, jolts of sensation flicking him repeatedly to make Dale do what Ronny wanted. Pulling him into the shadows, laughing as he pushed him—

Dale shook his head roughly, dispersing the image. He settled his gaze on Gabriel and Arthur once more, letting himself appreciate how prettily slender and tall Gabriel was as he frowned at the bag, how handsome and strong Arthur seemed as he waved his arms and spoke animatedly to his fiancé. Dale didn't consciously decide to start walking toward them, but he didn't stop himself once he realized what he'd done. They didn't appear to be doing something they'd mind him interrupting, and he desperately needed a distraction right now.

When they saw Dale, they smiled at him, waved, and then Gabriel sighed and gestured helplessly at what Dale saw now was a brown bag of steaming chestnuts.

"Do you have any idea how to eat these?" Gabriel held them toward him. "I bought them from a local vendor because I was trying to be polite, and now I have this bag of too-hot nuts I don't know what to do with."

Dale tugged his gloves from his fingers and tucked them in his pocket before withdrawing a nut from the top of the sack. "My grandparents had a chestnut tree on their farm in Wisconsin when I was growing up. They're rare in the United States, though this wasn't always the case. A blight in the early twentieth century wiped almost all of them out. They're doing what they can to repopulate them with a strain strengthened by an Asian variety, but it's going to take a long time to get back what we lost." He peeled one edge of the tough husk with a skill honed by years. The chestnuts hadn't been sliced through quite enough before they were roasted, and he had to get his pen knife out of his pocket to help them along the rest of the way. "Chestnuts are universal. Armies have survived sieges on them. They're part of special celebrations the world over and have been for centuries. Millennia, even."

He could feel Gabriel soaking in the story as only a librarian could. "I've always thought it was odd how we had a holiday song about them but we didn't know what they were. Now I understand why. I should have thought to look them up sooner."

Arthur leaned on a tree, watching idly as Dale peeled. "My great-grandpa talked about eating chestnuts at Christmas. I wonder where these came from, if they're so rare.

"They're starting to make a comeback, but demand far outstrips supply." Dale discarded one side of the husk and worked off the other side as well. "Different cultures have different legends about chestnuts." He sliced it in half to give them each a taste, passing the first half to Arthur, holding it out to drop it into his gloved hand. "In Japan they're used to celebrate the New Year, symbolizing both hard times and success." He extended the second half to Gabriel, but he was caught up listening, clutching the bag with both hands. Possessed by devilry, Dale didn't give the librarian time to extricate himself and popped the meat into Gabriel's mouth instead. "The early Christians believed they symbolized chastity."

Oh, but Dale liked the way the remark made Gabriel blush. He knew he needed to diffuse the flirt, though, to let Arthur know he wasn't actually making a play for his man.

Except Arthur only snorted and gave Dale a heavy wink, chestnut meat poking between his teeth as he reached into the bag for another nut. He swept the half Dale had peeled for him into his mouth with a wicked swipe of his tongue and bit into it smartly, giving it a few chews before replying. "Put us down for Japan, sweetheart."

Arthur peeled the chestnut, mimicking Dale's technique, holding his hand out for the pocketknife when the nut failed to comply as it had for Dale. Dale handed the tool over without a word, though he did note the way Arthur needlessly caressed his fingers as he collected the implement. Dale stroked his beard, trying to check his flicker of interest and stick to his earlier conviction Logan wasn't the place for such things. Especially with practically married men in Logan. Especially with practically married men whose fiancés were standing right fucking next to him.

Hoping for a reminder of why he should behave, he glanced at Gabriel—only to find Gabriel studying him with the same wary, careful gaze.

Wary, careful, tentatively *interested* gaze.

The world shifted beneath Dale's feet.

Arthur sliced the chestnut, carving it into thirds and splitting it between the three of them. He popped his part into his mouth, fed Gabriel the same way Dale had, and he did the same for Dale, though he took care to be extra sensual with his delivery of Dale's portion. "A shame we don't get chestnuts here too often, then. There's no reason they should be so rare, except they're not planted. Sounds like all they need to thrive is a bit of science, some common sense, and some care."

It was all simple enough, what he was saying, and yet Dale had never felt as if tree talk could strip him naked. He was working out how to call Arthur out and ask if he was getting propositioned with a bag of nuts and for what, exactly, when Gabriel whispered in a warning tone, "*Arthur.*"

Arthur rolled his eyes. "I was being cool, until you had to go and point it out."

Gabriel blushed as if someone had been roasting *him* on an open fire. He tucked the bag of chestnuts to his chest and pressed a mitten to his face. "Stop, you're making it worse."

Ignoring him, Arthur turned to Dale, the seduction veil lowered, though not entirely dropped. "Look. Let's be real. You've been giving both of us eyes one way or another."

"*Oh my God.*" Gabriel tried to make himself shorter.

Arthur patted him on the back and kept going. "And you're a tall drink of water, I'll grant you. So let's cut to the chase. You just flirting, or you interested?"

Stick to the plan. Tell him no. Except Dale's gaze kept tugging to poor Gabriel, who was mortified at Arthur's blunt approach. "Very interested. But I don't know if it's such a good idea, starting something in a small town."

His reply leached some of the tension from Gabriel. Arthur, however, seemed annoyed. "Oh, hell, that doesn't matter. It's not as if we're gonna fuck on the city square or anything."

Gabriel rounded on Arthur, looking ready to do murder. But when he raised his hand as if to strike, Arthur caught his wrist in a lightning-fast strike, grinning as he held him captive with a wink.

Dale's dick got a little hard, especially when Arthur raised an eyebrow at him. "You want to come play with us sometime before you leave for the Cities?"

Dale glanced around. They were in full view of the

town, but they were slightly separated, off on a snowy knoll behind the farthest ring of shops. It was risky and surreal. He reminded himself of all the reasons he should say no.

But Jesus, Gabriel and Arthur were one hell of a distraction from those reasons. Gabriel's pretty curls and the memory of what Arthur's tongue did to a piece of meat. Dale's thigh buzzed again, but Ronny's texts were no more annoying than a gnat at this point, because he had other, better prospects now. Ronny could fuck himself with his present.

Dale cleared his throat. "What type of play are we talking?"

Arthur's dark chuckle made Dale's knees waver, and when Arthur stepped close enough to run a subtle hand up his arm, Dale's legs buckled, however briefly. "I don't know, son. Why don't you tell me what you like?"

Dale's blood rushed to his groin, but enough of it lingered in his brain to remind him of Gabriel's nerves. They had to quit doing this out in the open. But part of him feared if they went anywhere private right now, Arthur would start something immediately. Dale paused, struggling to remember why exactly that was a bad thing.

He cleared his throat. "I'm pretty open-minded. Discretion is my bottom line, though. I'm not interested in being the subject of local gossip."

"Then it sounds as if we're all of the same mind."

Arthur's thumb massaged at Dale's elbow. "When do you leave town?"

With this prospect on the table, Dale was willing to stay through the New Year. "I'm flexible. I largely work remotely at this point, so I can stay in Logan as long as I'm needed here, or check in from the Cities. I have engagements tonight, tomorrow, and Monday night, but beyond then I'm free."

"We're booked Tuesday, but Wednesday we're open. How about you come over to our place? Show us your chestnuts."

It was Gabriel's curls, Dale decided. They'd hypnotized him. He stared at them, cock throbbing a happy hum in his pants as Arthur stroked his arm, and he threw his common sense out the window. "What time?"

"Six-ish? We'll feed you first." Arthur chuckled and swatted Dale's butt. "Wisconsin boy like you must eat venison, right?"

Dale kept his attention on Gabriel, who was long and lean and graceful as a gazelle. "Oh yeah. Anytime I can get it."

"Great. See you then."

Arthur linked arms with Gabriel and his bag of chestnuts and led him away.

Gabriel glanced over his shoulder, mortified, flustered…and eager.

Dale adjusted himself as discreetly as he could, relieved the phone in his pocket had finally gone quiet.

God in heaven, but he wished it were Wednesday.

As the Winter Wonderland festival wound to its successful close, Arthur stood at the back of the old elementary gym with his fiancé, family, and friends, and soaked it in.

An older, former school on the other side of town had been turned into low-rent apartments, but this place had been where Arthur went to school until Logan's enrollment had dipped low enough they'd had to consolidate with Pine Valley. Now this structure was the city council building and general catch-all meeting place for any and every event Logan couldn't fit in the American Legion or a church. Tonight Marcus's friends Laurie and Ed led Logan's finest in the waltz, rumba, and, at the moment, were giving the room a tango demonstration.

Arthur watched this from the side of the room, and beside him stood two new friends, Spenser and Tomás, whom Laurie and Ed had spoken of last year and had managed to coax up for the festival this time. They'd brought their son, Duon, and Tomás's parents and his nieces and nephews. They'd had reservations, apparently, about coming up to such a small town, worried about prejudice and discrimination, as Spenser was the single white person in their entire crew, but by all accounts they'd had nothing but a wonderful time all day. Renata, Tomás's mother, had fallen in love with the craft fair and engaged in a lengthy discussion of knitting techniques with one of the sellers who, by some miracle, knew Spanish. Tomás's father, José, and Arthur's best friend and business partner, Paul, had been huddled together for the last half hour, Paul struggling to resurrect his high school Spanish and José dredging up his best English so they could have a serious discussion about the Minnesota Wild's chances for the playoffs this hockey season. And the kids had a fantastic time because it was a festival and there were a million kid things to do and a Santa to visit in "his real house," Arthur had heard them whisper to each other.

It felt good to be having a festival in his hometown. He *missed* these kinds of community events. When he was a kid, it happened all the time. The Memorial Day bonfire. The Fourth of July parade and celebration in the park, with the fireworks at dusk. The parade had stopped happening when he was really young, but he had a dim memory of standing on a curb beside his mom, stamping his feet and dancing in time to the beat of the bass drum. The bass line had fascinated him. His mom had told him when he was older he could be in band if he wanted, and he could be the one to carry the drum, and he couldn't wait. Except by the time he got to school not only was the parade gone, so was the marching band. They barely had a music program at all now.

The tango demonstration ended, and the room erupted in applause. After Laurie and Ed took their bows, Laurie grabbed the mic from the stage behind him.

"Thank you so much for coming to the Winter Wonderland festival. Logan is such a wonderful town, and I know I speak for Ed and so many of us when I say we love any excuse we can get to come here and support your library, the Pine Valley Children's Home, and so many other great causes. In a moment we're going to announce the total raised, but first, let me thank—"

He cut off as Arthur's mother, Corrina, leaned over and whispered in his ear. He nodded, then resumed speaking. "I want to thank everyone who has donated their time and resources today, particularly Kyle Parks for his stunning ice sculptures in the city center. I understand he stayed up all night finishing some of the pieces. So don't miss your chance to thank him for his hard work, and remember, the best thanks you can give him is to make a donation to the Logan Library or to the Winter Wonderland Foundation. You can find links and addresses for those at the website, at the library itself, or in the back of the room on flyers near the cake, which I must warn you is almost gone. And we *will* announce the amount donated today, but before we do, we have to wait for the mayor. So until then, what do you say to a little more dancing?"

The room erupted in cheers and applause, though Arthur couldn't help noticing Tomás, who was standing beside him and juggling a weary six-year-old, frowned. "Ed can't keep dancing," he said to Spenser. "He was pushing it to tango as it was."

Arthur wondered why Ed couldn't dance, then remembered the former semipro football player was *former* because he'd had a serious neck injury.

Spenser bit the corner of his lip. "You could dance with him, yes? Or Duon?"

Duon held up his hands. "No way. I ain't dancing in front of all these white people."

Tomás shifted the sleepy boy in his arms. "Where's my mom? If I can pass off Ashton, I can get over there."

"Here, give him to me." Spenser held out his arms.

"He's heavy." Tomás jostled the boy gently. "Buddy, you're big enough to stand. Let Uncle Spenser take you to Abuela, okay?"

But before they could get any further in their plans, Laurie continued speaking. "I'd like to do something different this time. You're familiar, I'm sure, with the dollar dance at weddings, where the guests pay a dollar to dance with the happy couple? We'll do a variation of it now. Ed will collect the money, and the dancers will be me…" he made brief eye contact with Tomás, who nodded, "…Tomás Jimenez, from my studio in St. Paul, and of course your librarian, Gabriel Higgins."

Gabriel stiffened, choked on his sip of hot cider, and turned to Arthur with a wide, terrified gaze.

Arthur patted Gabriel on the back and took the cup from his hands. "You can do it, baby. You're a great dancer. Anyway, all you gotta do is stand there and smile."

Gabriel still looked rattled. "They could have *asked* me."

"I imagine this was Laurie punting on the fly, trying to make it seem planned. Dollars to donuts he apologizes after for putting you on the spot." He pulled his fiancé closer to plant a kiss on his cheek. "Hon, it's gonna be ninety percent little kids coming up to you anyway." He winked and shifted his hand to grip Gabriel's butt. "And me."

"You're right." Gabriel sighed. "I suppose I should get out there and do my civic duty or whatever this is." He leaned into Arthur's touch, bending slightly to speak into his ear. "But if I'm beset by Concerned Citizens for Logan or anything else unpleasant, I fully expect you to come rescue me."

"Always, honey. Always."

Arthur clapped with the rest of the town as Gabriel joined the other celebrity dancers, but nobody beamed with pride the way he did over the town librarian. Everyone queued up to dance with the gentlemen, but the line to Gabriel was longest and mostly filled with children clutching dollar bills and bouncing on their heels, smiling and staring wide-eyed at Arthur's fiancé as if he had personally hung every star in the sky. Linda Kay, Kyle's twin sister who had Down's syndrome, hesitated at Gabriel's line, but opted in the end for Tomás, waggling her eyebrows at Kyle when he came forward and quietly admonished her to behave herself during her dance. "I'll be good," she promised. "But he's sure a sexypants."

Arthur joined Gabriel's line out of loyalty, though he did agree with Linda Kay.

Kyle stayed with his sister, apparently not trusting her to keep her promise, but Kyle and Arthur's lines processed in parallel, so they chatted as they went.

"Too bad Laurie didn't call up your mom or someone," Kyle observed. "It's all women in these lines, except for us. Women and kids."

Arthur studied the sea of people waiting and saw Kyle was correct. "I guess this is the downside to him only knowing a bunch of gay men in a small town? I don't know. Something tells me he's killing time. I don't think he had the luxury of forethought here."

Kyle grinned. "I wished he'd have asked me. I would have suggested Penny Mattherson."

Arthur scratched his chin, trying to think of why she sounded familiar. "Penny Mattherson. She's Bob Mattherson's sister, right? Went out with Ottie Johnson back in the day?"

"Yep. Right up until she acknowledged she was a lesbian instead."

Arthur laughed. "So you wanted to have a full rainbow coalition on the dance floor?"

"Well, sure, but three gay men and one lesbian would hardly be a full representation." Kyle sighed wistfully. "I keep thinking of what Dale said at the city council meeting, about how we could be a draw because we're queer. I know it's not that simple, but I'd love to make even a little of it happen."

"It's not as if we don't already have a rainbow up here. We just have to gather it in...whatever you gather rainbows in. We should have a monthly LGBT supper club or something."

"That's a good idea." Dale Davidson's bright voice boomed over them, and Arthur and Kyle turned to find him standing in line with them.

"Oh, hi, Dale." Kyle shrugged. "I'd love to have a group, but I don't have time to organize it, and my schedule sucks. Maybe once I get to take my new shift, though it won't be a whole lot better. Besides, where would we have it?"

"They meet all over." Dale gestured to the gym around them. "Here would be a good place, though it might be big. Council room might be a bit stale, but it would work."

"Or the library." Arthur wanted it to be the library, actually, mostly because of family pride. "Maybe it could rotate. Because when the weather's nice, we could have it out at our place." He could see it in his mind's eye. Picnic tables set up on the ridge, him and Marcus working the grill, Gabriel chatting with the guests. God, he wanted to have them all over now. When they had the remodel done, they'd have room for that kind of thing inside the house too. Of course, once they started fostering, they'd also be full of kids.

Which was good. He wanted kids. Watching Spenser and Tomás wrestle their brood, however, had made him quietly glad they'd agreed on older kids only.

Hopefully kids less moody than Tomás's eldest niece, who was off in the corner weeping over something with her abuela. For what had to be the eighth time.

This hour.

Kyle frowned at Dale, glancing at him and then at the two queues forming on either side of him. "Are you in line, or...?"

Dale looked sheepish. "You caught me. I came up to talk to you guys in hopes I could slip in. I tried to get over here earlier, but those kids are fast. And they've cut off Gabriel's line."

Arthur bit back a grin as he gestured to the space in front of him. "Be my guest."

Dale inclined his head. "Thank you."

They were nearly to Gabriel now, and Arthur made eye contact with his fiancé, getting a smile and a wave in return. Dale got a smile and a blush, and when Dale and Kyle got to chatting about the ins and outs of how to start up a local LGBT support group, Arthur noticed Gabriel's gaze kept sliding over to Dale, mapping the muscles of Davidson's chest through his sweater.

Arthur grinned. This was so much more fun to think about than whether or not he was biting off more than he could chew by signing on to be a parent.

Last night in bed they'd had the best sex they'd had

in a long time while Arthur demanded Gabriel admit how much he was attracted to Dale. His fiancé had been stealing glances at the man ever since he'd shown up Wednesday night, and once Gabriel admitted he thought the guy was handsome, Arthur couldn't resist taking the fantasy to the extreme, teasing Gabriel until, in the throes of passion, he acknowledged he wanted to be fucked by Dale. Because they were playing, Arthur had pretended to threaten to call the man up and tell him, then settled for giving Gabriel a sound spanking instead.

Dale Davidson was fucking hot, and he turned both Gabriel and Arthur's cranks. He was almost as tall as Gabriel, but he was as wide as Arthur. He was blond, but a dull, dark blond, not the shiny light blond of Marcus's fiancé, Frankie. He had a granite jaw covered in a neatly trimmed full beard and mustache. His eyes were a soft blue, reminding Arthur of the Minnesota sky in summer. Paul had said Dale was like a combo between Chris Evans's Captain America and the Brawny paper towel man, and all this was truth. He looked as if he could bench-press a mountain, but he'd hold a door for you while he did it.

The man was a certified flirt with everyone from little old ladies to the stodgiest of councilmen, but whenever he flirted with Gabriel, he made a point to acknowledge Arthur as well so he knew Dale didn't have any dishonorable intentions on his man. He did this now as he danced with Gabriel, not settling for simply dancing in place with him as the children had but instead showing off his moves as he spun Gabriel around the floor, eliciting catcalls and laughter from the audience. Gabriel blushed and did his best to keep up, but he appeared to be having the time of his life.

Dale gazed at Gabriel as if he wanted the next spin to take them into a bedroom, but then he'd wink at Arthur, the gesture telegraphing, *Don't worry, man, I won't.*

Too bad the guy didn't know Arthur wouldn't mind one bit, so long as Gabriel came home again once they were finished.

Dale Davidson was handsome and polished, with all the city ways that gave Logan residents a thrill, but he was honest folks too. At least six different people had said as much to Arthur while Dale visited in the final preparation for the Winter Wonderland festival. Dale was a charmer, but he was a pleaser above all. Odds were good he'd carry that attitude into bed as well.

Oh, hell yes, Arthur wanted this experience for Gabriel. And he was going to make sure his baby got it. Arthur thought about how good they looked together dancing now, how good they'd look fucking on Wednesday night. He thought, too, about what a pretty picture Dale would make on his knees. Captain America/Brawny Man could fit into one hell of a submission fantasy.

When Dale's turn ended, he brought Gabriel back

to his station to a round of applause, and passed him, breathless and flushed, into Arthur's arms. Arthur accepted his fiancé's embrace with a grin.

"Nice moves there, buddy." He winked and drew Gabriel close, leading him in a slow, simple sway. "Bring them Wednesday."

With a grin, Dale saluted and disappeared into the crowd. But Arthur watched him go, and Gabriel had his eyes on him too.

Oh yeah. Wednesday was going to be all kinds of interesting.

Chapter Two

ALL DAY, GABRIEL had put on a good face. All day
he had behaved as if earlier in the afternoon
fiancé hadn't casually arranged a threesome for them
over a bag of chestnuts. With the man everyone was
already calling Logan's Santa. With the man Gabriel
had to work with professionally.

With the man Gabriel had struggled not to stare at
as it was. Now each time Dale smiled at him, all Gabriel could think was, *I'm going to have sex with this man.* It
took all his mental faculties to compose sentences, let
alone carry on as a functional human. So as soon as
they were away from the community center, as he
walked with Arthur back to where they'd parked behind Logan Repair, Gabriel gave Arthur a piece of his
mind.

"I can't believe you did that *on the town square* where
anyone could have heard you."

Arthur waved this away. "Nobody else was
around."

"They *might have been around.* And what would they have thought?"

"That we were gonna get hella lucky?"

Gabriel wanted to strangle him. "You do understand I work with children all day. People tend to not want to hear their local librarian was arranging orgies on the town square."

Arthur put a finger to his lips. "Hush, baby, keep your voice down. We're on Main Street. People might hear."

It was ten at night, they were almost to the shop, and literally no one was within fifty feet of them. "I'm going to strangle you."

Arthur unlocked the shop, pulled Gabriel inside, then shoved Gabriel hard against the door, seeking Gabriel with his mouth. "You're not gonna strangle me." He nuzzled Gabriel's neck, nipped at his collarbone. "You're gonna beg and scream while I strip you naked and fuck you over my desk."

Gabriel shivered at the rough words. It sounded perfect. But he wasn't giving in. "No. I'm angry with you."

"Too bad." Arthur hoisted Gabriel over his shoulder.

Gabriel shouted and pounded on Arthur's back, ordering Arthur to release him this instant, but when Arthur set him down in his office, locked the door, and came at him with a dark hunger in his gaze, Gabriel forgot he was resisting on principle and simply melted into his fiancé's arms, yelping as he dug his fingers into Arthur's hair, gripping it tight.

Gabriel gasped as Arthur undid his coat and pushed up his sweater to access the bare skin of his chest, trying one last time to argue. "He could have been offended. You were too bold."

"He's been eye-fucking you ever since he came to town, and if I so much as rub my thumb across my lip, he quakes like he wants to get on his knees for me. You admitted last night how much you were attracted to him. So stop complaining and show me how grateful you are that you're marrying a man who'll give you such a yummy Christmas present."

Arthur ran his tongue in slow, wicked circles around Gabriel's quivering navel, making it difficult for Gabriel to form a coherent counterargument. Or remember his own name. "It doesn't mean we have to actually *do* anything with…" He bit his lip and tipped his head back, parting his legs as Arthur fumbled with the fastenings of his jeans. "We don't… I…"

"He wants to fuck you, baby." Arthur whispered this along Gabriel's skin as he freed his cock from his briefs. "Lucky you, though. He wants to romance you first. The chestnut shit wasn't for me. It was to show you how smart he is. He wants to fuck your mind." Arthur thrust the tip of his tongue into Gabriel's belly button, making it go concave. "And then he wants to fuck your ass, slow and sweet, while he kisses your neck and you gasp against the sheets. While I watch. Or help."

Gabriel melted, joints failing as he imagined Dale doing what Arthur described. "Oh, God."

Arthur caught him, kissing his way down to Gabriel's waistband and pushing it aside. "But you're going to be up on your knees while he fucks you, because I'm going to be under your hips on the mattress, doing this."

Gabriel cried out as Arthur sucked him deep into his throat. He yanked on Arthur's hair, begging, almost sobbing, trying to thrust but finding his hips were pinned to the wall by Arthur's hand. Arthur's other hand fondled Gabriel's balls, tugging gently, distracting Gabriel as Arthur traced along his taint. Teased his hole, but didn't enter.

Pleasure raced through Gabriel, but Arthur was playing him like an instrument, winding him up but holding him back, keeping him from release. Gabriel knew what he was after. Knew what Arthur taunted him with. He wanted him to think about Dale fucking him, wanted him to be crazy with it, so crazy he wasn't nervous about whether or not it was okay. To stop worrying about whether or not it was cheating. To let go, to give into pleasure—with Arthur.

He'd done it the night before, Arthur torturing him until he'd confessed how attractive he found Dale to be, how much he cared for him as a person too. They'd been working with him the last few days in the final push for the Winter Wonderland festival, and Gabriel had become fond of him. He liked Dale's passion and his zeal coupled with his attention to detail, the insane moment with the chestnuts as exhibit A. Gabriel was impressed, too, that when he'd gone to talk about the Concerned Citizens, Dale had listened.

Dale had *liked* the binder. Usually people were exasperated or disinterested by Gabriel's thoroughness, but Dale had seemed impressed. Or he was simply being impressively polite, and either way, Gabriel approved.

This was the problem, actually, the thing he couldn't explain to Arthur. Somehow those fond feelings for Dale made him hesitate to take him to bed, and he didn't know why.

Arthur pulled his lips free of Gabriel's cock, his lips swollen, gaze lidded. "You're doing a whole lot of thinking, and it ain't about how great this blowjob is. And I know it's one hell of a blowjob."

Gabriel stroked his face. "I'm nervous. What if it changes things between us?"

Arthur kissed his fingers. "How would it change things? Tell me what you're afraid of."

"I don't know. That's the problem."

"Are you afraid of what I'll think of you if we do this? Because I promise you, it's not going to be an issue. You can spend the whole night fixated on him, let him fuck you six different ways, and I'll have nothing but a good time. Because it'll still be you and me together in the morning."

Gabriel wasn't worried about this exactly, though it felt as if this was near the edge of his fear. "What about Dale?"

"If he wants to stay for breakfast, he's welcome." When Gabriel glared at him, Arthur held up a hand, no longer teasing. "Sweetheart, he wouldn't have accepted the invitation if he didn't know the rules."

There. Maybe *that* was what was bothering Gabriel. "I don't think *I* know the rules."

"Easy enough to fix." Arthur stood, pulled Gabriel to him so he could place a kiss on his mouth and slide hands up and down the sides of his body. "The rules are whatever we make them. You and I want to take Dale into our bed for a night? For two nights? For a month? For the rest of our lives? We can do whatever we like. We're adults. This is our relationship, our life."

Gabriel had a vivid image of Arthur climbing into bed on one side of him and Dale behind him on the other, both closing in to make love to him, and it was incredibly distracting. "The rest of our lives?"

"Well, theoretically yes, but while I don't have anything against polyamory in theory, have even dated a few poly guys, I am not interested in being part of a thruple."

Gabriel quickly parsed the word *polyamory*. He'd heard it, possibly, didn't know it well enough to define it. Unpacking it, though, it appeared rather obvious. "Multiple…lovers?"

Arthur raised an eyebrow at him. "Am I about to

teach the librarian a word? Polyamorous means having multiple romantic relationships. I figured you'd have learned it in some fancy college class."

Gabriel ignored him, too interested in understanding. "You mean at once? Two girlfriends, boyfriends, and so on?"

"Yeah. I dated a guy once who was dating me and somebody else. Technically at the time I was also sleeping with Paul, who didn't care for any of it, mind you. There's a gal over in Hibbing who is married to a guy but has a girlfriend. And the husband has a different girlfriend. Sometimes they all play Euchre together. Polyamory isn't about sex, not primarily. It's about relationships. Being in love with more than one person at a time, or in relationships that could lead to love." Arthur trailed a finger down Gabriel's nose with a smile. "I can't believe I got to teach you about polyamory."

Gabriel could. He'd specifically avoided learning about anything to do with sex and relationships, until Arthur. Everything he'd come by had been what had fallen in front of him in books or by accident. But he liked this concept, polyamory. It was a rather democratic idea of sex. Free love, perhaps, but a more grown-up version?

Arthur kneaded his hip. "I'm not saying either one of us needs to start dating Dale. I'm saying we could, if we wanted, or we could just fuck him, because we get to do what we want."

Gabriel blinked at Arthur. "You're saying if I told you I wanted to date Dale in addition to marrying you, you'd be okay with it?"

His stomach felt strange as he asked the question, as if he'd spoken the forbidden aloud. He wanted to call the words back. But Arthur didn't seem upset. He lifted his eyebrows, then grinned. "I would."

"You wouldn't be jealous?"

Arthur shrugged. "Oh, I suspect I'd have to get used to the idea. But if you recall last year when we were first dating I said I couldn't bear the thought of sharing you, and now I'm nagging you into a three-way. Who knows? Maybe I'd get off on you dating somebody."

Ugh, the nasty feeling in Gabriel's gut was a knot in a rope. He kept talking, as if it might uncoil him. "But I wouldn't ever actually do it. I couldn't. Not in Logan. Not with my job. Not when we're talking about becoming foster parents."

Arthur's mouth thinned. "Why couldn't you? It's not as if you were in love with me and someone else at the same time it would make you a bad person. Who are any of those assholes to judge you? I won't let them."

"You couldn't stop them, Arthur." Talking was making the knot worse. Gabriel shook his head. "I don't want to talk about this anymore."

"You're right. Let's not talk." Arthur kissed him. "Let's think about all the ways Dale is going to fuck you on Wednesday. How I'm going to fuck him."

The image filled Gabriel's mind. Dale's hands, as large as Arthur's, moving over his body. Dale's mouth along his neck, his beard tickling the same as Arthur's. The two of them, kissing and touching, hands stroking, mouths claiming, bodies sliding...

Dale's smile, his bright blue eyes, the impishness of his grin as he popped the chestnut meat in Gabriel's mouth, looking cheeky, sexy...lonely...

The knot inside Gabriel tightened into a terrible ball, and he pushed it inside, let Arthur bury it deep as he divested him of his clothes and fucked him hard against the desk, chasing everything away but their bodies and their pleasure.

ARTHUR COULDN'T WAIT for Wednesday.

He wished they could have had Dale over sooner for a lot of reasons, not the least of which being Gabriel's nerves about the whole thing, though the more he thought about it, the more he appreciated a bit of time to sort out whether or not Gabriel was nervous because he was Gabriel or because he didn't want to go through with it. Arthur was fairly confident on it being the former, not the latter, but he didn't mind putting in homework. Especially since all his homework efforts so far ended up in him having seriously freaky sex with his fiancé. Yeah, no hardship there at all.

In the meantime, he also had plenty of work to do.

He and Paul had been charged with tearing down the remnants of the Winter Wonderland festival, putting decorations into storage, returning borrowed odds and ends to the rightful parties and so on. It kept them busy all Sunday afternoon, though they got plenty of clucks of the tongue from old-timers who had *views* about them working on a Sunday, but Arthur had more views about the extra work not cutting into his regular repair work that had built up while the festival took priority.

They also had to relocate some of the snow sculptures Paul's fiancé had made for the festival onto safer ground. A few had been auctioned off, a few couldn't be moved, and a few Kyle had insisted be reserved for specific spaces. Like the "Logan is Love" sculpture, the centerpiece of the event, was to be placed in front of the Logan Care center where he worked as a night nurse, though not facing the road but the windows, so the residents could see. Several other sculptures were scattered around the care center, also facing the windows. Two went to the library, one to Kyle's parents' place because it was Linda Kay's favorite—and guess who hauled them all?

"You could have asked Marcus to help us, at least," Arthur grumbled as he and Paul hauled yet another sculpture onto a flatbed truck.

"He's busy with Dale and the mayor with the post-festival stuff, I guess. Frankie is there too. And Kyle is sleeping because he has a shift tonight, before you get any ideas about saying he should be here helping." Paul pulled the cinch on the chain and cranked the lock into place. "Where's Gabriel?"

"I think he had the same meeting as the rest of them. What the hell do they have to talk about anyway? Damn party's over."

"It's for the Christmas Town plan, right? They're starting up on the Christmas in July thing Dale wanted to use as a pilot for the next phase."

Oh, right. "I guess they have to act now while he's here. Seems damn early, though."

"Well, they have more data now that they've had the festival. Number of attendees and so on. And it's not early, really. Only seven months away. It'd be nice to not have to plan the thing at the last minute, which you know will mean *we* plan it at the last minute."

"We did all right, I thought. Plenty of people from the Cities came up. Granted, a lot of them were friends of ours, or friends of theirs."

"Right, but this is how it starts." Paul wrested the last lock into place and stood back with a sigh. "Okay. We have to deliver this to the café, and then we're free and clear."

Arthur grinned. "This works out, because I could sure do with a hot beef sandwich and a cup of coffee right about now, which I'm betting we can get on the house in exchange for plunking this cute little ice princess in their parking lot."

This was, as it happened, exactly what transpired,

and soon Arthur and Paul were settled happily in a booth, watching the good people of Logan come and go through the cafe and past it on the street. A few people came up to Paul and congratulated him on his engagement to Kyle, which had happened at the festival, and they asked him when he intended to get married.

"Why do they keep asking if we've set a date?" Paul asked as soon as they left. "Do they honestly think we already set a date, when we've barely been engaged twenty-four hours?"

"They're still asking us, though we got engaged a year ago, so we're fair game, I guess." Arthur dragged a french fry through his mashed potatoes. "Probably we should set a date now that you're caught up in this marriage stuff too. Maybe the three of us should get married together. At Christmas, don't you think, since it's when we all got engaged?"

"I think if either of us set a date without our fiancés we wouldn't have fiancés a whole lot longer. I promised Kyle we'd have the wedding on my sister-in-law's birthday to make her angry, though I kind of hope he was joking." Paul sipped at his coffee. "It's not a bad idea, this hat-trick wedding at Christmas. I could see Kyle going for it, maybe. We'd need to talk to Frankie and Marcus too, though. I'd mention it to Frankie, not Marcus. If he likes it, Marcus will go along." He smiled, a slightly foggy but happy smile. "Seems weird we're all getting married now. Good, but weird. Guess we're all settling down finally."

Arthur couldn't resist. "Oh, not all of us are settling." He leaned forward, a wicked grin on his face as he glanced around to make sure no one else was listening. "We're going to have a *guest* on Wednesday, Gabriel and I. For dinner. And dessert."

Paul rolled his eyes. "Dale, right? I saw this coming."

Arthur was annoyed at how unimpressed Paul was. "Sorry to be so obvious." He frowned. "Wait, *were* we obvious?"

Paul shrugged. "We used to date, if you call what you and I were to each other dating. I know how you operate. Saw the way you guys were looking at one another. Though honestly, Dale was watching Gabriel more. I guess I saw the points of the triangle and drew the lines." He stole one of Arthur's fries. "Don't worry. Marcus doesn't have any idea."

Jesus wept, that would be a disaster. Marcus was a great guy, Arthur's oldest friend, but boy did he have rigid ideas about monogamy, helped along by the asshat who cheated on him for years while Marcus had lived with him in Minneapolis. "It's just a night of fun. Nothing to get excited about. Though I suppose with Dale coming up here for the Christmas-village thing, we could make it a regular habit." He waggled his eyebrows.

Paul did not waggle back. "Be careful, okay? I know you get off on these kinds of things, but Gabriel is tenderhearted."

Now Arthur was annoyed. "Are you trying to tell me you know my fiancé better than I do?"

"No. I'm saying I know *you* better than Gabriel does. You don't always think before you leap. You were always coaxing me into stuff like this, and you weren't always good at listening to me when I said I didn't want it. I'm saying make sure you're listening to him. That's all."

Arthur wanted to insist Paul didn't know what he was talking about, but he could remember all too easily the nervous look on Gabriel's face when they'd made love in the repair shop. How he'd asked so many questions. How he was still nervous.

"I'll make sure," he told Paul, and he meant it.

Paul lifted his coffee cup in salute. "Then here's to your Wednesday-night guest."

Chapter Three

GABRIEL COULD HAVE survived the Christmas in July planning meeting a lot more easily if he hadn't sat directly across from Dale the entire time.

The two times his future mother-in-law called on him for his opinion on something he'd been so absorbed in his own thoughts he hadn't had any idea what she'd said and had to ask her to repeat herself. He hadn't dared look at Dale to see if he suspected he was the reason for the distraction. In fact, Gabriel barely looked at Dale at all. He shouldn't have been surprised, though, to see the man weaving his way around the conference table once the meeting adjourned, coming for Gabriel.

Gabriel, not feeling particularly brave, attempted to make his escape, but Dale wasn't the only one trying to get his attention. Marcus and Frankie, who'd sat on either side of him and *hadn't* been distracted by thoughts of three-ways, kept Gabriel captive by their conversation. "Gabriel, do you think there are some grants for those cottage proposals Jennie Haverson had?"

Gabriel didn't know what cottage proposals they were talking about. "I'll go to the library and check." He tried to escape again.

Frankie put a hand on his arm. "I have some questions about the Main Street district. Everyone's getting ahead of themselves, dreaming of things we don't know can happen for sure. I mean, I'd *love* to have a nail salon in Logan. But how many tourists stop to have their nails done in a Christmas village? We need some demographics information. Do you know how to get that? Or maybe we should ask Dale."

"Ask Dale what?" a familiar voice boomed, and Gabriel sagged internally. Too late to escape.

Gabriel was accustomed to being taller than all of his friends, but Dale was as tall as he was, though twice as wide. Gabriel was fairly sure no one had ever called Dale Toothpick on the playground, or if they had, they'd apologize on their knees for it now. Gabriel had nothing to apologize for, but he'd get on his knees for the man for any excuse. God, but Dale was handsome. He had the *good boy* aesthetic going for him in about the same way Arthur had the *I'm going to get into so much trouble* thing down pat. Dale listened patiently as Marcus and Frankie repeated their questions, sometimes appearing pensive and rubbing his beard thoughtfully before giving a reply about statistics. Gabriel supposed he should be listening to the conversation, trying to think of grants and other helpful things.

All Gabriel had to contribute to the conversation was that Dale had a pretty pink mouth and bright teeth, and he liked the way they peeked out from Dale's beard and mustache.

Frankie glanced around the conference room, which was starting to empty. "Should we go to the house and continue this over tea and coffee? We don't have to talk shop. We can relax and congratulate each other on a job well done."

Here was Gabriel's chance to escape. "I should probably check in with Arthur."

Marcus jerked his head toward the street. "He's running around with Paul, delivering statues. If he's finished, my bet is they're cooling their heels at the cafe. I'll send them a text, though, tell them to come over when they're finished."

Thank you, small town, always knowing everyone's business. "I should probably go over my story-time notes for Monday."

Frankie gave him a scolding glare. "You need to *relax.*"

Gabriel fished out a smile, surrendering. "All right. Just for a bit."

They went to the city hall parking lot, the four of them walking together, but as they parted ways for their respective cars, Dale broke off and followed Gabriel. Once they were out of earshot of the others, he said, "Gabriel, I want to talk to you."

Gabriel marshaled himself, then turned around, trying to be as neutral as possible. "Yes?"

Dale put his hand on Gabriel's arm. "Let's take a drive."

Oh God. Gabriel wished he'd gotten the hell out of there before Dale found him. "Where...where are we going?"

"To Marcus and Frankie's." He added, sotto voce, "Slowly."

Oh God.

Dale climbed into the passenger side, and once the door was closed and they were enclosed in the silence, he spoke. "You're upset with me."

Gabriel fumbled with his keys. "I'm not upset with you." He dropped his keys on the floor and swore.

Dale picked them up, his knuckles brushing Gabriel's calf as he did so. It was a deliberate touch, and it made Gabriel shiver. And recoil against the door.

Dale handed him the keys with a sigh. "You are."

Gabriel took the keys, snatching them with a bit of annoyance, and put them in the ignition. "I'm not upset. I'm...unsettled. Nervous. But it's not a big deal."

"I don't like how you won't even look at me."

Gabriel continued backing the car up and maneuvering around Logan residents. "Well, I'm driving. It's not safe to look at you right now."

"That's not what I mean and you know it."

Gabriel pursed his lips and drew a deep breath as he pulled onto the street. He had to glance at Dale as he checked both ways. "I do."

"Is this because you don't want me to come Wednesday?"

Gabriel turned a deep shade of pink. "No."

"But it's about me coming Wednesday."

Gabriel wished he would stop saying *coming*. "It's truly not a big deal."

"It's a big deal to me that you can't look at me or talk to me."

He'd taken them down an odd side road, a back way to Marcus and Frankie's place, and they were in an area where there were no houses. Gabriel pulled over and put the car in park, the knot in his stomach from the night before blooming again.

"I avoid looking at you because you unsettle me." He hadn't meant to be so blunt in his confession and rushed to soften it. "Arthur paints an exciting picture of what Wednesday night will be like, and yes, I'm eager for it. The problem is, I'm attracted to you more than as a handsome someone to take to our bed for a night of fun. I'm still working out how to have those feelings, sleep with you, and then blithely brush them aside to be with Arthur." His face, his whole body, was hot not just with embarrassment, but with fear of exposure, and the center of his chest felt tight and cold. "I'm going to be with Arthur. And I won't lie to him."

"I wouldn't ever want you to lie to him." Dale regarded Gabriel with a strange expression, not quite predatory, but carefully, quietly eager. "For the record,

I have the same feelings about you."

Dizzy, Gabriel clutched the wheel. "What about Arthur?"

"I have different feelings about Arthur." Dale's smile was slow and wicked.

The whole world was abruptly strange, as if Gabriel had discovered another dimension he could open with his fingernail. It rippled before him, begging him to tug it open. But he was afraid. So afraid. "I don't think I can handle more than one relationship at a time."

Something flickered across Dale's face. Disappointment? Regret? Whatever it was, he snuffed it out quickly. "Do you want to call Wednesday off?"

Gabriel's grip on the steering wheel was so tight now his hands had no feeling in them. "I don't. But it feels like a horrible thing to say."

"Not at all. I'm certainly not going to complain about it. I only have one condition." He rested his hand on Gabriel's thigh, a gentle touch sending electricity racing through him. "I need you to start looking at me."

Gabriel glanced over at him. It was so hard. It would get more difficult, if he looked at him, to keep from...

Falling for him.

He swallowed against a sudden lump in his throat.

Dale raised an eyebrow, making it clear he knew exactly what Gabriel was thinking. "I didn't say I was going to make it *easy* on you."

No, he certainly was not. Gabriel decided he wouldn't, either. He put his hand on top of Dale's, the one that still rested on his thigh. "This one time. This Wednesday. With Arthur—with Arthur leading. And then we're done."

Dale turned his hand over, captured Gabriel's, and brought it to his lips. "Then I'll make sure I don't throw away my shot."

DALE HAD KNOWN Marcus for ten years. They'd met on the job, but they'd quickly become friends. Dale had always appreciated Marcus's no-nonsense approach to problems and his loyalty to his firm and to his friends. It had been a huge blow to Dale to discover Marcus's boyfriend had betrayed him by sleeping around. One, it hurt Marcus and ultimately drove him two hundred miles away, far enough all Dale could do was email him occasionally or catch him on his rare appearances on social media. More devastating, however, was how the cheating boyfriend had killed any chance for Dale to come out to Marcus, or at least it put up significant roadblocks to the hope Marcus would ever understand him.

He wasn't sure when, exactly, he'd understood he was poly, only that his sense of it was stronger than most other poly-identifying people he'd met. Too often he heard people declare themselves polyamorous as if it were some kind of rebellion, a social choice. All he knew was for him it wasn't a choice. Almost from the moment he'd understood he was pretty much only attracted to men, he'd also known he was attracted to more than one at once.

He'd always had multiple crushes, usually focusing them in different ways. One man would attract him because he seemed charming and gregarious, and Dale could imagine going on all manner of public dates with him, possibly playing with others if he were open to it. Another man would be quiet and reserved, and Dale would get lost in fantasies of mountain cabins and long weekends of making love, cooking together. Yes, he got a thrill from thinking about pursuing both men at the same time. Not in secret, but in tandem. To be able to talk to one man about the other, to feel his heart reaching for both lovers at the same time. The rush of it made him feel greater, more full. More human.

He had been the third in an evening's fun many, many times, and for some couples he was a regular feature. He was a bit of naughty fun, *for a good time call.* He didn't mind, to a point. But it upset him how Gabriel had put him in this same box, especially after admitting he had feelings for him. Essentially Gabriel could have let Dale into the relationship he'd wanted so desperately to have, but he'd chosen to dismiss it out of hand, no consideration, no conversation. It hurt, and he had no one to talk to about it. He didn't know anyone here but Marcus, and of course this was a subject with him he couldn't begin to broach.

Worse, he couldn't chase it away, not by taking a run down Logan's snowy streets in the early morning, not by absorbing himself for hours in the work he'd brought with him, or heading to the mayor's office on Monday afternoon and again Tuesday morning and spitballing more ideas for the project in his few free hours between regularly scheduled meetings.

To add insult to injury, Ronny hadn't let up on his texting. It wasn't constant—that wasn't how Ronny rolled. But it was consistent, enough Dale caught himself checking his phone sometimes, anxiously watching for another installment. Worried something lewd might pop up during a meeting, so he had to keep his phone face-down on the table. He'd made the mistake of replying to another text, telling Ronny he needed to lay off so Dale could work.

Send me a picture of your pretty little dick, and I'll think about it, had been Ronny's response. Dale had declined, but since then all the texts had been increasingly intense calls for Dale to go to the bathroom and photograph his junk so Ronny could make sure it was still in working order.

When a fresh round came in late Monday night, Dale almost sent one. Ronny was bad news, but Dale was restless and angry, and he knew there wasn't much the guy could do to him from Minneapolis. Maybe the exchange would make him feel good.

As soon as he'd had the thought he'd turned his phone off and hid it in the linen closet in the hall and hadn't let himself touch it until morning.

Between his frustration with Gabriel's refusal of him and his shame over nearly giving in to Ronny, by Tuesday Dale was pretty much a grumpy mess. That afternoon, before the final city council meeting, Marcus pulled Dale aside. "Is something wrong? You seem tense."

Dale ran a hand through his hair, trying to filter out a response. He was a shitty liar, and Marcus had a good bullshit detector. He decided a version of the truth would be best. "Trouble with a guy." *Three of them, but who's counting.*

Marcus raised his eyebrows. "Oh? I didn't know you were dating."

Dale shrugged. "Yeah, well. I'm not. He…wants to keep it casual." Dale's chest tightened, his throat thick and heavy. "I'm realizing, the longer I stay here, I don't. But there's no real way for me to change that. So I'm feeling down and out."

Marcus *harrumphed*. "Convince him to step it up. Woo him. You're a charming guy. You can do it."

Dale sighed. "It's complicated. Really complicated."

Marcus patted Dale on the shoulder and winked at him. "Then simplify it."

They went into the meeting, and technically Dale participated, but his mind drifted the entire time, thinking about what Marcus had said. Once they were adjourned and back at the house, he sat in the living room with Marcus and Frankie, watching their domestic bliss, letting it bleed into him, feeding his want, spurring his schemes.

Could he simplify it? What would this entail? Convincing Gabriel, yes, but convincing Arthur too. Neither task was a chore. Because he did want them both, in very different ways. For more than an evening's entertainment.

Was it selfish of him to tempt them into something more? Was it wicked to use Marcus's advice, knowing full well Marcus would see this as adultery, though Dale fully intended for there to be consent all around?

What *did* he want, exactly?

He thought of Gabriel, so taut and intense inside the car. Elegantly beautiful. Touching Dale's hand. The touch that still burned his skin. The glances that still fueled him. He thought of Arthur too, of the promise of his touch, his sensuality. But Dale had to admit, mostly he thought of Gabriel.

He thought of Ronny's texts, the slippery road into darkness he knew that path led to. He had a bad feeling about what waited for him once he went home to Minneapolis. To be honest, he didn't want to go. He wanted to stay here, to plan festivals in Logan and flirt with Gabriel and get winked at by Arthur.

Gabriel wanted it too. For one night. What Dale couldn't decide was if he had any right to try to nudge the one night into something more. Or what would happen next if he managed to succeed.

Chapter Four

ARTHUR MEANT TO do as he promised Paul and make sure Gabriel wasn't pressured about Wednesday, he really did. The problem was, Gabriel was hard to read on his best day, and he was exceptionally funky about this situation.

One of Arthur's favorite things about Gabriel was sometimes, especially when it came to sex, *no* meant *maybe* or possibly *yes, please, do that especially as I tell you not to.* So he knew he couldn't simply come out and say, "Look, baby, do you actually want to have this threesome or not?" Because when it came to sex, Gabriel had no fucking clue what he wanted. That was part of the fun, most days. However in this instance, Gabriel's contradictory nature was not as fun. As Wednesday afternoon turned into Wednesday evening and Arthur swung by to pick Gabriel up from work so they could stop by the grocery to get the last-minute things for dinner, he still couldn't read his partner, couldn't tell if he was about to lead them into a colossal mistake or not. And his time had almost run out to get his shit together.

He dug in on the way home, as they drove with the groceries on the truck seat between them. "Are you still okay with this?"

Gabriel, who had been lost in thought out the window, startled and turned to him. "Oh—tonight? Yes. I am. I'm nervous, but you're right, I'm sure it will be fun, once we get into it."

It wasn't exactly the excitement Arthur was going for. "We don't have to do it."

"Oh, I know." Gabriel frowned at him. "Are you saying you don't want to?"

"Hell no. I have so many ideas." Arthur decided maybe this was the problem, that they hadn't talked enough about it. "I really want to spank his ass. Can't decide if I want it over my knee or the bench."

Gabriel's smile tickled Arthur's insides. "The bench. You like to move around and admire your work."

Arthur felt a swell of pride. "I love how you don't mind when I play with other people. You've never even blinked."

"I know it's important to you." This was all he said, as if it were that simple. Arthur supposed it was, but it still meant a lot to him.

Why couldn't it be simple for Gabriel, then? What was going on, making it complicated?

He tried again. "What are you wanting to happen

tonight? I'm assuming you want me to drive."

"That would be best, yes."

"So you want me to decide everything? Are you feeling rough play? Sensual? Humiliation?"

Gabriel stiffened. "Not humiliation please."

Finally, a fucking reaction. "Good to know. Role-play? That okay?"

"Anything is fine, but not too rough, and not humiliation please."

"It's just, you don't sound excited." Arthur decided the best move would be to put his cards on the table, or the dash, since they were in the truck. "Paul said I can be pushy. He made me realize I might have gotten you into this and you didn't want to be here. Are you acting funny because I fucked up and you don't want this and I'm about to make shit bad between us by being an asshole like usual?"

Now Gabriel came out of his strange funk, turning to face Arthur in the seat. "No. *No.* Not at all. That's not what this is about. I'm just nervous. It's me, not you. I don't think I want to do this on a regular basis, but I do want to do it this one time. With you." He let out a breath, cast his eyes down, then deliberately met Arthur's gaze again. "I want to do this with you."

Arthur felt better, if not completely mollified. "All right then. Let's go get ready for our guest."

They prepped the meal together, tossing a salad, slicing potatoes to roast. Arthur had marinated the venison steaks during the day, and he had them ready now to put in the oven as soon as Dale arrived. "Why don't you pick out a bottle of wine?" he called to Gabriel as he pulled a stack of plates to set on the island beside the other bits of table service ready to be laid out.

"Do you mind if I open some now?"

Arthur paused with the plates halfway to the counter, then lowered them the rest of the way as he watched Gabriel select a bottle of wine from the rack. "No. Go on ahead."

He didn't quiz Gabriel anymore about the evening, but he noted how quickly Gabriel's glass of wine went down. Let him pour a second one, though it was a full half hour before Dale was due. Then and only then did Arthur, who was stone-cold sober, lead tipsy Gabriel to the living room and sat beside him on the sofa.

"What do you think of Dale?" he ventured as an opener.

He was surprised to find he hit so near the bull's-eye right off the bat. Gabriel fluttered and retreated into his wine before replying. "He's nice," he said, his tone belying the fact that he thought Dale was so much more than nice.

"He's pretty fucking hot. All those muscles."

"Mmm," Gabriel agreed, drinking more.

"And he's as tall as you. He could fuck you standing up with a whole different perspective than when I do it."

Gabriel drained his glass.

Arthur felt he was right in the thick of something important, but he was damned if he knew what it was. So what that Gabriel was attracted to Dale? Wasn't that the point of this? Was it because Gabriel was hung up on that, guilty about it? Probably. Maybe he needed a little tit for tat. "Of course I wouldn't mind seeing him on his knees in front of me. I like a big boy being obedient. Really turns me on. I want to fuck him with all those muscles bulging, him gasping and holding on to the couch. Maybe looking at you while he did it. Then maybe you come over and fuck his mouth. Or kneel in front of him."

Gabriel pressed the glass to his forehead. "Stop. *Stop.* He isn't even here yet."

"Yeah, well, baby, neither are you."

Gabriel turned to Arthur then, and he was shocked at the pain in his eyes, the fear, the tears.

Arthur couldn't breathe.

Gabriel leaned closer, slipped long fingers around Arthur's neck and drawing him into his orbit. "Arthur, I love you so much. I never want to do anything to hurt you, ever. You're everything to me. You taught me how to live, actually live, to come out of the shadows I'd told myself I had to exist in. You gave me friends, a family. I want to marry you and be your husband and build a life with you, have children with you like we planned. I would do anything to protect that. Do you understand? You are all I care about."

Paul had been right. Fucking hell, Paul had been

right. Arthur put his hand on Gabriel's cheek. "I'll call Dale and tell him we have to cancel."

He began to rise, but Gabriel grabbed his hand and pulled him down, regarding him with those same wild eyes. "That's the thing, Arthur. I don't want you to cancel."

Tires on snow and the slash of lights against the cabin preceded, by seconds, the sound of feet on the cabin stairs, and then a knock on the door. Arthur lingered for a moment with Gabriel, staring into his eyes, wondering what in the fucking hell he was supposed to do. When the knock came a second time, he acknowledged, at least to start, he had to answer the door and let in the other leg of this hot mess.

Dale stood beneath the porch light, cheeks reddened by the cold. He was hatless, well-groomed and smiling, though now that Arthur searched for it, the man looked as queasy and uncertain as Gabriel. He also had a bottle of wine in one hand, and in the other a bouquet of flowers.

"Hi." He waved the flowers slightly, as if they were a flag of truce.

"Come on in." Arthur stood aside to give him room, holding the door open. As he shut it behind his guest, he saw Gabriel had left the couch to greet Dale. He still seemed wary, but something had brightened in him as he smiled and greeted Dale.

Dale smiled back with the same intensity, holding out the flowers. "I thought you might like these."

Arthur watched Gabriel's eyes light up as he accepted the bouquet—and Arthur knew.

He hid his reaction as he hung up Dale's jacket, as he made a fuss over what a nice bottle of wine it was (he had no fucking idea) and took it to the rack before pouring a glass for Dale from the bottle Gabriel had already opened. He also paused at the liquor cabinet for a shot of whiskey, downing it before his conscience could point out alcohol never helped anybody solve their problems.

In that moment he didn't much care. He needed a crutch to help him through this minefield, because he had to process, really quickly, whether or not what he'd told Gabriel was true, that it didn't matter to him if a guy he was with needed to be with someone else. Or more to the point if this truth extended to the precious exception of Gabriel Higgins. Because he was almost completely certain Gabriel had feelings for Dale—and Dale had them for Gabriel in return.

In the end he decided the only way to make the decision about how he felt was to wait and see.

Clearing his throat, he brought Dale his wine and a glass of club soda for Gabriel, who frowned at him but didn't argue. With a lusty sigh, Arthur sipped the soda he'd grabbed for himself, as if the foundations of his world weren't shuddering and shaking beneath him. "So, Dale. Enjoying the eight million meetings Logan's finest have been putting you through?"

Dale smiled wryly over the top of his wine and

shrugged. "Honestly, so much of my life is meetings, I haven't noticed a difference except the people are nicer and more excited about my work."

Gabriel had been putting the flowers in a vase, but he lingered over them, fussing with the blooms. "Are you in the office most of the time, or do you ever work on sites you develop?"

Dale leaned on the edge of the counter, resting his elbows and canting his hips slightly as he watched Gabriel. "Oh, a bit of both. Depends on the type of job and the time of year. I only started Davidson Incorporated six months ago. Before that I worked in a different division of my parent company. I still work for them, but this has all been a new venture, the latter half of this year. I'm more independent and flexible. Right now I'm making less money, because I work on commission and I'm starting essentially from scratch, but I don't mind. I'm doing what I love. Though it's been a little more admin work since I became the head of my division. I miss my fieldwork."

Gabriel smiled as he listened to Dale talk. He still played with the petals, ostensibly looking at them, but his gaze was on the frame of Dale's crotch. Arthur had to admire the move. It was one of his favorites. Right now, though, he watched it with a question burning in his brain: did he mind that it was happening? Did he mind it, knowing Dale wanted more than Gabriel's body? Did he mind knowing Gabriel was so preoccupied with the man he'd been barely able to talk about it all week?

Was it enough that he'd had the outburst on the couch, the vow that Arthur came first? Did Arthur trust it?

He cleared his throat and turned away from the sight of the two of them. "Going to get cooking these steaks so we can eat, if that's all right with you folks." He said it a bit too loudly, and the *you folks* felt odd, like he was behaving as if they were the couple.

Perhaps he'd been too obvious, because Gabriel abandoned the flowers and came around to the other side of the oven, putting the appliance and Arthur between himself and Dale. "Arthur makes incredible venison steak. They're my favorite things in the world. He makes them better than any I've ever had."

"I can't wait to try them, then." There was so little challenge in Dale's reply he might as well have been on his back with his legs in the air.

Jesus, this shit was a mess and nobody was naked yet.

Arthur pulled the sizzling pan from the oven and placed it on the burner before carefully arranging the raw steak inside. "I'm fairly confident I can serve up meat to please the both of you." He laid the last steak in place, then nodded at Gabriel. "Sprinkle the bowl of spices I have ready over it while I wash my hands, will you?" He started to turn away, and then as an afterthought, maybe even as a test, he glanced at Dale and added, "Dale, why don't you give him a hand?"

He took his time at the sink, washing his hands slowly, deliberately not looking, giving them time to do whatever the hell they were going to do, or not do. He wasn't sure what it was he was going to see. He scrubbed his fingers, under his nails, along his knuckles, then simply played in the warm, wet stream until instinct told him it was time. Then he grabbed a towel, and as he dried his hands, he pivoted to give himself a view of the stove.

They stood side by side, bodies touching at the leg, the hip, the elbow, heads bent together as they dressed the steak. They spoke quietly, their voices murmurs, Dale's low and suggestive, Gabriel's higher and...well, Gabriel, something between admonishing and encouraging. Arthur had given them a test, and he had his answer. He hadn't been sure of what he was testing at first, but he had it now.

They had a spark. More than sexual attraction, more than casual interest. There was something pulling between the two of them. Something bigger and brighter than a single night of fun. A bit of tinder that could turn into a flame and become a raging fire.

It appeared as if the fire had already started.

Will this pull him away from me?

His whole life, Arthur had argued for others to trust in a wider vision of what relationships could be, what love could be. He wasn't poly, but he believed in polyamory. This idea that people could only ever love one person in their lives, as if they were shutting out

the rest of the world for them, was ridiculous. However-
er, as he stood in his kitchen, watching the man he
loved so much tentatively open his heart to another…well, for the first time Arthur understood what a
terrifying risk it was. Because for all Gabriel's promises
on the couch, there was potential for loss, wasn't there?
If Arthur let this keep going, if he didn't object, Dale
and Gabriel's relationship absolutely could make a
brighter spark than the one Arthur had with Gabriel.

And yet what kind of lover would he be if he said
no, you must choose this dimmer flame?

Was he afraid of this? Oh hell yes. He understood
now why Gabriel had been so distant and strange. He
knew what Gabriel had been trying to tell him too—
that Gabriel would push his feelings aside. Arthur was
going to insist Gabriel act on them. Even though it
scared Arthur. Even though it scared the both of them.
Because there was no way he was going to be the guy
who kept Gabriel from spreading his wings.

Even if Gabriel ultimately used those wings to fly
away.

Arthur cleared his throat, smiling and aching at
once to see them spring apart from each other as he
approached. "Let's get this business in the oven then,
and get things cooking."

Whistling to hide his fear, Arthur used potholders
to pick up the hot pan, put the steaks inside the oven,
and began to rewrite his plans.

GABRIEL FELT AS if he were on a knife's edge.

He was both annoyed with Arthur for cutting him off the wine and grateful. By the time he had food in him he'd sobered up enough to realize he was too loose, too free from the alcohol, but no longer drunk enough not to care. He was counting on Arthur to keep him in line. He was counting on Arthur for everything. He told himself so long as he treated this like a scene, so long as he did what Arthur told him to do and nothing more, he would be fine. It had been a mistake to agree to this, and yet he did not regret his choice. He would simply survive it, enjoy this one time, lean on Arthur, and never, ever do it again.

The knowledge that this was the *one time*, however, didn't help him, and it wasn't the thought of the up-coming sex that had him in knots. It was the frustration of realizing he'd enjoyed Dale bringing him flowers—knowing Dale had deliberately brought them for him alone—and this was it, there would be no more court-ing. He would like courting, actually. Arthur did some, but it was Arthur-style courting. His most successful apology had been a bag of frozen venison. Which had been an appreciated overture. But everything about Dale promised flowers were just the beginning. Wouldn't it be fun to see what else he would pull out of his charming bag of tricks?

Except of course that was ridiculous. Gabriel couldn't date Dale in Logan, not without calling it off with Arthur, and he wasn't doing that. Because Gabriel did love Arthur. Which meant there was no contest to be had here. He should have his meal, enjoy his sex, and shut the hell up.

Usually right about the time he'd get the argument settled in his head, Dale would smile, at him or simply in general, and the whole house of cards would tumble to the ground again. It helped nothing that through the whole dinner Arthur was nothing but the most wonderful, *sweetest* fiancé a man could ask for, attentive to both Gabriel and Dale, engaging them both in conversation, asking Dale about his Christmas.

"Will you have a celebration back in the Cities?"

Dale shrugged and cut into his steak. "Oh, I suppose I'll probably go over to my aunt's on Christmas Day for a bit. What about you guys?"

Arthur rolled his eyes. "You met my mother. Where do you think we'll be?"

Dale raised an eyebrow at Gabriel. "Not seeing your family?"

Gabriel wiped his mouth with his napkin and shook his head. "No, my family and I are estranged."

Dale frowned, sad for him. "I'm sorry to hear that."

Gabriel waved a hand. "It doesn't matter. This is my family, here in Logan. Arthur's, and the family I have in our friends."

Dale smiled. It was such an arresting expression. "You guys have such a wonderful group. You're so lucky."

"We are," Arthur said, "but we're your group now too. You'll be up here pretty frequently, I suspect, for the development project."

Dale cut a glance to Gabriel. "Oh—it might not always be me. I mean, it doesn't have to be me who works with Logan."

"Oh no, it absolutely does." Arthur leaned back in his chair. "You've built a rapport with us. The people here respect you. You've made connections here. You need to nurture them."

Dale wouldn't look away from Gabriel. "Probably not all the connections are welcome."

Gabriel focused on his plate, pushing a half-eaten bit of potato around. "It's not always a matter of you being welcome. Sometimes things don't work out, is all."

"And sometimes," Arthur said, his voice weirdly pointed, "things simply take time and care and patience, and attention. But that'll never work if you start sending surrogates up here." He put an arm over the back of Gabriel's chair. "I've wondered if some of us shouldn't come to Minneapolis too, on occasion. We can meet *your* people. I've been meaning to come down with Gabriel, in fact. Take a long weekend vacation. Maybe we could come sit in on your meetings for a change."

Dale brightened. "That would be great, actually, if you thought it would work."

Gabriel turned to Arthur, searching for where he'd

grown the extra head. "You hate the Cities."

Arthur looked annoyed. "I do not. They're not my favorite, no, but *you* care for them quite a bit. And it's been a long time since you were there. Plus it's like I said. We should do our part for Logan." When Gabriel opened his mouth to point out it would be more appropriate for the mayor to go, Arthur picked up a bit of venison from his plate and popped it into Gabriel's mouth. "Here you are, hon. I think you should chew on that."

Gabriel did, though he glared at Arthur while he did it.

Dale didn't miss Gabriel's reticence, and some of his eagerness abated. "It's all right. I need to diversify my projects. I don't know if I can devote all my time to Logan."

Gabriel scooped up Arthur's plate with his own. "Are you finished?" He reached for Dale's without letting him answer, then rose and took the stack to the kitchen. He plunked them on the counter and stood over them, shaking, and when Arthur came up behind him, he startled.

"Baby, you all right?" Warm, familiar arms slid around his middle, and a rough beard tickled his arm.

Gabriel shut his eyes and drew a deep breath. Everything was careening out of control. He'd made a mistake. He knew that now. He'd thought doing this would be a kind of exorcism, but it felt more like leaping into the oven. Or the fires of hell itself. Yes, he wanted Dale, but the thought of going through with this, of having this night of casual sex as if it didn't mean anything, of doing this without telling Arthur the whole truth of what he was feeling—if he did this, the awful feelings inside him would get worse, not better. In fact, they might never go away.

But he'd realized this too late, and there was no way out, no way to make it stop, no way to extricate himself without making a scene, because how did he say it? How did he explain?

Arthur turned him around, took his face in his hands. "Gabriel. Talk to me, right now. Tell me what you need."

The part of Gabriel's brain that had been taken over by rabid squirrels continued to scream. It careened off with his common sense and ability to make words into the dark of the night. But the part of him that had been Arthur's lover for a year, the part of him freest when in elbow tie or Hojōjutsu Ittatsu-ryū, responded not to the panic but to the firmness and the familiarity of the grip and the promise of safety it gave him. It summoned one word, the word it knew would tell Arthur to make everything okay. Because Arthur always made everything okay.

"Red," Gabriel whispered.

Arthur squeezed his shoulder, his hip, kissed the tear rolling down his cheek. Then he marched him to a kitchen stool, turned it to face out the back door, and plunked Gabriel onto it.

"Wait here. I'll deal with it." He kissed him once more, a firm pressure on his temple. "It's going to be fine. I'll fix it. I'll be right back. You sit here and take deep breaths. Nod if you understand."

Gabriel nodded. Then he did as Arthur asked. He sat on the stool and he waited, staring out the window into the blue-black of the yard, into the snowy night. He took deep breaths and didn't let himself react to hearing Arthur's low voice mingling with Dale's at the door. He didn't wipe away the tears as they fell, not until he heard the door shut and Arthur's feet cross the floor to where he sat, until Arthur stood beside him. Until they were alone, the two of them again.

"I'm sorry," Gabriel whispered, new tears falling now. "I'm so sorry."

"It's all right." Arthur helped him off the stool and held him close as he led him through the kitchen toward the stairs. "Let's get you into bed."

It wasn't all right, though. Gabriel was so much more than sorry. Sorry he'd ruined the evening. Sorry he'd made everything awkward. Sorry he'd ruined Arthur's fun.

Sorry he'd hurt Dale, that he hadn't had the courage to say goodbye.

Sorry doing the right thing didn't make the horrible knot inside him go away, that somehow it had only become bigger and tighter since Arthur had sent Dale home.

DALE WANTED TO go to Minneapolis straight from Arthur and Gabriel's place.

But of course he couldn't. He was staying at Marcus and Frankie's house while he was in town, and if he left at this hour, they'd want to know what was wrong. It was going to be difficult enough to keep them from seeing how upset he was regardless, and on the way back to their place he had to scrape up a mask so they couldn't tell. Except Marcus would know the second he saw him. So Dale lied, said he wasn't feeling well. Must be coming down with something.

Ronny texted him as he climbed into bed.

I'm not in the mood, he replied.

I'll put you in the mood, Ronny promised.

Dale didn't answer. But he didn't sleep, either.

Marcus and Frankie tried to get him to stay the next morning. Because he still didn't look good, they said, and they were worried. God, that punched him in the gut. It would have been nice to have them fuss over him, to have somewhere to stay, people to be with for Christmas. But he needed the distance, needed to get the hell out of this fucking postcard. Away from Logan.

Away from Arthur. Away from Gabriel.

Dale let Frankie give him peppermint tea, but he refused to stay, insisting he had a family thing, which he did, but he probably wasn't going to go. He waved his goodbyes, thanked them for their hospitality, and promised to text when he was home. Then he got the hell out of there and drove as fast as he dared until he hit the interstate, at which point he courted danger and went ninety all the way to the Twin Cities.

The first thing he did when he got in his condo was take a shower. A long, hot shower. When he got out, he turned the TV on, but all he could find was Christmas specials, because it was fucking Christmas Eve. He dug through his Blu-ray shelf and put on a mindless action movie, cranking the volume until the sound of shooting and men shouting filled the apartment. He went to his fridge, but he had nothing to eat. He'd been gone, had planned on letting Marcus and Frankie, or maybe Arthur and Gabriel, invite him for the holiday.

Stupid idiot, what did you think would happen? Where did you get the idea that this time it would be different?

He had a beer for dinner, because it was all he had, and had vodka for dessert.

When his phone buzzed at 10:30, this time he was too drunk to reply to Ronny's texts. So he called him.

"Don't text me," he slurred.

Ronny laughed, the familiar, cruel, silky sound carving the hollow in Dale's chest deeper. "You've been drinking. Mayberry not treating you well?"

Dale's nostrils flared. He plucked the vodka bottle from the counter and took a heavy swig. "I'm done with Logan."

"Are you telling me you're in the city? Well, well."

Dale went cold. And hot. He didn't understand how he could fear and yearn for Ronny at the same time. "I'm done with you too."

"But I'm not done with you. I told you. I have your present." He pitched his voice to a whisper. "It's big, honey."

He said *honey* like a tease. Mocking Dale, somehow, in a subtle manner he couldn't quite work out, especially drunk. But that was Ronny. He gave Dale so much of what he wanted, but the price was Dale always felt horrible after.

Yet what had Logan done for him? A week of sugar and spice and hope and love and gay men holding hands, of invitations made and rescinded.

Of Gabriel handing him everything, then snatching it away.

What was the difference, really? his vodka-soaked brain whispered. *At least with Ronny sometimes you get off.*

But even this drunk he remembered last Christmas. Or rather, he remembered how horrible it had felt to wake up in that hotel room *not* remembering. Unsure how he'd gotten there. Unsure what had happened. His body feeling off, wrong, subtly violated in ways he was afraid to ask about. Ronny laughing at him every time he'd tried.

"I'm coming over." Ronny's voice was muffled, and Dale knew he was moving through the house, down the hall, past his sleeping wife and children. "Leave your door unlocked. I want you naked in the middle of your floor, ass facing the door, waiting. But get ready, dirty boy. Santa knows what a bad, bad boy you are. He'll make sure this Christmas is better than the last one."

Dale's stomach lurched. "No."

"You want to play that game, do you? Fine. Keep your clothes on. You know how I love to tear them off." He hung up.

Dale stood in the middle of his kitchen, clutching the phone to his ear as the call ended with a series of beeps, then went silent. For several seconds he stood there, motionless, his alcohol-sodden mind racing as he tried to think of what to do.

Then, without actively deciding to do anything, he was moving. Grabbing his suitcase from Logan and heading out the door again, fumbling with his smartphone as he called up the Uber app. Except he didn't press it, not until he'd walked three blocks south onto a route Ronny would never take to get to his condo. He ducked into the shelter of an awning while he waited, his heartbeat thudding in his ears as he scanned the streets until the app told him his driver had arrived.

He found a small hotel in eastern St. Paul with a vacancy, a chain Ronny would never consider looking at, and he paid with cash, slipping the desk clerk an extra hundred dollars to let him avoid the credit card requirement. *You're being paranoid and crazy*, he told himself, and yet he couldn't stop glancing over his shoulder, couldn't relax until he'd shut the door to his room and thrown the deadbolt.

Though he lay on the bed, he didn't sleep, not one

moment of the night. He stared at the unfamiliar ceiling, heart still beating crazily, still aching from Logan, fear shaking rusty memories loose. He couldn't recall precisely what had happened last year on Christmas Eve, but the instinct to run from Ronny became stronger, the urge to forget and go back to the way things were evaporating as the cocktail of hurt and fear replaced the vodka. It had begun exactly this way. Dale lonely and alone, too drunk on Christmas Eve. Ronny calling him, coming over. Something starting as a simple scene, and then…

And then…

Every time he attempted to remember, something visceral in him revolted, keeping him from reaching into the place where the memory resided. Part of him wanted to trust this instinct and let sleeping dogs lie, but another part of him ran cold, thinking, *What in the world did he do to me? What did he make me do?*

He didn't know. All he could recall was Ronny's cold, wicked smile as he'd answered the door, and the terror and humiliation of waking up confused and alone in a strange place, unsure of what had happened.

Eventually he did sleep, a fitful catnap from dawn until housekeeping knocked on the door to let him know he needed to check out. He went to his aunt's house after all, though he didn't enjoy himself, and he didn't stay long. He returned to his condo, but he didn't linger there, only stopped long enough to get a change of clothes and his phone charger.

He slept in his office that night, in a sleeping bag on the floor. He did it for a few nights, in fact, and showered at the gym. He tried a few times to go back to his condo, but it took him four attempts to get into the elevator, and he felt like a caged animal inside his own home the entire time he was there. He called his real estate agent and put his condo on the market and had her find him a short-term rental until he could figure out what he wanted to buy instead. He managed to get his personal effects out in a few hours when he knew Ronny would be at work, then had a moving company handle the rest.

When she expressed her surprise at his wanting to sell, since he'd told her the condo had been his ideal metro space, he shrugged and said his ideal had changed.

Ronny continued to text, but Dale ignored him and concentrated on work. He delegated the Logan project to team members and searched for new ventures, focusing on putting the disappointments of life out of his mind.

Chapter Five

B Y FEBRUARY, ARTHUR was willing to acknowledge
he had a serious problem on his hands, and
worse, he had no clue how to solve it.

Oh, on the surface everything was fine. So fucking
fine he wanted to scream. Paul had spoken with Kyle,
who had spoken with Frankie, who had spoken with
Gabriel, and on New Year's Eve the six of them had
sat around Arthur's living room, sipping mulled wine
and planning their triple wedding for the following
Christmas. Gabriel had smiled and laughed, kissed
Arthur and made sweet love to him, and told him he
couldn't wait for another wonderful year with him. He
went to work at the library and stayed up too late at the
kitchen table preparing his county-wide famous story-
time lessons. He went over the cabin renovations with
Arthur whenever he asked him what he thought about
this detail or that major decision. He collected the
paperwork for the foster care license himself, even
though their worker had said they really couldn't have a

placement until they finished their renovations.

On the surface, Gabriel behaved as if nothing had ever happened. But the truth was, something had, and all Arthur had to do was look in his lover's eyes to see everything was an act. Gabriel was still upset. His feelings for Dale had shaken things loose in him he could not put into an orderly place. Arthur tried, once, to bring up Dale directly, and Gabriel had gone quiet for a day. So he followed Gabriel's lead. Let him try this route, to see if this made things okay.

It did not. A week before Valentine's Day, the tension had eaten so far into Arthur that when Paul asked him what he and Gabriel were doing for the holiday, Arthur simply sighed and said, "Fuck, I don't have any idea."

Paul set aside the wrench he'd been spinning idly in his hand and frowned. "Okay, wow. What was that about?"

Arthur was pretty sure it wasn't the best idea to air this dirty laundry, but he was equally sure he was out of shits to give about any of this anymore. "Do you remember at Christmas when you told me maybe we shouldn't have a threesome with Dale? Well, we didn't have it, but it still fucked shit up." He rubbed his hands over his face. "Maybe I pushed them to it? I don't know. Maybe it would have happened on its own, maybe their attraction would have stayed buried. The fact is, it didn't, and I don't know what to do. I don't know what the fuck to do. I'm losing him."

Paul's hand tightened on the workbench. "Are you saying Dale—wait, are you saying *Gabriel*—?"

"I'm saying they have feelings for each other. More than it's-fun-to-fuck-you feelings. Nothing happened, I don't think—and if it did, even if Gabriel breaks down tonight and confesses they fucked for a week on the library conference table, the only thing I'm going to be mad about is they didn't tell me first. But I know it didn't happen, that they're not together. You heard the mayor at the meeting the other day, flustered because Dale handed the Logan project off to someone else. Meanwhile, haven't you noticed how Gabriel is like a puppet pretending to be Gabriel?"

Paul scratched the side of his nose. "He has been weird, yeah. But no offense. Sometimes Gabriel is just weird."

"He's not weird with me, or at least he didn't used to be. He's depressed, and he won't talk to me about it." Arthur pulled a hand over his beard. It felt terrifying and relieving to say this stuff out loud, and now that he'd started, he couldn't stop. "I think Gabriel is poly. I think he's just figured it out, and I think he's trying to pretend he's not. And I think it's killing him. I can't make him stop, and—"

He stopped talking, stopped breathing for a second, until his vision got funky and blurry and Paul handed him a slightly dirty bandana. Arthur wiped his eyes, then let out a shuddering sigh and blew his nose.

"He's going to be okay." Paul put a hand on Arthur's shoulder. "So will you."

"Nothing fucking feels okay," Arthur said into the bandana, then blew his nose a second time.

"I can imagine." Paul twiddled his thumbs as he looked up at the rafters. "Okay. So. What do you think is the bigger issue, getting him to admit he's poly, or getting him back together with Dale?"

Arthur let out a few ragged breaths, trying to ground himself again. God, but he loved it when Paul helped him fix shit. "Probably both things need to happen, but A has to happen or B won't work. And B might not work at all, because I have a feeling he put the big hurt on Dale, given the guy is giving the whole *town* the silent treatment."

"Well, you know where you need to start. Pretty good Valentine's Day present, really, helping someone come out to themselves."

"Right, but how do I do that?"

"Oh, I've got some ideas." Paul patted the workbench, leaned forward, and with a sly grin, laid out his plan.

GABRIEL DIDN'T KNOW where they were going for Valentine's Day, only that it was a surprise.

He'd been ready for Arthur to tell him they were taking a weekend getaway, since the holiday fell on Sunday, but Arthur said no, they were staying in town. "Weather's too iffy this time of year to plan something away. Besides, what I've got in mind is best done here at home."

This was all Gabriel had to go on, and it wasn't much. Not that he cared particularly, which was becoming more and more of a problem. He was having a difficult time caring about anything. He would have preferred not to have Arthur's plans be a total surprise so he could work up a proper front. The last thing he wanted was for Arthur to think he was disappointed in him.

No. Gabriel was only disappointed in himself.

He had no hints, though, so he could not prepare, and in the end he had no warning. Since they were in town, Gabriel assumed whatever celebrating they'd do would be on the actual holiday, but on Saturday afternoon, when he was not-reading a book on the bed, mostly moving his eyes across the pages, Arthur came in around four o'clock and gently took the volume from his hands.

"All right. It's time for your present." Before Gabriel could draw in a breath to protest, Arthur wrapped a silk blindfold around his eyes and whispered in his ear. "You have two words, and you know which ones they are. Use them wisely."

Gabriel shivered, and he couldn't tell if it was fear or anticipation or what precisely it was, except it was the most he'd felt since the day before Christmas Eve. Arthur had made love to him plenty since then, but they hadn't played, and certainly not this game. This was an old favorite, though, Two Words. It wasn't that Gabriel couldn't say anything, but these were the only ones that mattered, the only ones Arthur would listen to, were the two that would make the game slow down or stop. Yellow and red.

Under normal circumstances this was an excuse for Gabriel to play *no*. To pretend he didn't want something and for Arthur to pretend to push past the resistance. It was a game they both enjoyed. Tonight, though, Gabriel said nothing at all as Arthur divested him of his clothes and led him carefully down the stairs.

"Only two words, and that's the only time I'm reminding you. It's time for your bath."

The main floor was warm, the furnace turned up high, the fire roaring, which wasn't an uncommon setup for this game. What wasn't usual was the large copper half bath in front of the hearth revealed when Arthur took the blindfold away, like something out of a Regency novel. It was full not only of water but soap, Gabriel's scented soap from the smell of things.

"Get in and let me wash you."

Gabriel climbed in, a little wobbly-legged, but he did as he was told. The water was warm and felt wonderful, as did Arthur's hands on him as he washed his hair, massaged his back and arms, then made him lie against the sloped edge and washed his legs too. They had to fold practically into his chest unless Arthur held them out of the water, but Gabriel didn't mind. It felt so good, both the water and the attention.

Maybe if he relaxed and gave into this, he could get over it. Maybe if he surrendered to Arthur, he could be okay.

Arthur washed every inch of his body, including the parts of him he hoped would feature more prominently later. By the time Arthur finished with him, Gabriel had an erection and followed him half-drunkenly as he shifted around the tub, eager to move on to whatever else he had in store.

Instead of taking the game to the next level, however, Arthur only settled him against the slope and rose, backing away. "I'm going to get changed and get your dinner. Rest here and wait for me."

Gabriel said nothing, because it wasn't his place to say anything. Which he appreciated so much right now. He shut his eyes and accepted his present, trying again to sink into it, hating the part of him that felt hollowed out. Maybe Arthur would fill the space. If he was good, if he was completely, utterly obedient, perhaps tonight would be the night it didn't matter anymore.

Perhaps tonight he could stop feeling like a horrible person, could stop feeling as if he were screwing a lid tighter and tighter onto a tiny monster who was screaming at him in a language he didn't understand, didn't want to understand.

He must have drifted asleep, or perhaps simply into subspace, because the next thing he knew Arthur had reappeared, wearing his leathers this time, his chaps and vest over the jeans Gabriel liked so much, the ones that outlined his cock with stitched arrows around a pouch. He had on his leather vest too, and his cap, and he had to be so hot, but he didn't complain, only held out a gigantic, fluffy white towel.

"Out of the water, Gabriel. Time for dinner."

He dried Gabriel off thoroughly, rubbing him down with a roughness that reddened his skin and made Gabriel buzz in a way he only did when he was playing sub to Arthur. He *was* feeling again, not all the way, but it was better. He hoped there was ropework ahead of him, or perhaps a spanking, something with a tiny bit of pain. He wished they could do it now, but no, Arthur led him to the couch, beside the coffee table strewn with nibbles, little cheeses and crackers and grapes and strawberries and some cured deer sausage. For a moment Gabriel got excited when Arthur produced a pair of nylon cuffs. But all that happened was he bound Gabriel's wrists before he began feeding him.

Gabriel ate, not really tasting, mostly chewing and swallowing between the sips of water Arthur made him take. Food hadn't had much flavor for him lately, not even venison, but he ate and pretended to appreciate the deer sausage because he knew Arthur would expect it. They didn't converse, which was fine. This was something to get through. Arthur stroked him while he ate, heightening his arousal, teasing him, and he welcomed it. He didn't whimper, didn't beg, didn't plead, because he was determined to be good. He would get past this. He would work with Arthur. He would make it through this.

He had to.

When Arthur took the food away, Gabriel thrilled, ready for the next part, only to groan aloud when Arthur produced a feather and pressed him backward onto the couch. Arthur laughed and straddled him, teasing his neck, his stomach, and his arms with the implement.

"What, you thought you could simply wait me out? Oh you know better than that. I'm not going to let you have anything until you're mad for it, honey. So you might as well settle in."

Gabriel writhed beneath the onslaught of sensation—it tickled, yes, but it was also just too much, more than he could take. "Please stop," he begged. Arthur ignored him, and Gabriel fought against it, even though he knew it was the game, knew how to make it stop. "It's too much. I can't. Stop it, damn it. *Stop.*"

"You don't get to escape feelings, Gabriel. That's not how this works."

Gabriel thought, for a terrifying moment, he was going to cry. He managed, at the last second, to turn it into rage. "You don't get to tell me how to feel. You don't get to tell me anything."

"I get to tell you everything, right now." He picked Gabriel up, swinging him into his arms as if he weighed nothing, and carried him to the table. "Time for my dinner."

He laid Gabriel flat on the dining room table, spread his legs, stuck a cushion he'd stashed on a nearby chair beneath Gabriel's ass, and dove in.

Gabriel shrieked, bound arms flailing, but he was like a beetle on its back as Arthur sucked, with zero ceremony, at his ass. It aroused him as much as it jarred him. He shouted, he swore, he kicked at Arthur's head, but within twenty seconds he was moaning and sobbing in desire, pleading for things he didn't know how to name.

Arthur built him to a fever pitch, not touching his cock, taking him nowhere near orgasm and yet arousing him to a height so insane Gabriel was begging him with a desperation beyond shame. He promised to blow Arthur, promised to eat *his* ass, promised to do whatever dirty thing he said, promised to do whatever he wanted if only he'd touch his cock, if only he'd fuck him, if only he'd let him come.

Finally, when Gabriel was so wrecked he was shaking, Arthur lifted his head. "So you'll do anything? Anything at all?"

Gabriel nodded vigorously, tears of exhaustion running down his cheeks. Somehow they'd stopped playing Two Words, but he wasn't going to point this out. All he wanted to do was be able to come.

Arthur's gaze focused. "All right. Close your eyes."

Gabriel did.

Arthur slid two fingers into Gabriel and sucked lightly over the tip of his cock. "Pretend it's him."

The words jolted Gabriel, and if he hadn't been so far under, they would have gutted him. *Yellow, say yellow,* a voice whispered in the back of his mind, but Arthur's mouth was on him, and he felt drugged, confused. Slightly betrayed, and also…sad. Because he couldn't help but do what Arthur said. He saw Dale in his mind's eye. Dale leaning over him, Dale pushing his thighs open, Dale—

"*Stop,*" he cried, his heart breaking.

Arthur released Gabriel's cock and kissed his way to his mouth. "It's all right. Listen to me. It's all right. I know, and *it's all right.*"

Gabriel was sobbing now. He clutched at Arthur, wrapping his legs around him until the pillow popped from under his ass and Arthur could pull him to the edge of the table and hold him tight. "I'm trying not to feel it." Gabriel buried his face in Arthur's neck. "I keep trying and I can't make it go away. I don't understand what happened. We didn't even d-do anything."

"Shh." Arthur wrapped a beefy arm around Gabriel as he kissed a tense divot of his neck. "It's all right. It's going to be okay. Trust me, baby."

"I love you so much. I can't lose you." Gabriel dug his fingers into Arthur's back. "I *won't* lose you."

Arthur tipped up Gabriel's chin. "You aren't going to lose me. This is because you're attracted to him, right? More than just because he's handsome. You're drawn to him. You're thinking, if you and I weren't together, you'd hope he'd ask you out."

Snakes of terror tightened in Gabriel's gut. He looked away.

Arthur kept his chin captive, compelling Gabriel to meet his gaze. "Hey. There's nothing to be ashamed of. All right?"

There was so much to be ashamed of. Gabriel forced himself to speak. "I wouldn't do anything, Arthur. You know that, right? It doesn't matter if I feel that way. I wouldn't ever do anything about it."

"But what if I said I wanted you to do something?"

Gabriel blinked at Arthur, trying to sort out the joke. Except it seemed somehow he was serious.

Arthur wrapped Gabriel's legs tighter around him and took Gabriel's whole face in his hands. "I love you more than I love anyone or anything in the world. You know that. But I don't love you like a thing I want to keep. I want to cheer you on. Help you soar. Keep you safe, yes, but help you grow too. One of the things I love about you is that you accept me for who I am, even though how I express myself in life and in sex is outside the lines of the way the rest of the world thinks is acceptable. I said let's bring in a fuck buddy, and you were all for it, so long as we were safe. You've not blinked when I go to BDSM events, knowing I'll do scenes with people."

"But those haven't involved sex," Gabriel pointed out. "Nudity sometimes, but not sex."

"You know damn well a strong scene can be ten times more intimate than fucking. But you don't mind.

Because you trust me. You trust us." He brushed his thumbs across Gabriel's cheekbones. "I'm telling you, if you're discovering your heart is complex enough it wants to fall in love with two people at once, I will not be the asshole who turns you away for wanting to be who you are."

Gabriel had stopped breathing at *fall in love with two people at once*, and by the time Arthur had finished talking, tears were rolling down Gabriel's face. "Arthur, I don't love him. I love *you*. It's just…silliness. If I leave it alone, it'll go away—"

Arthur's fingers threaded in Gabriel's hair, not hurting him, but holding tight. "I don't want you to wish any part of yourself away. You're too beautiful for that to happen." He had tears in his eyes too as he added, "And don't you *ever* try to do something like that for me."

Part of Gabriel screamed silently while another drifted quietly into the room. "But what are you saying? Are you telling me to date him instead? I told you, I don't want—"

"No, you beautiful idiot. Marry me *and* date him."

Gabriel traced Arthur's collarbone with a trembling finger. He made it sound so simple. "I never thought of myself as polyamorous."

"Baby, you barely thought of yourself as amorous full stop until me."

Gabriel felt dizzy. And terrified. Like he was at the seventh grade dance and two boys had agreed to take turns dancing with him before asking Gabriel to have incredibly hot sex with the pair of them in the parking lot. "I don't know the rules, though."

"I already told you. The rules are whatever we make them. What you've told me is your priority is marrying me and keeping our relationship healthy and safe while exploring this new one with Dale. Which is okay by me." He sucked on Gabriel's chin and trailed kisses along his jaw. "I want you to have this. I want to help you navigate this, if it makes you happy, if it makes you feel more whole."

Gabriel swallowed hard, as the last bit of awful surfaced. "I think it's too late. I think I hurt him."

"I think you may have too. But this happens sometimes, on the road to a relationship. So let's see what we can do to fix this pothole. Lucky for you, you're marrying a repairman."

Gabriel wrapped his arms around him, clutching him tight. "I love you so much, Arthur. So much."

"Love you too, baby." Arthur grabbed Gabriel's hips, tipped them up, and slid his thumbs to Gabriel's still-slick hole. "Gonna finish fucking you now."

He did, slow and sweet, and this time Gabriel didn't have any trouble accessing his feelings. It was only Arthur in Gabriel's head, but he knew the road ahead of them had something more, or at least the potential for it. He knew that whatever happened, Arthur would be with him. Arthur would be there, filling all the spaces, opening all the doors and windows, showing him the hollows and rooms he'd done his best to ignore.

Chapter Six

DALE FLICKED THE button on his radio impatiently, trying to find a station giving him weather, but all he got were rehashes of the same six country songs, either dirges about love doing the singer wrong or insanity about tractors or other rural vehicles. Meanwhile the sleet had turned to slush and was now full-blown snow. And he was still forty miles from Logan.

He hadn't wanted to come back at all, and he *certainly* hadn't wanted to come in time to get blindsided by a freak late-February snowstorm. But the Logan development had gone from sluggish to standstill, and none of his surrogates could get anywhere with any of the council members. Apparently the president of the library board had decided she was uncomfortable working with anyone but Dale. Dale would have happily pulled out of the project entirely, but his investors had put in enough money they'd have wanted to know why. And he certainly couldn't tell them. So here he was, hauling ass north to pat a little old lady on the head.

It was icing on the cake that the library president happened to be Arthur's mother.

There was another reason he'd taken off for Logan as well, that he'd packed up and gone with almost zero notice to anyone other than a note to the CEO of the parent corporation and his assistant and a quick check with Marcus that it was all right to use his guestroom for a few days to sort out the project. Because things with Ronny hadn't simply gotten out of hand. They had become so toxic Dale wasn't able to function.

He'd sold his condo, moved into a temporary lease on the other side of downtown, shopped at a new grocery store, and rarely left his office, but Ronny still managed to unnerve him at every turn. Dale had tried to end it. He'd stopped answering Ronny's texts, and when Ronny kept after him, he blocked his number. When Ronny got a burner and called from there, Dale got a new number and told his team he was having trouble with spammers. But of course Ronny got that number too, because all he had to do was tell someone at work he needed to update Dale about a project, and it began again. So Dale kept blocking, growing accustomed to his phone becoming a torture device.

When that didn't work, Ronny began haunting his office, stopping by and lingering around the front desk, bringing donuts for the team, chatting with them over coffee and giving Dale a distracted wave when he'd quick bolt through to make sure he wasn't the last one in the office alone with Ronny. No one else suspected. No one else knew. Ronny did, of course, and so did Dale. It had become almost all Dale could think about. There was something about the way Ronny regarded him, the glances he couldn't help taking as he disappeared around the corner. Those last looks reminded Dale no, he wasn't crazy. Every instinct he had told him Ronny had another shoe he meant to drop, and Dale lived in fear of discovering what it was. "I'm the cat, and you're my mouse," Ronny had often said when they played. It had been fun, once upon a time.

Ronny was still playing. But Dale wasn't having any fun at all.

This whole insanity with Ronny had affected Dale's ability to work, which meant he hadn't taken on new clients and was another reason he had to deal with Logan, as it was currently his only active project. When Dale started working remotely from home, Ronny got his new address from his assistant and would stop by his condo. Dale would hide in his bathroom, the door locked, but he could still hear Ronny's *tap, tap, tap.* "Don't be petulant, you ridiculous boy. This will never get better until we talk it through. Stop behaving like a child. I only want to talk. I still have your present, you know."

Dale refused to speak to him, to give Ronny so much as an inch back into his life.

When Logan had insisted he come back, Dale didn't want to go, but he also needed an escape, and between the two evils, Ronny or Logan, facing the misery of the town that had broken his heart seemed so much less awful than the man who was trying to crack his mind like an egg.

Dale talked himself into returning to Logan by rationalizing it. He could be in and out in a few days. A week at most. Marcus had assured him the spare room was his as long as he wanted it, and he'd be rigid about staying at the house and going to the city council meetings only. People would want to socialize, but he'd warn them his time was limited and he'd have to focus on business. He'd have to count on Arthur and Gabriel not wanting to see him keeping them away.

Gabriel. He gripped the wheel tighter. He'd promised himself he wasn't going to think about him.

Of course, he promised himself that every day, and he failed all the time, so why would driving in a blizzard on the way to the town where the guy lived be any different? Gabriel was clearly going to be an ache he nursed for a long time. Going to the scene of the crime wasn't going to make it any better.

As the snow got worse, he consoled himself with some black humor, that perhaps he wouldn't live to make it worse, perhaps he'd die in a ditch. God, but this would solve so many of his problems. If it wasn't such a final solution, he'd consider it.

He must have sent too much of that energy into the universe, though, because as soon as he turned onto the country road leading into Logan, careening off the road was exactly where he went. He hit a slick spot of snow, struck a drift, and the next thing he knew, his car was nose-deep in snow, ass in the air. It was a shallow ditch, and he didn't die, but his car wasn't going anywhere. Neither was he. He had no idea where he was, the roads were near whiteout conditions, and he was done.

He put in a call to emergency services, describing his last-known location as best he could, put on his hazards, and burrowed into his coat, settling in to wait, wishing he'd thought to bring winter gear. All he had was a thin jacket, which had been fine for the forty-degree weather in Minneapolis. He didn't even have a pair of gloves on him. He hoped the tow truck driver had a spare.

It wasn't a tow truck that came for him, though, and his rescue didn't come by the road. An erratic pair of lights zipped through the woods on the other side of the road, until he saw a pair of snowmobiles heading in his direction. He climbed out of the car and stumbled up the side of the bank to greet them, shielding his eyes from the sideways snow.

"Are you the rescue?" he shouted into the wind. "I called emergency services about fifteen minutes ago."

"Yeah, well, you're not exactly good with directions, now are you? Course, you ain't nowhere near as bad as Frankie."

Dread settled into Dale's stomach. "Arthur?"

Arthur pushed up his goggles and waggled his eyebrows. "And Paul. Logan Repair and, tonight, rescuers of underdressed city slickers in distress." He clucked his tongue as he looked Dale up and down. "Honey, I hope to shout your mama would never let you leave the house in a blizzard dressed like that."

This wasn't happening. This *wasn't happening.* "It's almost March."

"It's Minnesota." Arthur jerked his chin at the car. "You got anything you need in there?"

"My case in the trunk." He trudged toward the bank.

Arthur caught his arm, holding him fast. "Leave it. Paul, you fetch his bag, okay? You, bucko, are gonna climb on behind me and do your best not to turn into a popsicle on the way into town. I'm trying to remember if I have a spare hat in my saddlebag."

Dale would have protested, but Paul was already halfway to Dale's car, and besides, he was freezing, his legs stiff and aching. There wasn't much for him to do but follow Arthur to the snowmobile, where thankfully he did indeed produce a spare hat and a thin pair of gloves. He also unzipped his coveralls, peeled off a sweatshirt, and handed it to Dale. Dale took it wordlessly, in no position to refuse warmth.

It had been twenty years since Dale had ridden a snowmobile, and then as now, he'd sat behind a man. He'd been a boy then, and the man was his uncle, but it had been a glorious afternoon of speed and wind and cold in his face and turkey hunting. This experience was less appealing by a long shot. He was freezing, humiliated, furious, and thrown off his already fragile game by the loss of his car and the indignity of being hauled into town literally clinging to the man who was such a wonderful part of sending him out of it in the first place. Worst of all, Arthur was practically a furnace, smelling delicious and pulsing heat Dale both hated and could not turn away from. He was eager for this ride to be over. He intended to leap off this infernal machine, run up the steps to Marcus's house, and get the fuck away from this man before he waggled his goddamned eyebrows again.

He should have seen it coming, but he was so cold and tired, he didn't. Arthur didn't take him to Marcus's house. He took him to the repair shop. *Arthur's* repair shop.

Dale went inside because he couldn't stay in the cold another second, but as soon as Arthur came in and closed the door, Dale rounded on him. "Why the hell did you bring me here?"

Arthur wasn't waggling his eyebrows, and he wasn't smiling. Paul, Dale noticed, was also not following him into the shop. "Dale, you and I need to have a little chat."

Oh no. Dale shook a finger at him. "No. I'm not doing this. I'm cold, I'm tired, and I'm—"

He cut himself off as Arthur stalked toward him, backing him up until his legs hit a chair. Arthur put heavy hands on his shoulders and pushed him into it.

Grabbing the chair with Dale in it, he dragged him in front of a space heater. He flicked the heater on, then reached for a blanket, which he draped around Dale's shoulders. Afterward he perched on the edge of a workbench across from Dale and folded his arms.

"Like I said. We need to chat." He smiled, and it was a smile with a terrifying edge. "How ya been? Sleeping okay?"

Dale pulled the blanket tighter around his shoulders. "No."

"Glad to hear it."

Dale's nostrils flared. "Look, Arthur, I *did what you asked*. I went home. I left. I don't know why you're angry with me."

"I'm pissed at you because you fucking refuse to come up here or answer Marcus's phone calls, which means you sure as fuck won't answer mine, so how the hell am I supposed to fix this if I can't talk to you? I guess I should just be glad somebody upstairs loves me enough to deliver you to me in a snowstorm. I suppose this means I have to go to church Sunday, goddamn it."

God, Dale was so tired. "There's nothing to fix, all right? Logan will get its development. I came up here to straighten out whatever the hell the problem is. Then I'm leaving. Everyone gets what they want."

"No, that's not what everyone wants. There's one person in particular who's been increasingly miserable ever since Christmas, and I take it really fucking personally. If you say you don't want any part of this anymore, fine, it's your business. But you woke this tiger, buddy, so you're gonna help me figure out how to teach it how to…" Arthur waved his hand vaguely as his metaphor ran away from him, "…how to tiger."

Dale had not had enough sleep or possibly done enough acid to keep up with this conversation. "What in the hell are you talking about?"

Arthur held up his hands, glancing about the shop as if addressing an invisible audience with his exasperation. "What am I talking about? *Who* am I talking about, you mean? Who the fuck do you think I'm talking about? Gabriel, you dumb shit. Gabriel is miserable, Gabriel is a mess, Gabriel isn't over you, and you are going to help me fix him."

The world went quiet and soft and slightly blurry, until Arthur shook his shoulders.

"Dammit, Dale, do you understand what I'm telling you?"

Dale glanced warily around the room. "Did I…am I still in the ditch? Am I hallucinating? Is this what happens when you get hypothermia?"

Arthur laughed and bussed his forehead. "You dumb shit. Jesus, no. You're in my shop, and I'm telling you Gabriel has feelings for you and needs to see you. I want him to see you. Now it's your turn to tell me how you feel about that."

Dale stared at him for several seconds, then said, "A dream? I fell asleep in the car?"

"If you want, I can slap you, and you can decide if that happens in dreams." When Dale's tired flinch betrayed his interest, Arthur laughed. "For fuck's sake. Can you answer the goddamned question?"

Dale was so lost. "What was the question?"

"Do you still have feelings for Gabriel?"

Oh. That was one hell of a question. The one he'd been trying so hard to keep nailed shut inside a box. But he'd done a piss-poor job of keeping it sealed away, and the man in front of him had a wall full of tools behind him. "Yes."

Arthur smiled. "Good. That means you'll be open to talking to him."

Dale ran a hand through his hair. "I…I guess, but I still don't know. I mean, he seemed pretty against it, and he's right, how would we ever—?"

"Tonight. You're going to talk to him tonight."

Dale nearly knocked over the space heater in his scramble to get away from Arthur. "No! Jesus—*no!* I'm exhausted, I'm completely floored by what you told me, and—"

"Best time, the way I see it. If I give you until to-morrow, you'll have yourself all boxed up. Can't have that."

Arthur grabbed Dale's wrist, and Dale resisted him, holding on to the support pole beside him to keep himself in place. "Why are you doing this? Are you guys not together anymore?"

"Quite the contrary. We've set a wedding date

now."

"Then I don't understand—"

Arthur whirled on him, and Dale froze.

"Sure you do. You're poly. And so is Gabriel."

"And what are you?"

"Open-minded." Arthur winked and pried Dale's hand loose from the pole. "Come on, Prince Charming. There's a nervous librarian who needs rescuing."

GABRIEL DIDN'T MIND being in the library after closing. In fact, he rather liked it most of the time. He appreciated the chance to be in the quiet, to collect his thoughts from the day, to put to rights the fussy this and thats no one else ever paid attention to but he always noticed. Tonight, however, he didn't care to be there. He wanted to be at home with Arthur, but he couldn't until the boys came back from answering the emergency assistance call. What Gabriel should have done was go to Frankie and Marcus's house, or to the care center to wait with Kyle—anywhere but remain lingering here thinking about how tomorrow, Dale would be back.

Technically he would be back tonight, though odds were good he'd stopped somewhere because of the storm. His return had been Arthur's doing, though only Gabriel and Paul knew why he'd orchestrated it. Arthur had enlisted his mother in the scheme, but she didn't know the real reason they'd been so keen to draw Dale back to Logan. Gabriel felt guilty for that, for letting Arthur bring Dale back at all. But he'd rationalized it, saying at least he could apologize in person. He owed Dale that much. Perhaps Arthur was right, perhaps it would help them both move on. It still seemed like a great deal of manipulation to put the man through, but Gabriel was too tired to fight anyone anymore. He wanted this to be over.

Except he feared, deep in his heart, there was no over for this.

When the front door to the library rattled and heavy pounding sounded, Gabriel dropped the papers he'd been idly sorting on his desk and hurried to let Arthur in, relieved to finally be going home. He pushed the door open wide. "I was starting to get worried—"

It was Arthur standing beneath the snow-coated light, yes, bundled in his familiar coveralls and winter gear, but someone else was with him, and it wasn't Paul. Even with the snow and ice packing his beard, wearing Arthur's too-small hoodie underneath his not-nearly-warm-enough jacket, there was no mistaking the man standing beside Arthur as anyone but Dale Davidson.

Arthur pushed past Gabriel, leading Dale inside, stomping his boots on the mud mat inside the door as he shook the snow from his coveralls and pulled down his hood. "God, but it's a bitch out there. Damn shit's blowing sideways, and it's done being slushy. Gonna drift like all fuck, all night long. We're gonna take the

Ski-Doo home, baby, and leave your car here. I'll bring your emergency coveralls over from the shop on my way back. Text me when you're ready, but probably we need to be heading home inside of the next hour at the latest."

Gabriel recovered from his shock enough to panic as Arthur put his hood up. "Wait—you're leaving?" He cut a glance at Dale, who had his back to them both as he meticulously removed his snow-coated outer clothes.

Arthur tugged Gabriel low enough to place a snowy-mustache kiss on his lips. "It's going to be all right. Trust me. Call me if you need me, but first...talk to him."

He kissed Gabriel a second time, and then he pulled his hood low over his face, raised his balaclava over his nose, and disappeared out the door, leaving Gabriel alone with Dale.

Gabriel hugged his arms to himself as he watched Dale hang a scarf on a peg. The scarf was also Arthur's, and Gabriel realized outside the too-thin coat, all of Dale's gear had been commandeered from the shop. Dale's jeans were white with snow, and he looked as if he were some kind of dessert confection dusted in powdered sugar, though in the heat of the library foyer the snow had begun to form into clumps and fall off. The denim was soaked, and Dale shivered.

Awkwardness was forgotten as Gabriel went into nurturing mode. He strode to the supply closet, found one of the blankets he'd seen stored there, and brought it to Dale. "Take this and go into my office. You have to get out of those wet jeans or you'll catch your death. Wrap up in this while I go to my car and fetch the pair of sweatpants I have in my emergency kit. Did you not have a change of clothes with you?"

Dale accepted the blanket with shaking hands. He appeared utterly exhausted. "I do, somewhere. Paul had my case. I'm not even sure where it went."

Gabriel would have words later with Arthur for not taking proper care of Dale, but for now he had to climb into his boots and go get his duffel. He shooed Dale gently toward his office. "Go on. It's the room right behind the circulation desk. The light switch is beside the door. I'll drape your jeans over the radiator by the window, and they'll be dry before you know it." He buttoned his coat and tugged the hood over his head, checking his pocket for his keys. "I'll be right back."

It was indeed a nightmare outside, and he was grateful he wouldn't be driving home in the mess. He grabbed his bag from the trunk and hurried inside, hanging his coat up and stomping his boots on the mat before sliding into his shoes once more and hustling across the main entrance of the library to his office.

He rounded the corner just in time to see Dale facing away from him, bent over and stepping out of his jeans.

Gabriel froze, arrested by the sight. He'd known

Dale was beautiful, suspected he had a fine body beneath his clothes, but it was something else entirely to see the evidence with his own eyes. Arthur had muscles, yes, but as he liked to brag, they were real muscles coming from hard work and honest labor. Dale might do labor here and there, but the shapely, defined thighs and calves on display for Gabriel's viewing were muscles made by a gym membership and nothing else. Bright blue briefs with a white elastic band and high-cut sides showcased a taut, pert ass Gabriel had admired through the man's trousers many times, and yet seeing it now in nearly full glory made Gabriel want to fall on his knees in gratitude.

He was trying to decide if he should clear his throat or beat a quiet retreat when Dale hooked his thumbs into the waistband of his briefs and sent them to the floor as well.

Gabriel stared at the perfect, browned globes of Dale's ass and tried to remember to breathe.

Once Dale swathed himself in the blanket, wrapping it around his waist like a giant towel, Gabriel was able to move, though he stumbled the first few steps as he attempted to shake the erotic image of Dale disrobing from his mind. He knocked on the door before he entered, a ridiculous gesture as it was open and he'd just watched the man give an accidental strip show.

He forced a smile and held up the sweatpants before setting them on his desk. "Here you are. Go ahead and put them on while I take these." He picked up the jeans and the briefs, hands shaking as he remembered the ass they had so recently cradled.

This time as he departed and returned he took his time, giving Dale plenty of opportunity to put his clothes on. When he knocked on the door, Dale was dressed and sitting in the wingback chair in the corner, draped in the blanket and looking ready to fall asleep.

He perked up when Gabriel entered, sitting up and letting the blanket pool in his lap, which had the side effect of showing how much thinner Gabriel was than him, meaning especially without the bright blue briefs, the sweatpants strained across Dale's crotch and outlined his package. Gabriel deliberately swung his gaze to Dale's face and fixed it there.

He pulled his desk chair around and sat in it, placing his hands together on his lap. "I'm sorry if Arthur brought you here against your will. I can't imagine you wanted to come here."

"Oh—no, I wanted to come."

Gabriel beat down the hope in his chest. "I'm glad you're here, because there's something I've been wanting to say to you, and it's the sort of thing that needs to be said in person."

Dale leaned forward, some of his sleepiness sloughing away. "Yes? What did you want to tell me?"

Gabriel focused on his fingers, which were worrying each other in his lap. "I wanted to apologize for my behavior the last time we…the night you came to our house for dinner. I had something of a panic attack, which I don't know I could have done much to stop, to be perfectly honest, but I think either I hurt your feelings or offended you, and at the very least I was rude. I'm sorry my deficiency affected you in either a large or small way. I hope it wasn't the reason you decided not to be involved in Logan's development any longer, and if it was, I hope there's something I can do to either make up for it or assure you I'll stay out of your way so others don't have to suffer because of me. I know Arthur used his mother to get you up here so I could say this to you, but what they told you is true. This project isn't the same without you at the heart of it." His throat became thick, but he pressed on. "I don't want to be the reason Logan doesn't become Christmas Town."

Dale shifted slightly in his chair. "I'm not going to lie. Your reaction did hurt me. But your fiancé has been hard at work tonight, explaining some things."

Gabriel laughed, but it was mostly a sad sound, and he still couldn't look at Dale. "Arthur is obsessed with fixing this."

Dale reached across the space between them to touch Gabriel's knee. "He said what was meant to be a fun night between the three of us basically became you discovering you're polyamorous. Is that true?"

Gabriel drew a slow, ragged breath, let it out. Then nodded. "I didn't know what the word was until...all this." He wrapped his arms across his body, pulling his fist in tight to his heart. "I tried to shove it away. It worked about as well as declaring I wasn't gay when I was a teenager." He pursed his lips and shut his eyes. "I can't believe I have to go through this again. I keep telling myself I would have figured this out before now. That I'm making this up, trying to have cake and eat it too. I have literally done everything to make this go away—" His voice broke, and he stopped.

"But it won't," Dale finished for him.

This time Gabriel's laugh was nothing but black and full of bitterness, and laced with tears. He tipped his face to the ceiling. "I'm sorry, that was probably offensive, saying I've done all I could not to think of you."

"Well, since you're saying it didn't work, in a back-handed way it's actually pretty hot."

Dale slid off the chair and crept over to Gabriel on his knees. The blanket fell away, and the movements combined with the too-small pants highlighted every muscle the man had and the one not-insubstantial organ hanging free between his legs.

Gabriel choked on a smile and covered his eyes, though not so well that he couldn't watch each shift and bulge as Dale sidled beside him. "Those pants are obscene on you."

"I can take them off." Dale put a hand on Gabriel's thigh, inches away from his erection, which didn't seem to care much about his mental anguish or philosophical indecision. "You hurt me, yes. But I understand why, and the truth is, I still care about you. I want to be here one way or the other for you as you figure this out. I can be your friend who knows what you're going through, who can help you process this because I've been on this road too, and I know how difficult it is to go down it without someone to guide you." His hand slid ever so slightly higher on Gabriel's thigh. "Or, if you'll have me, I can be your first lover outside of Arthur."

Gabriel shut his eyes, his whole world dissolving to the pressure of Dale's hand on his thigh. Once again he had a sense of that seam of the universe presenting itself before him. A thin crack in his reality. He had the desire to paper over it, to fill the tear, but he knew now there was no repairing the break. The question was, did he do his best to maintain the damage it caused, or did he press upon its edges and let it lead him into a new world? Or was it simply a fantasy, and if he tried to widen it, it would bring down everything he knew?

Except he'd already tried standing still, tried ignoring it. Not going through this new door might mean drowning, no matter what he did.

He put his hand on Dale's, threading their fingers together. "I'm scared. That isn't going to change any time soon. But I'm also scared of what happens if I don't let myself pursue this part of myself." He brushed his thumb along the side of Dale's hand. "Arthur will be the first one to tell you I'm not always the easiest person to be in a relationship with. I'm fussy and neurotic. I panic. I contradict myself. I don't know if you really want to date me."

"I do." Dale pulled Gabriel to the floor so he knelt too, drawing their bodies together. Gabriel could feel his erection alongside his own. "Can you say the words, please?"

Gabriel nuzzled Dale's nose and took a deep breath with his eyes closed. "Y-yes. I would like to date you."

"There. That wasn't so hard, was it?" When Gabriel whimpered and gripped Dale's shoulders, he laughed. "All right, I know. It was terrifying. But it's done now." He ran his hands along Gabriel's back and over his ass. "Congratulations. You have a boyfriend, Gabriel Higgins. In addition to your fiancé."

Gabriel forced himself to keep breathing, in and out, one breath after another.

Dale rubbed his beard along Gabriel's cheek. "I'll come by tomorrow night. We'll set up some relationship rules, the three of us. Everyone can ask their questions and raise concerns. That's what Arthur thinks should happen, and I agree. Is this all right with you?" Gabriel nodded, and Dale kneaded his ass harder. "Excellent. Now...do you think, boyfriend, we could seal this arrangement with a little kiss?"

Gabriel clung to him, so dizzy he felt as if he were spiraling away through the library roof into the snowy sky. "Yes."

Dale kissed the spot beneath his ear, his tongue stealing out for a tiny lick. "Do you think you could handle it if the kiss got a bit...dirty?"

The seam of Gabriel's universe gleamed before him. He pressed his fingertip on it, feeling the pulse of the new world beneath his thumb. "Yes."

Cradling Gabriel's face, Dale dragged his lips along Gabriel's jaw and captured his mouth in a kiss.

This isn't Arthur's kiss. Gabriel was critically aware of this as Dale delved inside. There was a beard and a mustache, and it was a man kissing him, but for the first few seconds all Gabriel could think of was that this was not the man he had said he would marry.

Then he thought of how *that* man had, in fact, brought him *this* man, knowing this kiss was going to happen, had in fact orchestrated every part of it. Arthur had delivered Dale to him like a gift, or rather like the world's most complicated antidepressant, because Arthur had seen Gabriel hurting and had done all he could to make it stop. Suddenly Gabriel was not simply kissing another man. He was kissing another man because the man he loved had told him he believed it was the best thing for him to do right now.

Gabriel pressed the bright crack in his universe…and pushed through to the other side.

He wrapped his arms around Dale and surrendered to the kiss, leaving behind his fears and insecurities about what they were doing, about what it meant and whether or not it was the right thing to do. Gabriel kissed Dale because his heart hurt so much when he kept it from reaching for this man, because unleashing himself to Dale was the first time in months he didn't feel as if he had stone pits inside his stomach. When Dale pulled him in tighter, encouraging him to rub against his now-iron-thick erection, Gabriel did so with abandon, lost to the dome of joy and safety he'd found in this space, in this moment, with this man.

Dale broke the kiss abruptly, clutching Gabriel's shoulders and pressing their foreheads together. "We have to stop, or I'm going to push you to the floor and take you here and now." Before Gabriel could say he wouldn't mind that, Dale nipped his upper lip. "We need to have that meeting with Arthur. After everything the man did to set this up, I'm going to respect him by waiting until we've set some ground rules before I send you back to him smelling like my spunk."

Gabriel clung to Dale as he came down from his high. "I need to text him. We have to get home before this storm gets so bad we're sleeping in the shop."

Dale kissed Gabriel's temple and tugged at one of Gabriel's curls. "I can't wait for tomorrow night. Do you think there's a chance we can christen this relationship with that three-way we should have had at Christmas?"

The world beyond the fissure kept growing and growing, getting brighter and brighter. Gabriel hoped it could stay that way. "Sounds good to me."

Chapter Seven

THE STORM SUBSIDED in the middle of the night, and though it would take road crews most of the morning to get things cleared up, the day dawned bright and sunny, as if there hadn't been forty mile an hour winds and crazy snowfall only a few hours earlier. It was late by the time Arthur finally came home, after helping Paul rescue another stranded motorist once they delivered Dale to Marcus and Frankie's house. Arthur and Gabriel barely had time to process everything that had happened, and they mostly made grateful love to one another before falling into bed.

Despite the hard work and scant hours of sleep, Arthur woke early, brimming with energy and purpose. Gabriel, not so much. It took three tries to rouse him from the cocoon of their bed, and it didn't take Arthur long to see that, as he had suspected would happen, some of his fiancé's shadows had returned in the light of day. Arthur didn't let it worry him too much. He simply herded Gabriel through his morning routine and drove them both into work, humming and reaching across the bench of the truck to take Gabriel's hand on occasion.

"Remember. I'm taking care of things," Arthur reminded him.

"It doesn't seem very adult. I'm the one having the polyamorous relationship, and I can't manage it without help."

"There's no litmus test here. You get to run your relationship your own way. The only people who get a say in this are you, me, and Dale."

"I'm afraid I'm going to make a mess of it again. I'm afraid I'll panic and I'll upset him, and this time you won't be able to lure him back."

"That's why I'm going to go talk to him today. Before the three of us meet tonight." The question Arthur kept meaning to ask about Dale hung in the air, and he decided no, it was too much for Gabriel right now. So he tabled it, drove his librarian to the library, and kissed him goodbye. He didn't go to work, though. He went to Maple Avenue, where Marcus and Frankie lived.

Frankie had already left for the salon, but Marcus was still home when Arthur arrived, and he smiled in surprise as he greeted him at the door. "Hey there. Didn't expect to see you by this morning. What can I do for you? I was about to head in to work, but I can call in and hold my nine o'clock."

Arthur kept his hands in his pockets and did his best to play it cool. He could bluff a lot of people, but his best friend since second grade was a tough sell. "Here to see your houseguest, as a matter of fact."

Marcus blinked. "That so? Is there a meeting I didn't get told about?"

"Nope. Just gonna kidnap him for the day." He laid out a plan as quickly as he could. "With the blizzard, the council won't be meeting this morning like they'd originally planned, so he's got some free time. Thought he was probably overdue for some ice fishing."

Marcus gave him a knowing grin. "Paul know about this plan?"

Paul would be getting a call in about five minutes. "I'll owe him a favor."

Laughing, Marcus clapped him on the back. "Dale's upstairs, fussing on his laptop as usual. You'd think he was a computer hacker, the way he hunches over that thing." He grabbed his coat from a peg by the door. "Pull the door shut when you leave."

Dale was indeed upstairs in one of the guest bedrooms, so absorbed in his work that he didn't glance up until Arthur cleared his throat twice. He looked up as if from a daze, not unlike the ones Gabriel went into when he was working on a story-hour plan, and he even had on a pair of reading glasses Arthur had never seen him wearing before. At first Dale blinked at Arthur in confusion, then straightened and stood awkwardly. "Arthur. I didn't—Hi."

Arthur jerked his head at the hallway. "Come on. We're going ice fishing, you and me."

"Okay." Dale ran his hands over his hair, gaze darting from his closet to his bed, then to Arthur. "Am…am I in trouble?"

Arthur noted the color draining from the man's face and realized what he'd been thinking. He laughed, though it wasn't funny at all. "Jesus, no. I really meant we were going ice fishing. Not that I was going to murder you and drop you in the lake."

Dale blushed and glanced away, rueful. "Sorry. It's just, I was reading *American Gods* last week, and—"

"*Hush.*" Arthur held up a hand and glared at him. "Damn it, Gabriel's still reading that to me. We weren't in a rush because we had plenty of time before it came out on STARZ, but I don't need anybody spoiling anything, thank you." He nodded at the closet. "You got an outfit better suited for sitting out in the middle of a frozen lake, get into it. I'm gonna go raid Frankie's fridge and make a phone call."

He left Dale to get changed, and on the way down the stairs he dialed Paul. His business partner picked up on the second ring. "Where the hell are you? I've been waiting for you to get in here so we can go out on a call."

Arthur winced. "About that. Something has come up."

"What? Goddamn it, Arthur—"

"Paul, I need to work on this thing with Gabriel and Dale right now."

Paul paused. "Wait—so it worked? It's official?

They're a thing?"

"Sort of. It's new. It's fragile. It's weird, and they need me. Gabriel needs me. I need to take this time. I owe you, I know. But I need today. I'll make it up to you, I promise."

When Paul finally spoke again, his voice was soft, gentle as a lamb. "Take the rest of the week. And you don't owe me anything."

Arthur's heart swelled, and his throat got a little thick. "Thank you."

"Give my love to Gabriel, and tell him it will be okay. Same goes for you. If anybody can navigate this, it's you."

Paul hung up, and Arthur leaned on the doorway, allowing himself a moment to wallow in feelings. Then he straightened, pushed his phone into his pocket, and went about looting the kitchen for supplies. He didn't feel bad taking the food, since half the time he and Paul and Marcus went hunting they emptied *his* pantry. So a box full of sandwiches, some bottles of beer, a bag of chips, and a thermos of coffee wasn't going to put anybody out.

Dale came into the kitchen just as the coffeepot finished percolating and Arthur was screwing the thermos top on. He had on older jeans and a beat-up Wisconsin Badgers sweatshirt. Arthur put the thermos in the box beside the rest of the supplies. "You ready to go?"

Dale looked ready to go through the window,

mostly, but he nodded. "Sure. You driving?"

Fuck yes, he was driving. "There's a nice spot a mile north of my cabin, on Big Bear Lake. Got a lean-to, gas heater, camp stools, the works."

"Okay."

Dale followed him to the truck, taking the box and holding it on his lap as Arthur climbed in and started to drive.

"You've been ice fishing before, right? I mean, I assumed. Wisconsin's got lakes."

"Oh, yeah. With my grandpa. And my dad, once."

Arthur glanced at Dale as he drove. "You're pretty far away from your family."

"Actually, I shifted over to a different section of it. My mom's side. Her brother offered me a spot in the family business before it got bought out. I stayed in when most of them moved on to California. Started as an architect. Worked my way into running my own division."

Arthur couldn't decide if he wanted to calm him down yet or not. Part of him liked the guy on edge, nervous. All right, part of him wanted to put the guy on his knees. There, he'd said it. This was what he'd wanted to talk to Gabriel about, doing scenes with Dale, and he could tell it was going to be an issue before the end of the day was done. It couldn't be simple, could it. They couldn't just have a nice three-way and be done with it. They couldn't have an easy arrangement where Gabriel had a hot boyfriend in the city. No, Gabriel wanted Arthur to manage his boyfriend for him, and Gabriel's boyfriend kept looking at Arthur like he wanted managing in a way that wasn't quite what Gabriel had meant. God help him but Arthur wanted it too.

Maybe he was the one who should jump in the icy lake.

He shook off the need and put himself back in control. "They don't have a problem with you being gay, do they?"

Dale shrugged. "Maybe a little?"

"So I imagine you haven't sprung it on them you're poly to boot."

Dale's laugh was bitter. "Are you kidding? I don't tell anybody."

"Not a healthy way to live your life."

"Yeah, well, not a whole lot of other options."

"So are you seeing anyone else right now?"

Dale paused, rubbing his beard. "Not really."

"Sounds like a story I'd enjoy hearing fleshed out."

Dale sighed. "There's a guy. From work. It's…complicated, but it's over now."

"Sounds as if it was a good move. Bad ending?"

"Bad everything. I guess some of it was all right. It wasn't ever dating. All D/s, but mostly mistakes."

Arthur's senses went on alert, but he maintained his calm. "Oh? How do you mean?"

"I knew he was married, and…well, I'm not gonna be shy about it. I have kind of a thing for married guys.

Coupled guys. Always been attracted to people who are already with someone. Don't know why, it's just how I roll. He said he was bi, said she knew about me, that it was all on the level."

Oh, fuck, Arthur saw where this was going. "But it was all horseshit, and she had no clue."

"*All* of it was horseshit. He admitted early on he wasn't bisexual, that it was the kink he was after. Should have been my first clue he was bad news, that he'd begun the relationship under false pretenses. But no, his wife has no idea either. He's a manipulative bastard. And he's mean. Twisted and mean. I don't mind a little humiliation, but he went too far, and..." He shut down. "It's done now. It took me a long time to end it, and I went back to him a few times more than I should have, but I'm finished now. I don't want a fucked-up relationship anymore. I want to make this work with Gabriel."

Arthur shifted the truck into a lower gear. "Hold on. We're heading onto the ice."

The nice thing about the snowy winter was that the ice had frozen solid months ago, and they'd had their ice hut set up since late October, had been driving out to greet it since Thanksgiving. They only had a handful of weeks yet before they had to dismantle or the Department of Natural Resources would fine them for having a structure on the ice, but they could still get out there now, and the ice was holding solid enough that driving wasn't an issue at all, not yet. It had snowed, obviously, since the last time they'd been out, but he could see his tracks, and it wasn't long before they were parked beside the hut, hauling the box of food inside, and setting up two of the camp stools.

"This is a great setup," Dale said, glancing around as Arthur arranged their poles and bait and fiddled with the heater.

"Yeah, it's our retreat, the boys and I. By that, of course, I mean Marcus and Paul and me. Gabriel and Kyle and Frankie aren't so much for the fishing, or the hunting. Which is fine."

"I miss getting out in nature." Dale planted himself on his stool as one who had done this before, baiting his line with skill and ease. "I try to run in the park when I can, but that isn't often, and it's not the same. I like sitting in the quiet, being with friends."

They settled in, set up their gear, and cast their lines. "You have a good group of friends, in the Cities? Or you one of those married to your job?"

"I'm not a hermit, but I don't have a group the way you guys up here do, no." Dale looked out of the lean-to's opening, staring out across the frozen lake. "It's got to be gorgeous out here in the summer."

"Beautiful year-round." Arthur caught the look in Dale's eye and rolled his. "Hell, don't you go developing my fishing hole."

Dale grinned. "All right. But you've got to show me somewhere just as beautiful then. The places the mayor and his buddies kept taking me in December weren't doing it for me. If I'm going to bring people way out here into the sticks and put them in cabins, it's got to be for a view that makes it worth the trip."

"Fair enough." Arthur leaned back and rubbed his beard. This was why they needed this guy spearheading the project. "You want a lake, and some nice timber around it, but some flat area for your cabins and resort?"

"And I want to be able to get them into your Christmas village easily enough." He grimaced. "Something is missing still. I know Gabriel said you brought me up here on a ruse, but I'll admit, going over the files this morning, my team hasn't been giving this the attention they should. I'm going to stay here long enough this time to figure it out."

"You should talk with the guys. Marcus and Frankie, Paul and Kyle, Gabriel. Our gang. We're good at brainstorming this kind of thing."

"I will. But I want to wrestle with it myself first. It's kind of how I operate."

They lapsed into silence for a bit. Arthur got a yellow perch, but it was pretty tiny, so they put it back and took a break to eat their sandwiches. It was at that point Arthur decided it was time to bring up what he'd actually dragged the man out here to discuss.

"So, there's a slight adjustment you need to know about, as far as dating Gabriel."

Dale looked up, immediately nervous. "If he's changed his mind, or if you have—"

Arthur held up his hand. "Slow down, sailor, and let me finish. Like I said before, this is really new to Gabriel, this poly business. What's not new is my boy, he overthinks everything to death. And he has a terrible fear of rejection. But at the same time, I think it's good for him to explore this with you. So we talked, and the compromise we came to is tonight, and maybe these first few weeks, he needs me to be the fulcrum, for lack of a better term. Until he gets used to having his feet wet, you'll check in with me if you want to set up times to meet him, and he'll require some time with me after your dates to process. I suspect this will go away eventually and faster than he's thinking it will right now. But you're also going to need to be ready to call me in if all of a sudden he panics. You okay with that?"

Dale blinked for a moment. This clearly hadn't been what he'd expected. "Yeah. I mean—sure, it's not a problem." And then there it was. He shifted his feet, glanced up with his head still tilted down, his expression cautious, open, inviting. "I mean...I'm not against... You're welcome to..."

Arthur allowed himself a moment, congratulating himself for seeing this coming six miles off. "As far as hearts-and-flowers relationships go, I'm a one-man-at-a-time guy, though I don't mind multiple men in my bed for fun, and I don't have an issue being with a guy who has several romantic relationships at once." He let out a heavy breath. "Now. I wouldn't say no to some nice playtime with you on the regular. *But*," he added quickly when Dale brightened again, "we're not taking this conversation any further without Gabriel. Because what you're going to learn is keeping that man happy is everything to me. I don't care how pretty you might sing for me when I paddle you or how good you might sit for me if I asked. If it's going to upset Gabriel, it's not happening. Understood?"

Dale nodded. "Gabriel is lucky to have someone like you."

"It's exactly the other way around." Arthur picked up his line. "Let's give these fish a few more chances to dance, and then I gotta get back and put some steaks on. And you need to go get yourself prettied up. You have a gentleman to impress."

Smiling, Dale picked up his line as well. "Yes, sir."

THE DAY DRAGGED on longer than any day had ever dragged in Gabriel's life. He was so nervous and eager at the same time, he thought he might explode. But once Arthur came to collect him at five, he calmed down. In the truck on the way home, Arthur held Gabriel's hand. Gabriel clung to it like a lifeline. "Maybe we shouldn't start this. Maybe this is the wrong way to go, beginning with sex."

"Oh, no. With you? You want to get this out of the way first thing. You remember how we started."

Yes, Gabriel did. A fight in his living room because Arthur had barged into his house, and they'd ended up fucking on the couch. With Arthur teasing him into consensual non-con sex. He hadn't known what such a thing was, but Arthur had helped him name the dark, shameful thing he'd always wanted. The same as he was helping him now.

He drew a deep breath and let it out.

Arthur rubbed Gabriel's forearm. "It's going to be fine. I have the steaks marinating, salad tossed, potatoes in the oven. Wine picked out I know you like, though you only get two glasses, one before dinner and one during. You can fuss over the music. I laid some clothes out on the bed I thought might do, and I bought some nice things for your bath. You should take a book in with you, and the first glass of wine."

Gabriel felt so dizzy. "Are we just going to…how do we do this? Eat, do dishes, fuck?"

"You let me drive, baby. Your job is to relax and do what I tell you tonight, and enjoy a nice night with me and this man you're thinking of trying out."

It seemed impossible for everything to be this simple, and yet with Arthur at the helm, this was exactly what happened. He ended up pouring the wine for Gabriel, handing him a book to take to the bathtub, making him sit with both on the closed toilet seat while Arthur drew him a scented bath. He looked ready to usher Gabriel through getting undressed as well, but at this point Gabriel recovered enough to put down the things in his hands and kiss Arthur on the lips. "No. I'm fine. Thank you."

The bath was calming, giving him the quiet space he needed to gather himself. It helped that he could hear Arthur in the other room, fussing with pans, humming to himself as he worked. When Gabriel emerged from the bath, Arthur stuck his head around the corner, raising one eyebrow at him. "You all right? Want me to come help you get dressed?"

"I'll be right there."

"If you change your mind, holler. I'm chopping things. Adding some vegetables to the salad and a few herbs to the potatoes. Dale texted and said he was bringing some bread."

"I'll be okay." Gabriel was damp in his cotton dressing gown, but he lingered to kiss Arthur sweetly. "Thank you again, for everything. I'm sorry you keep having to nurse me through my freakouts."

Arthur winked at him. "That's the part you're not getting. I *like* how you need me to nurse you through your freakouts." He nipped Gabriel's bottom lip and smacked his hip lightly. "Go on. Get dressed already."

Arthur had indeed laid out several outfits on their bed, and none of them were ones Gabriel would have picked. He would have gone with a sweater, but Arthur had selected dressier button-downs, all which went with a light suede jacket and a pair of pale blue jeans. Gabriel felt ridiculous wearing a jacket in his own home for a casual meal with Arthur and another man, but he supposed it *was* a date.

There were shoes at the foot of the bed too, which

also seemed ludicrous, but he put the whole of it on, tucked the options he hadn't selected away, and came downstairs, ready for inspection. Arthur glanced up from the kitchen counter and ran his gaze over him critically.

"Yes, that looks perfect, I think. Do you agree?"

Gabriel brushed self-consciously at the jacket. "I feel overdressed."

"Still willing to trust me?"

Gabriel nodded.

Arthur smiled, pleased. "Then you're dressed, we're ready, and I do believe we can sneak in another chapter of *American Gods* before he gets here."

They sat on the sofa, before the fire Arthur already had banked and crackling, and Arthur put his head in Gabriel's lap and shut his eyes, listening as Gabriel read aloud. It was one of Arthur's greatest pleasures, having Gabriel read to him, and Gabriel enjoyed it as well, because it was a way to share some of his favorite novels with his partner. It came with the benefit of Arthur's constant interjections, and this evening's installment was no exception. They were at chapter eight, in the middle of the part where Shadow was talking to Jacquel about souls, when the sound of tires on snow preceded the flash of headlights across the yard and the slamming of a car door. Gabriel clutched the book tightly in his hand.

Arthur put a hand over the top of his and kissed his cheek. "It's going to be fine. Nothing will happen that you don't want. Remind me you know how to make things slow down."

Gabriel drew a slow breath. "Yellow."

"And if you need things to stop?"

"Red." He turned his hand over and threaded his fingers with Arthur's.

As the knock sounded on the door, Arthur tipped Gabriel's chin up and kissed him slowly, sweetly, but with an ownership and sense of safety that wrapped around Gabriel and brought him home.

Then Arthur rose, catching Gabriel's hand and leading him along as they went together to greet their guest.

Chapter Eight

DALE STOOD OUTSIDE Arthur and Gabriel's door clutching a bottle of wine, a loaf of bread, and an incredibly unsettled stomach.

He couldn't remember the last time he'd been this nervous for a date. He'd never dated a couple before, to start, even though Arthur had made it clear this was about Gabriel and he was only along to supervise. He told himself this was a ridiculous overreaction and he was reading too much into this intense attraction to Gabriel and needed to chill out…and then the door opened. Gabriel smiled shyly at him, and Dale spun dizzily into the stratosphere, his rational arguments abandoned in the snowbank behind him.

"Come on in." Arthur stepped back and extended an arm, welcoming Dale into the cabin. "This looks excellent. Where in the world did you get the bread?"

"I made it, actually. It's whole wheat garlic rosemary." He'd asked Frankie what Gabriel's favorite flavors were and had spent the afternoon fussing with the perfect loaf. He'd abandoned three not-quite-satisfactory attempts at the house. He kissed Gabriel on the cheek, lingering long enough to inhale the scent of the man mingling with the bread.

Gabriel blushed prettily as he took the bread. "I can't wait to eat it. Let me wrap it up to keep it warm."

He hurried to the kitchen, and as he disappeared, Dale glanced at Arthur, who winked and grinned at him before following Gabriel with the wine.

Arthur poured Dale a glass from an already opened bottle. "Excuse the mess in the corner there. We're about to start our first round of renovations in a few weeks, and that's the corner Gabriel's relegated my construction junk to, as he puts it."

Dale eyed the construction junk with interest. "What kind of renovations?"

Arthur pulled a roll of architect plans from a shelf and spread them on the table. "We're adding several bedrooms, expanding the kitchen, extending several rooms on the main floor as well. We want to keep the feel, but we need more space."

Dale set his wine down and ran his fingers over the plans, seeing them with an architect's eye. "Wow. These are some pretty intense renos. Who are you hiring?"

Arthur gave him an incredulous look. "Myself and Paul, obviously. You think I could afford a contractor for this?"

Dale shook his head at the plans. "Yeah, but…all

right, will you at least call me if you get stuck? I can pull a few favors for you. And don't go placing any orders for supplies until you talk to me. I can get you in on my bulk purchase orders. Save you a mint there alone. I don't mind pitching in here and there with some elbow grease, either. I don't usually do the hammering and nailing, but I do know how." He lifted the top page of the plans and studied the second floor, noting the number of bedrooms. "What are you doing with so much house?"

Gabriel answered, chin lifted defiantly. "We're going to adopt children."

Dale didn't have a chance to figure out how he wanted to respond before Arthur patted his shoulder. "I'm going to go put those steaks on." And with that, he disappeared into the kitchen. Which granted wasn't a separate room, just the other side of the counter, but now Dale was alone with Gabriel, who was clutching his wineglass and regarding him warily, waiting to see what Dale thought of his plan to build a huge house and fill it with children.

The thing was, Dale didn't know what he thought of it. He tried to play it loose. "Sounds pretty exciting. Are you talking overseas adoption, surrogate, or something else?"

"Foster care. We want to put an emphasis on older children, since they're harder to place. We'd *like* to make it clear we'd be a welcoming home for LGBT children, but we haven't filled out the paperwork yet."

"Wow." Dale shook his head, rubbing his beard ruefully. "*Wow.* That's pretty amazing."

"We both wanted children, but it isn't so much about raising a baby or even a little child. I work with children every day at the library, and Arthur has a nephew he adores." Gabriel tapped the paper, an intense look on his face as he stared at the plans. "What we want more than anything is to help youth. How that happens isn't important. It's more about passing things on. Sharing our lives, I suppose."

"You don't need to defend the choice. It's an incredible one." Dale bit the inside of his lip as he weighed his next words. "I hope you don't think less of me if it's not a choice I personally want to make."

Gabriel blinked and shifted his attention to Dale. "What? Oh, heavens no. Neither Marcus and Frankie nor Paul and Kyle seem interested in children, and we don't hold it against them. There's a lesbian couple, though, who visits the library from Pine Valley, and they're also about to take the foster parent classes. So it isn't as if we'll be the only queer family in the county." He pushed his glasses higher on his nose. "It's important for children to see different kinds of families. Especially in these remote areas. It's so difficult when you know you're not the same as everyone else. Seeing someone else who doesn't fit society's mold...if *they* find happiness, if a queer child sees that, it can give them the hope they need to make it through."

Dale leaned on the counter behind him, cradling his

wineglass in his hands. "When I was growing up in Deansville, I couldn't wait to get away. I felt like the fucking cuckoo, and it was just a matter of time before they found out my secrets."

"But not everyone is able to leave, or wants to. There should be ways for people to be different and stay."

He was so beautiful and passionate. Dale wanted him to keep talking, keep arguing. "How do you keep them safe? Small towns will always turn on people like us."

"Everywhere will always turn on us. You can drown in a city if you don't know how to navigate it. You can suffocate in a small town or a suburb or a skyscraper. You have to have your community, or it doesn't matter where you are. You're simply dressing up a different version of being alone."

That blow hit home, and this time it was Dale who retreated into his drink, thinking about all the evenings he passed through crowds of people without speaking to anyone, when he barely spoke to his secretary, let alone the few friends who still tried to reach him. *And you wonder why Ronny is able to get you to dance like a puppet on his string.*

Gabriel softened and put down his wine. "I'm sorry, I didn't mean to get carried away."

Dale held up his hand. "No. It was a fair point."

Gabriel gestured to the rest of the room. "Would you care for an official tour?"

"I'd love one."

They started for the living room area, but Arthur called Gabriel into the kitchen for a quick word, leaving Dale to admire the open space alone for a few minutes. Dale lingered at an extensive line of bookshelves on the far side of the fireplace, and this is where Gabriel found him when he returned.

Gabriel approached him with an arch expression on his face as he stroked the spine of a nearby volume. "I heard you nearly spoiled *American Gods* for Arthur this afternoon."

Dale laughed. "I didn't mean to. But I'm jealous that you read aloud to each other. I don't know if anyone's done that to me."

"Well, your parents did when you were little, yes?"

"No, not really."

Gabriel's eyes went wide, and his jaw fell open. "You're joking."

"I'm not. I was a caboose, and everyone worked."

"But someone at daycare read to you, surely? A teacher?"

Dale shrugged. "Maybe. I don't remember it, though."

Gabriel still appeared scandalized, but in a quiet, wounded way, as if he were trying to be polite about how to deal with Dale confessing his family had left him out in the rain every evening while they ate dinner in front of a warm fire. "Do...do you enjoy reading to yourself?"

"Oh, yes. I like nonfiction mostly, though I pepper in fiction too. Nonfiction is my jam. A bit of memoir, some biography—I'd read Chernow's *Hamilton* before Lin-Manuel Miranda made a musical out of it—but mostly I enjoy books about history or aspects of it. One of my favorites is *To Rule the Waves* by Arthur Herman. Have you read it?"

Gabriel leaned against the bookshelf. "No, I haven't heard of it. What's it about?"

"It's basically the history of the world through the lens of the British Navy. *So good.* Changes how you look at everything. You won't believe how it alters the Boston Tea Party. And World War II? He details so many decisions and factors that add perspective. I also went on this kick where I read every book I could about the East India Company, sometimes reading old nonfiction books about it, written in other decades. I've done that for other topics too. Starts to change everything, because of course history isn't ever anything but a modern lens we use to look backward. So what happens when you pick up the lens they used in the 1950s to examine the 1850s?"

Gabriel smiled. "You start to see what the lens was made of?"

"Yes, and in a way you couldn't if you'd tried to do it then. Like the sexism and gender typing from ages past, and internalized homophobia. I wonder if they'll study our time and see the heteronormative systems and find them repulsive. I hope they'd see the assumed monogamy as at least rude, but I'm not getting my hopes up."

Gabriel glanced away, but he seemed shy, not uncomfortable. "Would you like to see the rest of the house?"

He gave Dale the tour, though there wasn't much to show. The cabin was small, and mostly one room except for the bathroom and then the upstairs, which Gabriel did take Dale up to. He led him to a window overlooking a beautiful snow-filled meadow backlit with the dark sparkle of evergreen trees. In the distance, the faint dance of northern lights played above the tree line.

"Wow. What a view."

Gabriel hugged his arms over his body, staring out into the blue-black night. "Sometimes if I'm overwhelmed I come up here and simply stare out this glass, and it centers me. I love living here, and I love this view. Arthur promised me the renovations wouldn't ruin it."

"I got enough of a glimpse of those plans to see this part. They won't. They'll make it better, if anything."

Gabriel turned to him, smiling. "Good to hear."

It was a pristine, perfect moment. Dale wanted to lean in and kiss him, to back him into the corner and bury his face in his neck, to drink in the scent of him. The feeling came back, the same one that had chased him all afternoon, the sense of giddiness. Except now

Gabriel was in front of him, feeding it.

"God, but I want to kiss you."

Gabriel's gaze hooded. He didn't move, but his body language changed. Opened. Invited. "You can."

Dale's blood hummed, cock thickening in his pants. He cast a glance toward the stairs. "I thought... He said the rules..."

Gabriel's cheeks stained with color, but he seemed eager, not embarrassed. "This is what he called me into the kitchen to discuss. He predicted we'd end up here and this would happen. We discussed it, he says it's all right, and so do I. No penetration is the rule until we're together, all three of us." He unfolded his arms, the blush of his cheeks spreading to his neck, but his resolve didn't waver. "So. Like I said. You're welcome to kiss me. Unless you'd rather I kiss you."

Dale blinked. Smiled a slow, surprised grin. "I wouldn't say no."

Gabriel closed the distance between them. Pressed long fingers against Dale's chest. "I'm still nervous."

Dale could feel him, the heat of him, the intensity of him. Smell him, all of it. He'd forgotten his wine somewhere, but it was irrelevant. He was drunk on Gabriel. "Of kissing me?"

"Of doing this. It still doesn't seem like it can be okay." He bit his lip and shut his eyes on a long blink. "But it's ridiculous. Why is it easier to think about fucking you with Arthur than dating you while also marrying Arthur?"

Dale put his hand on the bedpost to steady himself. "I don't know, but you're turning me on so much right now I think I'm going to explode. I really hope you decide it's okay."

Gabriel opened his eyes, smiled softly, and touched Dale's cheek. "Oh, I have."

Then he leaned forward and pressed his lips to Dale's.

It was the most perfect, wondrous kiss Dale had ever been given. Nothing in his memory could compare to the deliciousness of the kiss, to the way Gabriel embraced him so gently. Never had anyone tilted Dale's face to make slow, sweet love to his mouth. Gabriel's kiss thrilled Dale, but it tortured him too, because he knew he couldn't surrender to the feelings Gabriel inspired in him, not yet. Because what he wanted was to throw Gabriel on the bed and grind into him, push away his clothes and thrust into his body. He wanted this man with a hunger rising from his bones. He couldn't pour it into Gabriel's gentle kiss, and so he kept his wildness contained. All Dale allowed himself was to put a hand on Gabriel's hip, gripping him and kneading as Gabriel deepened the kiss. Dale stroked Gabriel's face, his neck, the line of his ears. His cock throbbed and ached, and he let the yearning stand, his focus on soaking in the wonder of Gabriel's kiss.

When Gabriel finally broke away, they nuzzled their noses, smiling, pressing their foreheads together.

"I like you," Dale whispered.

"I like you too." Gabriel threaded their fingers. "What do we do next, after tonight? Because I don't want this to end."

Dale kissed Gabriel's knuckles. "After this, we'll see each other. We text. We set up dates."

"What about when you go back to Minneapolis?"

Dale never wanted to go back to Minneapolis. "Then we Skype and set up times when I come here, or you come to me, or we meet in Duluth. But I'm thinking of staying up here for a while. I have...several projects here I'm working on."

Gabriel smiled and lifted his head to meet his gaze. "I'm a project, am I?"

"A wonderful, beautiful one. Though I have another question for you, actually." He ran a finger down Gabriel's collarbone. "I wouldn't mind doing a few scenes with Arthur. With or without you. I told him I'd ask you for permission. He said you wouldn't mind, but it was important to me that you know. If you don't want me to, I won't. They don't have to be sexual. It's more about power and control, for me."

Gabriel seemed surprised, but pleased. And turned on. "Oh—it would be fine. Well. Isn't this working out."

"Isn't it just." Dale caught Gabriel's bottom lip, sucking it lightly. Then drew on it again, sucking a little harder.

This time their kiss was more carnal, but still not the unleashing Dale needed, which was in a way an even more exquisite torture. He stroked Gabriel's ass insistently, kneading at the flesh as he thrust deeper into his mouth. When Gabriel began to make sweet noises that sent them both over the edge, Dale backed him into the corner he'd been eyeing earlier and slid a palm up his front, slipping a hand inside his jacket in search of a nipple.

"Go soft for me, sweetheart," he murmured into Gabriel's lips. "Open and let me in." He rolled his thumb over a bud while his other hand trailed fingers to Gabriel's rump, hitching a leg up and fingering his crease, seeking the heat of his hole through his jeans. "Will you let me in, honey?"

Gabriel clung to him, shaking and going slack. "I…" He whimpered as Dale stole into his mouth.

"Give me your tongue," Dale demanded, first tangling with it, then sucking as Gabriel surrendered to him. He rocked his pelvis into Gabriel, shifting his hand to unbutton his jeans, unzip him. He broke the kiss but stayed near his mouth, as his fingers played along Gabriel's waistband. "Let me touch you."

Gabriel kept his eyes shut but didn't fight him, only sought his mouth as Dale continued to work open his trousers. Dale groaned as Gabriel's length filled his hand, and he broke the kiss to take in the sight.

"So beautiful." He ran his hand down the shaft. "So beautiful."

He jacked Gabriel slowly as they kissed, drinking in every gasp and sigh. Eventually, though, he had to stop, burying his face in Gabriel's neck, kissing him between confessions. "I want to push you on the bed and suck you dry. Right now. I want you to ride me and let me watch that long, beautiful body dance over me."

Gabriel shuddered too. "Arthur…we need to wait for Arthur."

Dale stroked him more insistently, sending him closer to the edge. "You said no penetration. Would he allow oral?"

Gabriel's head rolled back and forth against the wall, eyes screwed shut. "Yes."

"Would he let me get you off, Gabriel? Would he let me take you in my mouth and make you come?"

A shudder. "Yes."

"Would you like that, baby?"

Another tremor, and a slouch of surrender as Gabriel thrust into Dale's hand. "Yes."

Dale gave Gabriel a long, maddening stroke, rubbing his thumb over the head. Then another. He kept going until Gabriel was clutching him, mewling.

Then he gave up and went to his knees.

Gabriel made one cry of protest before Dale took the cock deep into his throat. Slow velvet sliding over his tongue, gasps mingling with the precome and the push of the rod in and out of his heat.

A call came from the distance, Arthur. "All right, boys. Dinner's ready." Dale could tell Arthur knew what they were doing, that he knew Dale was upstairs making out with Gabriel. The thrill of it all rushed him, made him suck harder, faster. Gabriel whimpered, pulled at his hair. Dale opened his throat more, took him farther in, flicked his tongue over sensitive places to urge the orgasm out of him.

When it came, he swallowed it down, learning the taste of Gabriel along with everything else about him. Dale sucked until Gabriel was spent, then licked him clean after and tucked him away. Rose on slightly shaking feet and kissed Gabriel with spunk still on his lips.

"You okay?"

Gabriel nodded, breathing heavily.

Dale finished putting him back together and took his hand. "Let's go have some dinner."

GABRIEL HAD NOT expected to be blown in his bedroom before dinner. He'd hoped for a kiss, maybe some petting. Even though Arthur had specifically given him permission for a blowjob, though, to give or to get, he'd written it off as too far too fast. But obviously his fiancé had seen it coming. Pardon the pun.

The sly grin and the wink Arthur gave before he slid a hand over Gabriel's backside said he knew exactly what they'd done and was glad. He also kept touching Gabriel, being extra attentive to him as they took their places at the table. It occurred to Gabriel that Arthur never behaved this way, not unless Gabriel was upset, but Gabriel wasn't upset right now, only a little overwhelmed. This was Arthur being a doting partner in front of another man. A man who had just blown Gabriel in Arthur and Gabriel's bedroom.

Goodness. Gabriel swayed in his seat.

Dale put a hand on Gabriel's other leg, appearing concerned. "Are you all right?"

Now the two of them were touching him, sending their heat, their intensity into him, both of them laser-focused on his comfort, his needs, his pleasure. Suddenly he had a clear idea of how this evening was going to go. Gabriel held up his hands and let out an unsteady breath. "I'm fine. Shall we eat?"

He was relieved to find they settled into a rather normal meal, giving him a respite to collect himself. His body was a little sleepy from the orgasm, and he declined his second glass of wine, opting for water instead. The food was familiar, simple, and delicious. In the year they'd been together, Arthur had perfected the set of spices for venison steak, knowing just what and how much to season with to bring out the flavor in a way that made the meat exactly right. It was the same meal as the disastrous first dinner between the three of them—had it been deliberate? Arthur's way of giving them a complete do-over? Probably. Except all Gabriel needed from the spread was the steak. The potatoes and salad, as far as he was concerned, were there for show—though he did try Dale's bread, since he'd gone through the trouble to make it himself and since it happened to be Gabriel's favorite.

It was quite good, in fact, especially since Arthur had kept it warm in the oven. Gabriel slathered it with butter and ate several large pieces, to the point that he put himself in a conundrum of which did he finish, his meat or his bread.

Arthur nudged him with his elbow. "Don't make yourself so full you're sick. Plenty more coming later."

Gabriel understood what he meant by more—activity, not dinner, but Dale said, "Oh, is there dessert?"

Arthur didn't move his gaze from Gabriel's. "Yeah, I was thinking some cream."

Gabriel blushed scarlet.

Dale chuckled and eased into his seat. "Goddamn, Arthur, but I love how you don't muck around."

"Not something I'm known for, no." Arthur poked at the last few potatoes on his plate and swept up the remaining juices with the crust of his bread. "And since we've brought it up now, let's lay out some rules for this evening's entertainment. First, as a reminder, I'm making all of them. Second, and most important, if anybody doesn't like what's going on or needs us to ease up, we use yellow and red." He rested a hand on Gabriel's shoulder and toyed with a lock of his hair. "Gabriel does enjoy, in the right circumstances, saying no when he means *go*. But obviously it's a risky game, and if we end up going there tonight, you'll be following my lead, Mr. Davidson."

Dale nodded, his expression hooded. "Yes, sir."

Arthur glanced across their plates. "It looks like we're all pretty much finished. Let's get this table cleared, shall we? And then we can have a little fun."

Gabriel carried the bread to the counter, because it was the only thing he dared carry for fear he'd drop it in his shaking hands. He wasn't fearful, really, simply so stimulated and primed, aware both Arthur and Dale were focused on *him*. It made him excited, but it was overwhelming too. Part of him wanted to throw up his hands and tell them to leave the leftovers, for God's sake, but for the first time ever he hadn't finished his steak, and he watched it go into the fridge, thinking of when he would like to eat it next.

Then everything was put away, and they were heading into the living room.

Here we go.

Arthur led Gabriel, putting a hand in the small of his back, but once they were at the couch, he moved to the overstuffed chair opposite and arranged himself with his leg crossed over his knee as he nodded to Dale. "How about you sit there with my honey on the couch, kiss him a bit, undo his shirt. Take the jacket off first, but leave the shirt on. I'll sit here and enjoy watching you make out with him, undressing him. Sound all right to the two of you?"

Dale grinned wolfishly at Gabriel before moving behind him to slide the jacket from his shoulders. "I'm good. Gabriel?"

Gabriel couldn't answer, only let his shoulders roll

and arms go slack as Dale peeled the coat away and laid it carefully over the stair rail. Gabriel took Dale's hand, followed him around the couch, heart pounding. He allowed Dale to seat him on the sofa and settle him into his arms, tip his head back for a kiss.

Gabriel opened his mouth, fitting his lips to Dale's and meeting his tongue when it stole inside. For a moment he was aware Arthur watched, but then he simply rode the sensation, the wet lushness, the pressure, the way it made him so dizzy, so beyond himself to be kissed like that. Dale's hand slid into Gabriel's shirt, undoing the buttons, moving his palm over Gabriel's skin. Gabriel held still for him, letting him explore his body. When Dale broke the kiss and trailed his mouth and beard along Gabriel's jaw and cheekbones, his neck, Gabriel tipped his head to help Dale on his path, breath hitching as Dale began to nip and bite at his collarbone.

"Push his shirt away farther on his shoulder so I can see his nipple." When Gabriel jolted at Arthur's voice, Arthur laughed. "Yeah, baby, you forgot I was here, didn't you? Oh, Dale, honey, pinch that nipple for me. Let me watch you do it."

Gabriel tried to roll his shoulder forward, but Dale pushed it back, kissing him briefly before pulling away enough that he too was watching while he raised thumb and forefinger and pinched Gabriel's nipple, tight enough to make him gasp.

"Do it again," Arthur said.

Dale did. Gabriel whimpered, sagging into Dale, quavering. He felt the pinches through his whole body, into his cock which, truth be told, was still tender from coming earlier. Dale pinched him once more, tugging this time. Gabriel cried out softly but held still, waiting.

"Oh God," Dale whispered. Then he bent and took Gabriel's nipple into his mouth.

He knelt, pushing the shirt panels far to the sides so he could capture the other nipple. Gabriel tried not to writhe beneath him, tried to hold still—why, he wasn't sure, only somehow he had it in his head he was to be still unless he was told to move. Or perhaps it was that he didn't want them to see him react? He didn't know. All he did know was his nipple was made of ten million nerve endings, Dale's mouth was soft and wet, and he sucked so hard while tracing with his tongue that Gabriel wanted to sob. As Dale pinched the other nipple, Gabriel nearly did weep.

"Keep going. Very nice, Dale. I like your slow and steady approach. You'll wear him down. Spread your legs for him, Gabriel. Let him get right up in there and make you crazy."

Gabriel didn't want to spread his legs and let Dale make him crazy. Except, of course, he did, but this panic was in the way.

"Let him in." Arthur's voice was closer now, not quite beside him on the couch, but near the couch somewhere, as if he stood behind it. "Dale, unzip him, open his legs."

Dale backed away from Gabriel, leaving his nipples sensitized and pert and in one case, quite wet. Gabriel watched him, belly quavering, as Dale opened Gabriel's knees, unbuttoned his jeans, and unzipped them.

"Take them off."

Gabriel tensed, but Arthur's hands came down on his shoulders as Dale removed Gabriel's shoes and tugged his jeans off. Jeans and socks and shoes came away, and then Gabriel sat in his undone shirt and his briefs while the two of them crowded around him, fully dressed and eyeing him like wolves. Dale did indeed regard Gabriel as if he would consume him. He stroked Gabriel's legs, threading his fingers in the hair, skimming his palms over the knees, back up Gabriel's thighs. Parted them wide, and Gabriel thought Dale would remove his underwear too, but Dale only ran his hands up Gabriel's chest, to his nipples, where he circled them with his thumbs, plucked them both, tugging until he pulled a gasp from Gabriel. Then another.

Arthur remained behind Gabriel, watching. "You can go harder."

Gabriel mewed in protest, then reached up to hold on to Arthur's arms as Dale dragged agonized pleas out of Gabriel. He shivered, twisted, then cried out, "No, stop."

Dale paused, relaxing his pressure.

Dizzy, Gabriel blinked in confusion.

Arthur forced the pressure of Dale's hand back,

doubling it, making Gabriel yelp.

"Remember, no doesn't mean no." Arthur put his hand over Dale's other as well, increasing the grip there too, and Gabriel almost came off the couch. "Oh, but this isn't a bad game, is it, baby? Kiss him, Dale. Hard."

Gabriel barely had time to draw breath before his mouth was full of Dale—and there Gabriel was, Arthur behind him, helping Dale knead his nipples into peaks of pain as Dale fucked him with his tongue.

"Get your cock out." Arthur kept working Gabriel's nipples as Dale's hands slipped away, and Gabriel didn't let Dale break their kiss. "Gabriel, you get out yours. There you go. Dale, line them up. Slow. Fuck him slow."

Gabriel wasn't sure how exactly they maneuvered—at some point Arthur let him go, and it was only Dale pressing over him, pushing him into the couch, lining their cocks together and gripping them tight. Slow he was indeed, maddeningly so, and the more Gabriel thrust up and tried to urge him on, the slower he went. He rubbed his thumb over their cockheads, kissed his way down Gabriel's throat, ground circles with his pelvis, but he wouldn't go faster. Not even when Gabriel was practically in tears, begging him.

Dale abruptly hissed and jerked, and when Gabriel opened his eyes, he saw Arthur behind Dale, looking wicked. Dale's arms tensed, his eyes shut. Letting out a breath, Dale kissed Gabriel deeply and quickened his pace, tightening his grip until they both came.

Gabriel lay exhausted on the couch, unable to move.

Dale climbed off him, winded, but he watched Arthur as he came around. Met Arthur's gaze as he spoke. "I want to suck you off. Will you let me?"

Arthur raised an eyebrow in question at Gabriel.

Gabriel could barely move, let alone respond. He nodded and waved a hand weakly.

Arthur stood an arm's reach away, and Dale knelt before him, undoing his pants with rapt attention. It was the first time Dale hadn't been focused on Gabriel, which was a little...not alarming, but different. It was hot, though, to see him take Arthur in his mouth. To watch Arthur be masterful to him instead.

But he couldn't get it out of his head how Arthur had checked with him. To see if it was okay.

Arthur grabbed a fistful of Dale's hair, guiding Dale's mouth up and down while keeping his face turned up, his gaze focused on Arthur. "There's a good boy. That's right. There's a good boy, getting his cock. But you want more than that, don't you. You want to sit pretty for me. You want me to make you do all the wicked things, don't you, sweetheart?"

Dale made a muffled sound around Arthur's cock and sucked more desperately. Gabriel's cock was too spent to rise, but desire swelled in him all the same, and he watched, transfixed, as his fiancé mastered his lover.

Arthur pumped his cock deep into Dale's throat, making him choke, smiling as Dale didn't fight him. "Yeah, baby, I know what you want. I see it every time you look at me. You want me to give you stripes across your ass. You want me to truss you up and torture you until you weep. Some of it you want other people to see, but most of it, you just want someone to do to you. You want someone to know all the twisted shit inside your head, dish it out and show it to you. Isn't that right?" More sounds around Arthur's dick, more intense sucking. Arthur pulled almost affectionately at Dale's hair, then cut a casual glance at Gabriel. "Baby, go upstairs and get my small trunk from the closet. Bring it here for me."

Gabriel rose from the couch, dizzy and disoriented, but he followed Arthur's command and went up the stairs in a kind of dream state. He knew the trunk, a small black one with silver buckles Arthur took with him for scenes in Duluth. When Gabriel returned with the case in hand, he almost stumbled, because in the time he had been gone, Arthur had rearranged himself and Dale, and now Dale was splayed over an ottoman, still sucking Arthur's cock, his knees on either side of the piece of furniture, exposing his hole and his balls to Gabriel as he came into the room.

Arthur grinned at Gabriel as he entered, reaching over Dale's back to run his fingers down his crack. "Keeps himself in good shape, your boy. You know how to pick 'em, hon. Like the view I gave you there?"

Gabriel had to swallow several times before he could speak. He couldn't take his eyes off Dale, stumbled toward him in a fever as he passed Arthur the trunk. Arthur set it beside him, undid the clasp one-handed, and passed Gabriel a bottle of lube. He didn't release it, though, and they held it together as Gabriel met Arthur's gaze.

Arthur regarded him coolly, with the hard, commanding stare that could always send Gabriel so deep. But question lurked in there too. "What do you think, baby? You wanna play with your new boy? Or you want to keep it sweet between you two? Semisweet, anyway." When Gabriel cut a quick glance to Dale, as if he would pop off Arthur's dick and give his opinion, Arthur massaged Dale's head and smiled. "Oh, lover-boy here is good either way. He just wants you, sweetheart. He wants you and your sweetness and hotness and everything between, and he wants this, all dirty and raw and almost cold. He got a twofer in us, and he's so fucking excited, honey. Right now he's so happy he could squeal. And I'm gonna make him squeal before we're done here. Question is, do you want to help him get there, or leave it to me?"

Gabriel regarded Dale again, saw him so submissive, so lost—the same space he liked to go to. He thought about letting Arthur command him to help Dale get there too, of being under Arthur's spell with him. Of establishing this as their baseline, that when the three of them were together, this was what they did.

Leaning forward, Gabriel kissed Arthur's knee. "I want to help, please."

Arthur let go of the lube and ruffled Dale's hair. Threaded his fingers, tugged, just a bit. Then he let him go. "Go on behind him and get him ready."

Chapter Nine

GABRIEL DID AS Arthur told him, moving into place behind Dale, remembering seeing this same beautiful ass exposed in his office in the library. He wanted to lick it, caress it, map it with his hands. But Arthur had told Gabriel to get Dale ready. He glanced up at his fiancé in silent question.

Arthur still had his cool expression on, but he winked. "You can play a bit first."

Gabriel didn't waste any time. He splayed his hands over Dale's taut backside, shivering as he discovered yes, those muscles were as deliciously firm as they looked. Best yet, when he kneaded slightly, Dale moaned against Arthur's groin. He'd been redirected from his cock to Arthur's balls now, had one of the heavy sacs in his mouth. Gabriel massaged the smooth, delicious planes of Dale's ass, sliding his thumbs up and down the crevice of his crack, running his fingertip around the puckered, quivering hole.

"Give your boyfriend a kiss, baby."

Gabriel felt a ridiculous thrill at the word. *My boy-friend.* He felt heady too that *his boyfriend* was playing so dirty with him. Would they play dirty together, the two of them alone, as well? His heart soared as he bent, running his nose along the same path his fingers had taken, his tongue stealing out to taste the salty skin.

Then he reached Dale's hole, shut his eyes, opened his mouth, and kissed it.

He had done something similar to Arthur once. One night, during a blizzard as it happened, Arthur had slid to the edge of the couch and made Gabriel eat him out for what had felt like hours but in reality had been only fifteen or twenty minutes. Slow and thorough, though, Arthur had insisted. He had been in a dirty mood, and apparently he was in one now, because he said the same things to Gabriel as he had then.

"Make love to his hole, baby. Show Dale how sweet you think his ass is. There you go. Nice and slow. Use your tongue. Give his hole a big old kiss. Now hook your thumbs in there, sweetheart, and open him. That's right. Make those sounds I like. I bet Dale enjoys them too. Show him, Dale. Show him you like his kisses."

Dale made little squeals, the ones Arthur had promised Gabriel Dale would make, and Gabriel felt a thrill that he'd been the one to make them happen. When Arthur told him to lube Dale's ass, pushing his fingers inside, Gabriel did, but he kissed the base of Dale's spine the whole time, licking it as he opened Dale wider.

Then Arthur tugged Dale off his balls by the hair. "Stand up, boy. Gabriel, you lay on the floor. Go slick your cock while you wait."

Gabriel did as he was told, then watched as Arthur helped Dale turn around over the ottoman. He couldn't see what happened from where he lay on the floor, but he heard a series of cracks and Dale's muffled gasps and cries as he counted to ten, then twenty, then thirty. There was a shuffling, murmured instruction from Arthur, and then Dale was crawling over the top of Gabriel, naked, lost to subspace, hard as a rock.

He stared down at Gabriel, his gaze a mixture of fondness, wonder, lust, and disorientation, until suddenly it transformed into sharp focus and near pain, his whole body tightening, his eyes shutting. Gabriel could see Arthur over Dale's shoulder. Arthur appeared to be fucking Dale and yet was standing too straight. He twisted his wrist, and Dale gasped, bending closer to Gabriel, shaking.

"Kiss him," Arthur commanded as he pushed a dildo into Dale once more. "Kiss your lover while I work this inside you. That's what you want. You know you want it. Feel this in you, giving you what you want, and feel him under you. Slide your body against him. Fuck your tongue into his mouth. Gabriel, you lie there and let him have you."

Gabriel did. He shut his eyes and gave himself to Dale's kiss, gave over to letting Dale claim his body, shuddering with him every time Arthur made him tremble and moan. At some point Arthur stopped, and Gabriel could feel the dildo brushing his own balls as Dale caught their cocks together and thrust into him, fucking him into the floor. Gabriel came just before Dale, and they collapsed together, a heap of arms and legs on the rug.

Dale was the first to lift his head, look around, still catching his breath. "Arthur went upstairs, I think."

"He's giving us a moment." Gabriel smoothed hair from Dale's eyes. "That was amazing."

Dale gazed down at him, full of adoration. "It was like nothing that has ever happened to me. And this was our first date." He ran his knuckles down Gabriel's cheek. "It would have taken me six months to work up the courage to let you know I liked things so kinky."

Gabriel smiled. "There are perks to being in a relationship with Arthur."

Dale kissed Gabriel's nose, his cheek, the corner of his mouth. "There are perks to being in a relationship with you."

Gabriel pulled his boyfriend onto the floor beside him and kissed him back. For a very long time.

DALE ENDED UP staying the night, which was what Arthur had predicted, and he was glad. By unspoken agreement, Dale slept downstairs, and though Gabriel stayed with him for a good hour, he came to bed with

Arthur before dawn. They didn't speak, but they did make love—Gabriel had come twice with Dale, but he urged Arthur into fucking him once it was the two of them, and Arthur certainly wasn't going to say no to that. He suspected Gabriel needed to reconnect with Arthur, to re-cement their own relationship.

In the morning, Arthur had intended to make breakfast, but he woke to find Dale in the kitchen far ahead of him, coffee brewing, chopping vegetables, and frying up ground venison. He smiled over his shoulder at Arthur as he came into the kitchen. "Good morning."

Arthur came up behind him and ran a hand over his ass. Dale tensed, but didn't hiss. Arthur nodded in approval. "You're not too sore?"

"Nope. Some nice souvenirs, but that's it." Dale gave him a sly half grin. "That was amazing. Thank you."

Arthur waggled his eyebrows. "Thank *you*." He patted Dale on the shoulder. "I'll go wake lazybones. We'll lay out some plans and ground rules for this horse-and-pony show while you make us whatever you're making us here."

"Omelets." Dale popped a raw green pepper into his mouth. "You have a *ton* of venison in your freezer."

"I have a man upstairs who gives me the best sex in the world every time I feed it to him. I keep us well stocked."

Dale saluted with the handle of the knife. "Noted."

Arthur left Dale to the cooking, feeling rather pleased with how this was working out. He definitely didn't want to live as a thruple still, but having Dale around on occasion to play chef wasn't a bad perk. He hummed to himself as he went back up the stairs, smiled as he burrowed under the covers next to Gabriel and began the process of kissing him awake.

It took some doing, but whispered reminders that Dale was downstairs and they had a lot of decisions to make got some consciousness in him. Gabriel had taken the day off from the library, and thanks to Paul, Arthur had some time on his hands as well. Dale probably had to put in some time with the council members, since that was ostensibly the reason he'd come to Logan but hadn't done a thing with yet.

The three of them enjoyed a lovely domestic morning, and it wasn't awkward, not really. No more than new things were. Arthur kind of hung back, letting them have their space, but he appreciated that both Dale and Gabriel would go out of their way to include him in their conversations, and Gabriel, to be honest, gave Arthur far more relationship-like touches than he did Dale. Which made sense, Arthur supposed. They'd been together longer. He paid him more attention than he usually did, however, and Arthur noticed.

It wasn't exactly news, because he'd heard his poly friends talk about it, but the reality of how much conscious work this multiway thing was going to be dawned on Arthur like a sunrise. He'd never been one for advanced classes in school, but he felt as if he'd landed in Relationship Calculus 101.

"So," he began, once they'd finished their omelets and had settled into their second cups of coffee. "How do we want to set this up? How do you two want to start?"

Gabriel and Dale glanced at one another like high school boys preparing to go to the prom. Dale rubbed his thumb along his beard bashfully. "I'm open. I get it's going to be a challenge for a lot of reasons. The long-distance thing isn't going to be a party. But when I'm here, we're going to need to be discreet because it's Logan."

"Discreet is putting it mildly." Arthur lifted a finger. "This town knows if I sneeze in an underground bunker. If you stop by the library to see Gabriel and you smile at him wrong, people will whisper. You touch his hand and he ducks his head, people will start making up stories. There *will* be stories. You're not going to get around them. Hell, there've been rumors I'm doing Kyle on the side with Paul."

Gabriel drew back, blinking. "There *are*? Why? Who's saying this?"

Arthur waved a hand. "Idiots. This is the thing, though. We're gay men in a small town. They all think we're oversexed maniacs as it is. I think maybe Marcus and Frankie have been written off as the good gays, but I wouldn't put it past people to talk about them too. People assume I'm still doing Paul. People assume all sorts of shit. This is what I'm saying, though. There's no way they're going to miss what's going on between the two of you. They want us to be the Real Gay Housewives of St. Louis County. They want drama and all that shit, and you're going to give them seeds to sow the nonsense in."

Gabriel frowned over his coffee cup. "You're right. I hadn't thought about it, but you're right. And every time they insinuate it, we'll panic, because they'll be stepping on truths. And we'll make it worse." He ran a hand through his hair. "So what you're saying is this is going to be a disaster? That we'll be found out for sure?"

Arthur raised an eyebrow at Dale. "Son, you're the player on the board who's been past Go already. What's your experience here? How have you handled this before?"

Dale dropped his gaze to the table, abruptly awkward. "My experience hasn't been the best model."

Well that was just wonderful. "We'll have to forge forward on our own smarts, then. I'd say let's take this slow and careful. Be mindful, the two of you, when you're in town together, at least at first. I know it blows, because it's being in the closet all over again, but it's not for Logan, is it? It's for you. Either one of you feel ready to weather the ride of this new car as well as the whispers and stares and questions and assumptions of this town?"

"No," Gabriel said without hesitation.

Dale shook his head. "It would devastate the development. It would do some damage to me at my job as well. A lot, actually. Because they'd see it as adultery, me getting involved with a soon-to-be married man."

Arthur scratched his arm absently. "Right. So this is why we're operating on the down-low for now. The people who know are the three of us and Paul. And to be honest, I'd guess Kyle, as Paul's probably told him in confidence. Frankie doesn't know, and Marcus sure as hell has no clue. You'll want to keep him in the dark as long as you can."

Dale nodded, but Gabriel frowned. "Why?"

Arthur realized that though the six of them were close, there were things not all of them knew. "The guy Marcus dated before Frankie, when Marcus lived in the Cities, cheated on him. Rampantly, for years, and he was glib about it when he was caught. Obviously this isn't the same thing. But it's going to take some talking to explain this to him."

Gabriel sighed. "I don't like keeping secrets from our friends."

"I know, baby. But for now, I think it's best. Let's give the two of you some space to be together first." Arthur tapped his finger on the table, thinking. "The bitch is you can't be together in town. You could rent something in Logan cheap without raising suspicion, but the trick is it has to be somewhere people won't see Gabriel going in and out of at night, which is when I assume you'd want to be having quality time together when you were up here. Paul's old duplex is open on the other side, and I'm pretty sure he's going to move in with Kyle's family any second now so they can do the remodel on that little house out back Kyle is so set they move into, but you can't meet up with Gabriel there. You could bring him in under the cover of darkness at three in the morning with a team of ninjas and my mother would still know about it by breakfast, and she lives in the country."

Gabriel shook his head. "That's not true. Kyle made all those snow penises and no one knew he was doing it."

Dale blinked at him. "Snow penises?"

Arthur waved a hand. "Later. Okay, that's a good point. Maybe the duplex is remote enough. But you'd have to get over there without a car. Though I guess there's the back access. What would be better would be for me to pick you up after, in the morning, on the way to work. We'd have to make an early go of it, and you'd have to hang out at the shop a bit, but we could make it work."

Gabriel slumped in his chair. "I feel like we're planning a siege, not a polyamorous romance."

"Welcome to Logan, Minnesota." Arthur leaned over, pulled a legal pad and pen from a drawer in his construction notes, and began making a makeshift calendar. "That's getting ahead of ourselves, anyway. First thing is, how long are you staying this round, Dale?"

Dale settled his elbows on the table. "Originally I'd planned to get in here and get out. But now I'm thinking I could take a few weeks. I might have to go get some things, straighten up, and so on. Maybe I could even stretch my stay to a couple of months, or through the summer."

"Nice." Arthur graphed out a month on the legal pad. "All right. So I'm thinking what we want here is a schedule. Right now this is a new thing, and you guys need to put in some introductory time, so I'm willing to let you hog my boy a bit, Dale." He ran a hand down Gabriel's arm. "Just come to me after and reconnect so I know we're still good."

Gabriel leaned over and kissed his cheek. "Of course."

Arthur looked at Dale. "Now. You expressed some interest in having some playtime with me. You want to schedule that too?"

Dale's gaze darkened with interest. "Yes, please."

"And I'm assuming you want the bulk of that just the two of us?" When Dale nodded, Arthur made a few more notes beneath his makeshift calendar. "Okay. That's the two of you covered. For my part, I would like to request we repeat last night on a regular basis. One, it was hot as all fuck, and two, I think it could be good for us to connect and keep up with each other. You guys all right with that?"

They both agreed, but Arthur noted Gabriel especially seemed pleased, content, and cared for. Arthur cracked his knuckles and squared his shoulders. "All right. Let's schedule this bitch."

It took them a good half hour to do just the first week, and this was because everyone had to keep getting out their phones and planners. Dale had to call and check meetings and even create a few. There was also the struggle of Dale and Gabriel *wanting* to get together as often as possible initially, and yet not really being able to without giving away the game. Unless they went out of town or came to the cabin, there was nowhere for them to meet.

Dale got frustrated. "I need to rent the damn duplex."

"You need to get back to the Cities and get your shit," Arthur pointed out. "Let me talk to Paul, see if you can get the duplex squared away this week. But you could also plan a mini getaway in Duluth. See a movie. Have dinner. Stay in a hotel."

Gabriel was staring at the construction paraphernalia. "You know, that could work. We could say we're getting supplies for the remodel."

Arthur snorted. "How about you *do* get some supplies for the remodel? Two-for-one deal. Hammer and nail and hammer and nail."

Dale caught Gabriel's fingers, twining them with his. "I'd love for you to come down to the Cities sometime. Not when I go to get my stuff, but sometime for a long weekend."

"Sounds wonderful," Gabriel said.

They were damn cute, Arthur had to admit. He was proud of himself that he was kind of their godfather helping them get together. But at the same time, he was also keenly aware what they needed right now was space alone, without him. He wished there were somewhere for him to escape so they could have a lingering moment to cap off this first date. He supposed there was—the whole goddamned outdoors. He rose from the table, clearing his throat.

"I'm going to go enjoy this nice crisp winter morning. Probably take a walk around the lake." He rubbed his belly and quirked a smile. "Need a dog, you know that? Should go to the shelter and see about getting one. Some eager old idiot to run around the snow while I walk. I have this sudden urge to take a lot of walks."

Gabriel smiled and rose, capturing Arthur's face and kissing him, a lingering, grateful kiss. "Thank you. I love you, so much."

Arthur kissed him back, stroked his face, tugged at one of his curls. "I love you too."

Chapter Ten

DALE HAD BEEN to Duluth several times, but for jobs, never for a date.

He wanted to take Gabriel somewhere special, somewhere to wow him, but it was hard when all Dale knew were office buildings, construction sites, and a few stiff restaurants. He was compromised too by not being able to ask anyone for ideas except Arthur or Paul, and he didn't exactly want to go to either of them. Arthur would have been happy to help, but Dale wanted to find something Arthur *didn't* know about and hadn't already showed Gabriel. Paul might have been an option, but Dale didn't know the man well enough. He wasn't sure how well he actually was taking this idea of Gabriel dating Dale and marrying Arthur too. So he got together with his pal Google, and he hunted down every tourist and art and culture site in Duluth. It didn't take him long to find what he was looking for: Zeitgeist Center for Arts and Community.

It was a performing arts center, cafe, and movie

theater, with community spaces nearby, and watching the informational videos on the website had the hairs standing up on Dale's arms. Yes, it was a promotional video designed to raise money and sell the center, but it was a good video and it was doing its job. It was similar to what he'd done with a project in Minneapolis, though this seemed more coordinated and more community based. It was also, he realized, what was missing from the Logan development.

Bread and roses, the man in the video said. Sustenance and art both. It was a bit of what they were trying for in Logan, but they were so fixated on the development at the moment. Maybe they should push for more art. Maybe *that* was the sell. Jesus...it would bring the LGBT element they wanted as well, not just the idea of inclusion, but that it was more art based. Why hadn't he thought of this? Obviously he wouldn't sell the idea this way precisely to the town, but he could sell it in the Cities. A gay-friendly environment, a small town with an arts scene.

Buzzing with ideas, he booked dinner and theater tickets for the days in May they'd agreed would be Gabriel's and his big first weekend getaway. Which he hoped to God wouldn't also be their first solo date, since it turned out Paul hadn't moved in completely with Kyle yet. The two of them were flopping back and forth between their places while they did construction on the house behind Kyle's parents' main farmhouse, and to everyone's surprise, Paul hadn't told Kyle a thing about Gabriel and Dale, saying he thought it would be good to keep things quiet for the moment. So Gabriel and Dale were reduced to skipping out of town and parking like a pair of teenagers to neck in the backseat. It had been fun for ten minutes. Now it was frustrating.

Dale shut the laptop and rose from the desk, putting the computer in his suitcase with the rest of his things. Frankie appeared in the doorway to his room with a cup of tea and a sad smile. "I know you'll be right back, but we're going to miss you. It's practical, you taking Mrs. Michealson's old place, but we've enjoyed having you as a guest."

"I've enjoyed being your guest." He zipped the suitcase shut. "But if I'm going to stay here for the summer, which is my intent, I'm going to be more productive in my own space." This was the truth. He also wanted to be able to have Gabriel over to watch a movie, read together, and have wild sex on every piece of furniture. And who knew what sort of games Arthur would have for him. Yes, his own space was a must.

"I know." Frankie sighed and pushed off the doorframe. "At least you'll be in town. And actually, there's something I'd been meaning to talk to you about. Kyle was telling me you two had talked about starting an LGBT club. I'd love to be a part of that."

"Sure. We'd talked about it meeting lots of places, but we'd decided the best first place would be the library. I could talk to Gabriel." He felt a flush of self-consciousness, thinking perhaps he shouldn't have mentioned Gabriel. God, this was going to be an awkward game. Arthur was right, negotiating a secret poly relationship in Logan was chess-in-space levels of complicated.

"I'd love to do a potluck. Do you think he'd be okay with food in the library? We could do games and dinner. It would be nice to have it in a church basement, but I don't know how it would go over, either with the church or the attendees." Frankie tapped the side of his mug. "I'll think on it."

"You do that." Dale hefted his suitcase from the bed. "Right now I have a lot of driving to do."

It was a three-hour drive from Logan to his condo in downtown Minneapolis, but he made the trip in record time. He hadn't ever completely unpacked, so a lot of things he moved wholesale in boxes into his car, packing it full. What he needed from there was clothes, though he did make sure to pack books and movies and, pausing in his bedroom closet, some of his favorite toys. He poked through his cupboards for dishes and did a once-over of his furniture, but in the end he decided he'd get new things from stores up there, because he didn't need much and he didn't want to haul things back and forth. Arthur had said he'd get his mom on the case for things like furniture and dishes and a TV, so really, he was set. In the morning all he'd have to do was grab his suitcase and go. He'd be back in Logan before lunch.

When he went by his office, they were happy to see him, and he sat with the field supervisor's team for fifteen minutes, getting caught up on office gossip and other projects his subordinates had started for their own commissions. He gave them his contact information, reassured them he'd be in touch, and left.

Then he went to the main Kivino complex.

He hadn't been by the main offices in over half a year, and he wouldn't have come by now, but he had to swing through the CEO's office and play politics, and he needed to find a few physical files his team had reminded him of, supporting documents from a case they'd worked on three years ago not unlike the Logan project. He told himself it was a huge office building. He hadn't announced his arrival, and he wouldn't stay long. There was no reason he should run into Ronny. None whatsoever.

He made a quick sweep through the main cubicle area before he ducked into Mr. Overfeld's suite, saying hello to everyone, but he kept it as brief as possible, telling them the truth, that he had to get going. Then he went to the CEO's suite and told him he planned to take an extended leave to focus on the Logan project alone. He'd expected to have to do a little arguing, but the man was only pleased.

"The project has been floundering. I'm glad to see you're taking an interest in it again. Do you need any other team members up there with you?"

"Maybe later, but at the moment I think it's a waste

of resources. I can patch in remotely to meetings and come down here as necessary to meet with investors. Also, I had a germ of an idea I wanted to run by you. It's the bare fleck of a thing right now, but I think this might be the angle we've been missing." He told him about the Zeitgeist Center, about the bread-and-roses concept, about his desire to try to transfer the city's vision to Logan. "I don't know how it works yet, but everything in me says this is the right direction."

Overfeld nodded. "I like where you're going with this." He slapped Dale on the back. "Get some good fishing in for me, you hear?"

He was in the clear then, nothing left to do but gather up the files. One stop in the archives, and he was on his way to Logan, to freedom.

But once in the archives, he'd forgotten himself. He got in the zone, lost to the world, so focused on searching for ways to bolster his project he saw nothing, heard nothing. He forgot. Tricked himself into thinking it was safe space, and he forgot.

His only warning was a click of shoes, a waft of familiar cologne. Then hands snaked around his chest, arms caging him in place. "Hello, sweetheart."

Ronny's silky voice sent a shiver down Dale's spine.

Dale told himself to move, but fear held him immobile. His mind raced as he tried to climb out of his research bubble, to escape, but a larger part of him refused to leave his soft place. *Stay here. Wait him out,* it whispered. The two voices warred inside him, and in his indecision, he remained.

Ronny's fingers trailed to Dale's nipples, teasing them into peaks. "You've been avoiding me. Deliberately."

Dale shut his eyes, setting his teeth as he went rigid. "I've been busy."

"You're hiding. It's boring. This game where you pretend you don't want what I give you is tired." Though Dale was careful not to react to Ronny's touch, Ronny continued to tease Dale's nipples through his shirt, as if Dale's stillness were part of the fun. "You used to love this game. It was the break room on the twenty-third floor, but the game was the same."

He tugged Dale's nipples hard enough to make him gasp, sending a dark treacle drip of sensation through Dale that made his dick twitch and his stomach heave. "Stop."

He knew it was the wrong thing to say the second it came out of his mouth. Laughing, Ronny pressed his erection into Dale's crack and licked the back of his neck. "You don't want me to stop. You need this, sweetheart. You were made for this."

Dale twisted free and tried to loom over Ronny. It should have worked. He was taller than him, and bigger. "I don't need this from you. Not anymore."

He wished he could have said the words with more bravery. He wished he could have shoved him, punched him, and run. He told himself this was the meeting at Logan and Ronny was the Concerned Citizens. He could dismiss him. He could leave.

Ronny had a strange darkness that pulled Dale in, a draw he'd never been able to understand—it was why Dale avoided him, because he was so afraid simply seeing the man would put him back under the spell—but in that moment, Dale was able to resist Ronny's orbit. He thought of Gabriel, of Arthur, of Logan, and he let them pull him instead. *You cannot have me*, he whispered in his heart, and tried to push past the man so insistent on drawing him into his pit.

If Ronny had grabbed him, he'd have shaken him off. If he'd tugged on him, Dale would have fought back. But this was the problem with Ronny. He'd always been far too clever for his own good, and too patient. When Dale came past him, he didn't lay so much as a finger on him. He simply held up his smartphone, arm out, eye level, blocking Dale's path.

On the phone's screen was a photo of Dale strapped to a bench, covered in welts, mouth dripping with cum, ass full of an obscenely wide plug.

Dale staggered into the filing cabinet and slid down the side, the handles digging into his back.

Ronny put an arm around his waist, a gentle, help-ful gesture. He cradled Dale to his side as he flipped through photo after photo, each one more graphic than the last. "I have more at home on my hard drive." Ronny's voice sounded wistful, proud. "Oh, here's a video. This is good. You'll want to see this."

Dale didn't want to see it, but he was too shocked,

too numb to breathe, let alone object, and so he could do nothing but watch. Watch himself suck Ronny's cock. Watch himself beg for it. He had no recollection of this, but it was clearly him in the video. Except he was acting like a crazed whore. Erratic. His mind refused to accept it was him he watched, and yet every so often the camera would zoom in on his face. There was no denying the truth. This was him.

When the camera zoomed in yet another time, Dale got a good look at his bloodshot eyes beneath a reindeer headband. *Christmas.* This was from Christmas, when he'd woken up in the hotel room with the feeling something bad had happened.

He grabbed the phone and hit pause, staring at his own eyes. Dull, enlarged pupils, bloodshot. His gut twisted so tightly he hunched forward. "You drugged me. Last Christmas you drugged me, then *took video of me.*"

"You had a *wonderful* time." Ronny patted his hip. "I've been trying to show you this for a year. But you're so petulant. If you'd have finished your drink at this year's office Christmas party, we could have had this conversation sooner."

Dale blinked, replaying the Christmas party encounter. He remembered being drunk in the hallway. Letting Ronny kiss him. Ronny insisting he have a drink, but Dale had said no and gone home.

How many more photos would he have if I'd finished that drink?

Horrified, shaking with revulsion, Dale tried to get away from Ronny. But he'd lost his determination from earlier. His soft bubble had popped, his lifeline of Logan lost. All he could see were those photos. The video. The drink. Ronny's traps everywhere. He pulled, but without his strength, and Ronny held him fast.

"Stop being ridiculous." Ronny stopped the video and showed Dale more photos, a parade of Dale displaying himself in a drugged, erotic haze. "You accepted the drug willingly. You knew I took the photos."

Dale would never have taken a drug, not unless he was so drunk and so far under Ronny he wasn't thinking straight. "I want you to delete these. Delete them, all of them. And then I never want to see you again."

Ronny laughed, and the sound sent shivers down Dale's spine. "What's it worth to you?"

Dale blinked. Then his stomach lurched, sick, as he realized what Ronny was doing. "Don't," he whispered.

Ronny pushed Dale into the cabinet and ran the phone down the center of Dale's chest, digging the metal of the case into his sternum. "I thought about sending a few to Overfeld. Wonder what he'd think of his golden boy if he knew he could stuff three dildos in his ass at once."

Fear, rage, and hot shame pierced Dale. "*Don't.*"

Ronny's smile was cold and terrible. "Then turn around, put your hands on the cabinet, and be a good boy while I have a little fun with your tits." He winked.

"You can tell me to stop, though, if you want. It's so much more fun when you tell me no."

Dale froze in place, bile in his throat. *Stop.* The word was on his lips, but Ronny had just said he'd only laugh at it. *Push him off and run*, another part of his brain urged him. He could do it. He was bigger than Ronny, outweighed him by at least thirty pounds, and *he* used his gym membership. All he had to do was push back. All he had to do, and he could get out of here. Punch the bastard out, grab his phone, and run.

He couldn't do it.

Mother of God, but he couldn't make himself do it.

His breath caught, and though the room was in fact overly warm, Dale was abruptly cold.

"Turn around," Ronny ordered.

Dale turned around, put his hands on the cabinet. He jolted when he felt Ronny's hands on him, moving over then under his shirt, tugging it out of his trousers. "Stop," he whispered.

Ronny laughed.

Time became slippery, all Dale's senses disconnected and strange. At first he trembled, and then it was as if a switch flipped and he folded into himself. He was aware of his body, knew it was responding to what Ronny did to it, but his brain checked out. *Just be quiet, and it will be over soon. Just wait, and it will be over.* He made himself a space inside himself, a shelter like Arthur's hut on the ice. It kept him safe, but he was all too aware that outside of his safe space, terrible things were happening. Pain, so much pain. Things he should be stopping. Things he didn't know how to stop.

Don't think. Just wait for it to be over. Wait for it to get over, and then you can leave. If you don't react, if you give him as little as possible, if all he has is your body, maybe he'll leave.

Pictures, he has so many pictures of me. And video. What will he do with them?

Don't think about them. There aren't any pictures here. Safe space. Be in this safe space. No one can get you here.

Dale remained in his cocoon for a long time. He didn't know how long. All he knew was the sound of someone knocking on the door blew through his mental cocoon like a cannon, jolted him back to the room and awareness of what was happening with a sick rush. His pants were at his ankles. His nipples stung, but Ronny's hands weren't there. Something was clipped to them. His ass hurt, and when Ronny swore and released him, Dale felt him removing two fingers out of him, slick with nothing more than spit.

Shaking, Dale sank into the file cabinet. Whatever was on his nipples pinched him, made him gasp.

Ronny winked at him, grabbed one, and tweaked it until Dale had to bite his tongue to keep from crying out. "We'll finish this later," Ronny said, and disappeared through the aisles toward the door.

Dale touched his chest, moving his shirt aside to reveal two binder clips, one fastened to each of his nipples. He tugged them off one at a time, gasping against the pain. He winced as he crouched to pull up his trousers, trying to fasten them quickly, but his hands couldn't stop trembling.

You have to get out of here, a voice whispered inside his brain. *You have to get out of here in case he comes back.*

Still fastening his belt, he wove his way through the files until he could exit without talking to whoever had entered, striding down the hall as quickly as he could, his mind whirring at ninety miles an hour, plotting a course to get out of the building without being seen.

Without running into Ronny again. Without giving him another chance.

He wanted to weep with relief when he burst out the side door and saw his car in the parking lot, but he didn't let himself take the luxury. He got in, ran by his condo to grab his suitcase, terrified the whole time Ronny would appear. But there was no sign of Ronny when he left. No sign of anyone.

He'd made it. He was free.

Even so, he drove fifteen miles over the speed limit for an hour out of town, and he kept glancing in his rearview mirror, searching for Ronny's car. When he stopped at Moose Lake to go to the bathroom and grab a sandwich, he came out of the men's room with his stomach in knots, half expecting to see Ronny waiting for him in the parking lot. More than half, to be honest.

It was ridiculous, he knew. But goddamn if he could shake the sick feeling that this wasn't over.

He ended up only eating three bites of the sandwich, and one swig of the coffee almost sent him back into the bathroom to puke everything up. He bought a Sprite instead, sipping it with a shaking hand as he continued his desperate drive north.

He nearly headed down the road for Gabriel and Arthur's place, but he felt too sick inside his skin. He needed a night of sleep, he told himself, and he'd be all right. Just a bit more space, and he could put Ronny out of his head.

He ended up at Marcus and Frankie's without really planning to go there. It was almost ten, but he couldn't do anything about that now. He went up the walk, but the two of them had already opened the front door and were coming onto the porch to meet him. They seemed surprised, but they welcomed him without question.

"Well how about that," Marcus said. "Didn't figure you back until tomorrow."

Frankie regarded him with concern. "Are you all right? Did something happen?"

Something screamed, briefly, in the back of Dale's mind. *I'm not. I'm not okay. I'm so incredibly not okay. So much has happened, and I'll never be safe again.* But he couldn't speak the words, so he forced a smile, managing to look simply a little tired. "Rough day at the office. I kind of made an impulse decision to come at the last minute. Hope that's all right."

"Always." Frankie put an arm around his shoulder. "Marcus, go to the car and get his things, okay?"

Dale let Frankie lead him inside, the familiar smell of their house sending waves of healing through him.

He took deep breaths and shut his eyes for a moment as Frankie fussed over him.

It would be all right now. He was gone, it was over. Everything would be all right.

Except he still couldn't shake the feeling that there was something on his skin. Inside of it. And whenever he thought of it, each time it moved against him, all he wanted to do was cry.

ARTHUR HADN'T EVEN poured his coffee when he got the call from his mother. "Why didn't you tell me Dale was coming back last night? I would have had his duplex ready."

Arthur blinked and rubbed his face, switching the phone to his other ear so he could better wrangle the carafe. "What are you talking about?"

"Patty called me and said Susan saw him pull up to Marcus and Frankie's place late last night. You told me he was staying in the Cities and coming this afternoon."

That's exactly what Dale had told him he was doing. Arthur put his coffee cup down and frowned at the wall. "Something must have come up." Except he couldn't fucking figure out what the hell would have. More to the point, he had no idea why Dale had gone to Marcus's place instead of coming to the cabin.

He let his mother carry on a bit so she didn't get suspicious of anything, then extricated himself and went upstairs to wake Gabriel. "Hey, baby, did Dale tell you he was coming to town last night?"

Gabriel lifted his head sleepily. "No, he's not coming back until around three, he said."

"You mind checking your phone quick to see if he sent you any texts?"

Groaning, Gabriel picked up his phone. "No. He said he probably wouldn't be in contact much because he was so focused on getting packed up and out of there. Though it's weird he didn't text last night. But he said he knew it was your evening, and he didn't want to interrupt."

"Apparently part of the reason he was quiet was because he was driving here. He's at Marcus and Frankie's, according to my mother."

Gabriel sat up on his arms, blinking at Arthur, still half asleep. "What?"

Arthur ruffled his hair. "You know what? This is your day off. You sleep in, and I'll go see what's going on."

"Okay." Gabriel pulled the comforter over his head.

Arthur put his coffee in a travel mug and swung through the cafe for some donuts to go, then tucked the box under his arm as he went up Frankie and Marcus's walk. He almost knocked on the door, then thought better of it and doubled back around to the garage, where he saw both their cars were gone but Dale's was still out front. He let himself in through the side door, noted the house was silent, that Dale's boots were by the front door, then settled in at Frankie's kitchen table to eat a donut and drink his coffee. He didn't know what was going on, but he had a funny feeling something was off, and he knew he'd deal with the situation more smoothly with food in his stomach and caffeine in his blood.

Once he was done eating, he put his plate in the dishwasher so Marcus wouldn't bitch, then went up-stairs to see if he could find Dale.

Dale was asleep in one of the spare rooms, and when Arthur knocked on the door, he startled awake. He turned over and regarded Arthur blearily. "Arthur? What are you doing here?"

"Coming to see why the gossip mill felt the need to let me know you were in town early." The uneasy feeling in his gut intensified. Dale looked like he'd been out all night drinking, which Arthur was fairly sure he hadn't done.

Dale groaned and sat up, rubbing his eyes. Arthur watched him carefully, trying to read the signs Dale didn't want him to see. Something had happened in the Cities, he'd put money on it. Something had sent him running in the middle of the night, something he didn't want Arthur or Gabriel to know he was working through. Something had kept him up half the night.

Oh fucking hell, but Arthur had a bad feeling about this.

He knew better than to push on the wound, though, at least not right now. "I've got a box of donuts downstairs I'm willing to share. I'll put some coffee on for you while you have your morning piss and splash a little water on your face."

Dale touched his stomach as if unhappy to be reminded it existed. "I'm not really hungry."

"Well, you've got to eat. I'll put some of Frankie's peppermint tea in to steep if your stomach's upset." He patted Dale's shoulder, noting how this made him flinch. "How about a hot shower for you."

"I need to sleep. I didn't get to bed until late."

"I hate to break it to you, but my mother is going to appear on your doorstep inside the next hour with an army of Women's Circle ladies eager to deck out your duplex."

When Dale only buried his face in his hands, Arthur sighed and sat on the edge of the bed.

"All right." He dropped the false cheer and put a thread of command into his tone. "I suck at this game, so you know. I'm better at laying it on the line. Shit went down in Minneapolis. Don't tell me it didn't. I'm not going to make you talk about it—yet—but I am going to be real with you and point out it's going to be rough to get others to give you space. You're not hiding it as well as you think."

Dale's shoulders shook, and he pinched the bridge of his nose. Arthur's gut twisted as he saw a tear slip out from Dale's tightly shut eyes. "I keep trying to climb on top of it, to push it behind me, but I can't. I don't know why. I'm sorry."

"You don't have anything to be sorry for, I'm fairly sure of that." He patted Dale's leg through the blanket, noting the twitch again. His mind raced to try to guess what happened, but nothing made sense. All Dale had done was go home, and then into work.

He went cold as he remembered what Dale had confessed at the ice fishing hut, about the guy at work. He remembered the look in Dale's eye, the sense of unease the story had given Arthur. *No. No, let me be wrong.*

Except as much as it made him sick to his stomach, he was fairly sure he wasn't.

He shut his eyes, drew a breath. Then he left Dale's room, went back downstairs, and pulled out his phone.

His mom answered on the first ring. It took him several minutes to convince her no, she should *not* be right over, and yes, she should leave Dale alone today. Once he had her taken care of, he went to the garage and called Paul.

"Hey. Pauly." God, his voice was shaking. "I need to call in."

He waited for Paul to give him shit, but Paul didn't miss a beat. "What's wrong?"

"Complicated. I don't know yet. But I'm pretty sure I'm going to need to be alone with you and a six-pack later."

"Gabriel okay? You okay?"

"Yeah." He hesitated, then decided he was going to end up spilling it all to Paul regardless, whether he found anything out or not. "Something's going on with Dale. And I have a bad feeling I know what. Going to take the morning and see what I can do to try and…fuck, I don't know. Hopefully not fuck shit up."

"You'll do fine." He paused. "Holler if you need me, okay?"

"I will. Oh…and I know this is weird, but Gabriel doesn't know about this yet. Probably best to keep him in the dark for now. Until I get the story out of Dale." He bit his cheek. "I hate that I just said that."

"I know what you're saying. It only sounded shit because you don't always have the most grace about the way you phrase things. Or much grace period, really."

The ribbing made Arthur laugh. "Thanks, asshole."

"Anytime. Good luck."

Arthur hung up and went back inside.

He heard the shower running, which was a good sign. His belly grumbled, finished with the donut and ready for a real breakfast, so he poked around until he found the fixings for a nice set of scrambled eggs. He made enough for Dale, figuring he'd bully him into eating a few, and he was plating them when the man himself came in.

Dale had a good mask on now, and Arthur realized Dale had a decent one on all the time, actually. He could see the cracks because he was looking for them, but anyone poking around would think he was tired and write it off. When Arthur passed Dale a plate of food, he didn't reject it, but when they sat at the table, he didn't eat either, only pushed things around.

Right. Arthur knew how to play this one.

He chewed the bite he'd put in his mouth, then speared a new forkful. "So, yesterday I went to go fishing with Paul, and we damn near put the truck through the ice. We're good on foot to go out on the lake, but checking the weather forecast, I'm here to tell you, I'm thinking we're got another few weeks at best for fishing, no matter what the DNR says." He held the fork to Dale's lips, not pushing, only holding it in front of his mouth. "Since you've got a morning free, I thought you might like to go out with me. Let some of Logan's finest fresh air clear that pretty head of yours."

Dale didn't move for a long moment, but eventually he accepted the food, chewed, then nodded. "Sure."

Arthur ate a few more bites, but when Dale continued to not feed himself, Arthur put another forkful in front of his mouth again. "You still planning on moving into the duplex today, or you thinking you might want to hang out here a bit? I know Frankie and Marcus wouldn't mind."

Dale accepted the bite once more, but he took longer to answer this time. "I still want to move in, yes."

Okay then. Arthur ran a finger around the rim of his coffee cup, considering his next move. "Eat your food."

He noted how obediently Dale fell to the task. He

was fairly sure if he'd lightened his tone and said *please,* Dale would have told him he wasn't hungry, but here he was, eating, because Arthur had used his daddy voice on him. Arthur made a note to be careful with Dale. Arthur was far too used to Gabriel, who loved to argue. Not Dale. Dale didn't want you to know how eager he was to please you, but that's who he was. Eager to please you. Oh, so eager. He had mentioned playing "a little," but he craved it pretty hard, from everything Arthur had witnessed.

Oh, sweet baby, if that fucker hurt you, I'm going to break him in half.

They didn't say much through the rest of their breakfast, and Arthur let them lapse into companionable silence as they packed up lunches and stopped by the shop to get gear. Dale tensed as they went down the road to the cabin, which was the point at which Arthur acknowledged how real shit was about to get, but he pretended he hadn't noticed and only turned down a side road that would take them to the lake without going anywhere near the house. And yes, as soon as Dale realized he wasn't going to have to see Gabriel, he got calmer, but a peek out of the corner of Arthur's eye also revealed Dale'd gotten that hollowed-out thing going on again.

Arthur was going to kill the fucker in Minneapolis with a rusty spoon and make him eat his own stomach while he died. He tried to check himself, to tell himself he didn't know anything yet, but somehow he already knew.

It was a nice walk out to the shed, and the day was so pleasant that normally Arthur would have moved the hut to the side and enjoyed the fresh air. Something told him Dale could do with walls around him, though, so they set up the stools and the heater and got comfortable. No fish were biting, but he didn't care, because it wasn't the fish in the water he was trying to catch.

After a few hours of occasional idle chatter and a whole lot of heavy silence, he said, "You're going to have to talk to me about it eventually. And we're going to have six different messes if you try to carry on in front of Gabriel like this."

Dale stared into the hole in the ice as if he wished he could dive into it. "It's stupid. Nothing really happened."

The words came out a raw whisper, making it fucking obvious something sure as hell had happened, but Arthur made himself exercise the patience no one ever thought he had and combed through the words. Nothing *really*, so something happened, but not as bad as it could have. But whatever it was had shaken him all to hell.

Arthur pulled his line from the ice, then removed Dale's as well. He faced Dale, sitting with his hands on his own thighs. "Okay. We're going to have a scene right now, you and me, except it's not going to have a single thing to do with sex. Your clothes stay on. Nothing about this is your body. All the mind, all about control. Because that's your kink, isn't it? You like some dirty fun, and you love getting done, but what turns your crank is giving up the keys. I know we're still in the getting-to-know-you phase, but I hope you know you can trust me to never abuse that. I'm going to do my damnedest to prove it to you today. Because I'm going to ask you to go under for me, so I can help you calm down. But I'm going to also ask you what happened."

Dale shut his eyes, nodding. "I don't know what you mean, though, go under."

So that's how little he'd played. He didn't even know the terms, or didn't know how to connect the dots. "Subspace, baby. Like hypnosis, maybe—you let go a bit, stop driving the bus. You do it pretty easily. You were doing it at Marcus's house. It doesn't take much with you, I'm realizing. The right tone of voice is almost enough. You've probably moved up the ranks at jobs your whole life, because you're a pleaser, and you deliver. But there's an edge to the sword. It's easy to abuse that kind of person too."

Dale stiffened, looking ill. Arthur swallowed his own bile and kept his voice soothing, as if he hadn't triggered the land mine he'd hoped wasn't there. "Shh, it's all right. It's all good. Just you and me in an ice hut. Sit up nice and straight for me on your chair, but relax those hands. There you go. Good posture. You were a Boy Scout, weren't you, baby? That's right. Never met a man more prepared. Well right now there's nothing to prepare. Sit here, relax, and take deep breaths for me. There you go. In and out."

Arthur talked nonsense to Dale a bit longer. Led him through some simple exercises in the chair, had him touch his nose with his index finger, open and shut his mouth, dumb stuff to get him compliant. Wasn't hard, but Arthur made sure Dale was smoothly, firmly under him. Then he started on the questions.

"Talk to me, boy. Tell me about Wisconsin. Tell me again where you grew up."

"Deansville. And then Sun Prairie."

"Right, that's right. And where'd you go to college?"

"Marquette."

He did a whole damn interview, asking inane questions until Dale was so soft he answered everything without thinking. Then Arthur dove in. "Here we go, baby. Yellow to slow down. Red to stop. Tell me about the guy you played with in Minneapolis. *Keep your eyes closed,*" he said when Dale tried to open them.

Dale became visibly upset, but he still had his sub haze going, and he maintained. "H-his name is Ronny."

"Is he your boss?"

"No. He used to be in my department, but I got promoted."

"When did the playing start?" When Dale showed signs of stress, Arthur added, "No judgment, honey, but I need to hear the answers. Also, you're not feeling things this afternoon. You're just answering me. You don't have to feel things if you don't want to. You can push the feelings away."

Dale kept his eyes closed. "I can't. The feelings are everywhere."

Arthur huffed. "Let me show you the power of your sweet, sweet subspace." He lifted his palm, splayed his fingers, then used his other hand to guide Dale's mirror hand to his. "Who's in charge of you, Dale?"

"You are."

"Who's in charge of your feelings, Dale?"

A slight hesitation, then, "You are."

"When you have feelings you can't control, you are to push them through your hand into mine. I will take them. That's my job. I make the rules. I take the feelings. Do you understand?"

He frowned, then nodded slowly.

Arthur kept his palm flat to Dale's. "When did the playing start?"

"A few months after I first got promoted out of his department." He pushed gently on Arthur's hand, then opened his eyes and looked at it in surprise. "How—?"

"Eyes shut," Arthur ordered.

Dale shut his eyes.

"Talk me through how the playing got started. What kind it was. What you thought of it at first. Push on my hand when you need to."

Dale took his time, pausing often to discharge feeling into Arthur's palm. "I don't remember how it began anymore. At a party, I think. I'd been drinking, so had he." Hard pressure. "It was in the back of the room. He felt me up, and no one else could see. It was exciting. But then the next day he cornered me in the copy room at the office, and it was strange."

"Did you ever date him?"

Dale shook his head. "It's never been about sex. He's not gay, not even bi. He's married. Has a family."

Jesus. They always were, the sick freak shows. "It was about power and control. You were the big, strong man everyone liked, who got his promotion. And he discovered he could manipulate and control you."

Dale pressed into Arthur's hand. "Yes, but...but..."

Arthur's heart broke. "Shh, it's all right. It's okay."

"It's not. It's not." Dale pushed so hard he nearly knocked Arthur over.

"It is." Arthur laced their fingers together and held Dale's hand tight. "It's all right." Dale let out a ragged breath, near-sob, and Arthur rubbed his thumb along the side of Dale's hand. "Breathe. Deep breaths."

"It's sick," he whispered.

"Ronny? Yes, he's a sick fucker who should have his testicles turned inside out and shoved down his throat through his nose."

"*Me.*"

"You? No, not you. You're a wonderful, charming, sexy, big-hearted man my fiancé is falling in love with and I am quite fond of too. But you also, my dear, are an abuse survivor, and if the shadows in your eyes are telling me the right story, a survivor of sexual assault as well."

Dale tried to open his eyes, but the command not to had him conflicted. Arthur squeezed his hand, lowered it to his lap, but didn't let go. "Open your eyes and look at me."

Dale did. "I…I'm not…I told you, I didn't ever have…"

"Were you coerced into sexual positions with him when you didn't want to be in them?"

Dale hesitated, then nodded.

"Were you ever hurt getting into any of these positions, or did he ever hurt you because you wouldn't get into them?"

Dale shut his eyes in a painful blink, then gave another nod.

"Did he make you feel less than human in a way that wasn't part of play, in something that extended beyond consensual fun of a game?"

Again, Dale nodded.

"Did he threaten to expose you if you tried to end contact, threatening your job or your relationships with friends or loved ones?"

Dale glanced away. Then he nodded once more.

Arthur squeezed his hand. Whispered, "Look at me."

Dale did, his eyes glazed with tears.

Arthur fought to keep his voice steady and clear. "Everything you said yes to means you confirmed you are a victim of abuse. You want to know how I know that? Because I belong to a leather community, real BDSM, and we take our practice seriously. I took an online class, had Gabriel help me do research, and did a lecture for our group last summer on care and consent. I know about what I rattled off to you because it's what a good Dom knows. You didn't have a good Dom. You didn't have a Dom. You had an abuser. So you need to stop anything you're doing right now that puts any blame for what happened on you and turn it all back around on him where it belongs. And you need to let me hook you up with this counselor lady I know in Duluth. She'll talk to you over Skype if you want, once you've met her in person, if you're rural. Which right now you are."

Dale looked wrecked, but he held Arthur's hand tight, and when he spoke, things were coming out of him, not trying to stay bottled in. "I tried to get away. I couldn't. I don't know why. I should have been able to overpower him. I'm bigger than he is. But I couldn't make myself move."

"Because it's not always about who's big and strong on the outside." Arthur rubbed Dale's knee. "It's all right. Remember we're okay now. We're out here on the ice, just you and me. We're safe. Not even fish here today."

Dale shut his eyes, taking slow, deep breaths without being prompted. "That's why I came straight here.

I feel safe here. But I couldn't face Gabriel. I still can't. I feel dirty."

"You're not dirty. You're perfect. Beautiful. I think you *should* see Gabriel. I think he would be good for you."

Dale's grip on Arthur's hand tightened. "I'm afraid I'll freak out during sex."

"That fear could get worse the longer you feed it. Do you want me along for the trip? To make sure?"

Dale flushed. "That makes me sound ridiculous."

"It makes you sound like my sub who is an abuse survivor needing his Dom for a leg up."

"But he'll want to know why."

"Yes. And at some point, if you intend for this to be more than a summer fling, you'll probably have to tell him. Because I have news for you. Wounds don't tickle. But you don't have to tell him tonight. Or anytime soon. You tell him when you're ready to share this wound with him. And if you tell him you need him to wait to hear it, he'll wait."

"You didn't wait."

"Well, I'm a pushy bastard. You needed someone to help you out of the hole, and I think I was the only one who could tell you were in one. You were going to keep trying to convince us all you were fine."

Dale said nothing, but his guilty expression confirmed that yes, this had been his plan.

Arthur stroked his hand. "If you're all right with it, I can tell Gabriel I know the story and he needs to be patient with you."

"He won't be upset?"

Arthur wasn't sure. "I'm pretty sure I can persuade him."

Dale sagged slightly. He'd come out of subspace a great deal, but he was calmer now. "I do want to see him. I was so excited. I found a perfect place for our date."

"Then tell him about it. Don't let this fucker take that away from either of you. Remember, Dale, the thing with power play is it's all about consent. You still give it. This guy conned you into handing it over, but you're on to him now. He doesn't get anything more. He doesn't get your first date with Gabriel. He doesn't get this day on the ice with me. He doesn't get Logan. You decide what he gets to keep and what he doesn't. You're the one in control. He only gets to keep what you give him. Never let him trick you into believing otherwise."

He knew he'd triggered some land mine again, because Dale got his haunted look back, retreating into himself.

Arthur snapped to attention. "Breathe, Dale. Sit up straight. Breathe. Stay with me. There you go. Now tell me what just happened. What did I say and what did you think about that made you swallow yourself into a black hole?"

Dale clung to Arthur's hand so tightly Arthur began to lose feeling. "Pictures," Dale whispered. "He has pictures."

Chapter Eleven

G ABRIEL HAD A vague memory of Arthur waking
him to tell him Dale was in town early, and he
thought he'd possibly been asked to check his phone
for texts, but once he was fully conscious, he didn't
have texts from anyone, Arthur or Dale, and no one
was home. Arthur wasn't answering his phone or
replying to texts, but this wasn't a new phenomenon,
so after taking a shower, Gabriel got dressed and went
into town in search of him. He was surprised to find
Paul's car but not Arthur's at the shop, and he went
inside to see what was going on.

Paul was fiddling with an old refrigerator, but he
stopped when he saw Gabriel. "Hey there. Looking for
Arthur?"

"I am. Dale too. Did I hear right that he came back
early?"

"Think so." Paul cleaned his hands on a rag. "Haven't seen him yet, though. Or Arthur. He called in,
said he had to take care of something."

Gabriel flattened his lips. "Well, if he shows up or texts you, will you tell him to call me?" He checked his watch. "I've got to go. I'm due to meet Frankie and Kyle at the salon. We're going to start doing the planning for the wedding."

"Sounds good. Have fun."

He worried on the way to Frankie's salon, but he told himself there wasn't any reason to fret. Not until he arrived and Frankie mentioned how concerned he was about Dale.

"He came in so late, not a text, not a phone call." Frankie was styling Kyle's hair while he told the story, trying out a new product and showing Kyle a few ways to use it, meeting Gabriel's gaze in the mirror while he worked. "We heard a car in the street, wondered who it was, and it was him! But he looked awful. He said it was a rough day at the office. I'd say it was something terrible, from the expression on his face. I gave him tea and put him to bed, but I don't think he slept much until early in the morning."

Gabriel was torn between being upset Dale hadn't come to him and being worried over what had happened. "Is he at the house now?" His mind raced, trying to find an excuse that would let him go over.

"No, he was gone when Marcus went home for lunch. I assume he went to a council meeting or something." He patted Kyle's shoulders and smiled into the mirror. "What do you think?"

Kyle preened, turning his head this way and that

before smiling coyly at his reflection. "It's cute. I like it. How much is it for the bottle?"

Frankie waved a hand. "On the house. I still owe you a birthday present." He washed his hands in the sink and nodded toward the back. "I have the books all laid out. Gabriel, do you want to flip the *closed* sign around, and we'll get started?"

Gabriel saw to the sign, all the while sending texts, first to Arthur, then to Dale, and then, finally, to Paul. None of them answered. He followed the other two into Frankie's workroom, and for almost ninety seconds pretended he gave a damn about place settings and venues and themes and color schemes. Then he gave up and stood.

"Actually, I'm sorry. I have to go."

Frankie looked surprised and annoyed. "Gabriel, we've been planning this for *weeks*. We can't ever get a day we're all free, and I cancelled two appointments for this."

I don't care. "I'm sorry."

He didn't make it out the front door, though, before Kyle caught up with him. "Hey." He held loosely on to Gabriel's arm, frowning. "What's going on? You're clearly upset. How can we help?"

Gabriel would love to vent to his best friends how his boyfriend had come back to town without telling him and his fiancé had also gone missing. How he had this suspicion they were together and he wasn't jealous that they were having sex, but he was hurt they'd excluded him or worried something was wrong, and in that case hurt also they'd excluded him, and mostly confused and jumbled and hating how alone he felt right now because he couldn't tell anyone. "I'm sorry. You can't."

"Did Arthur do something?"

Gabriel held up a hand, used the other to push on the door, and left.

He drove too fast to the shop, then almost screamed in frustration because Paul's truck wasn't there anymore either, so he couldn't grill him like he'd planned. He drove around town aimlessly, swearing under his breath and being increasingly irrationally upset until he reached the point he was worked up simply because he was worked up.

Until he saw Dale's car, and Arthur's truck, and Corrina's car, all parked at the duplex.

He turned around in a red haze, parked alongside Corrina's car and got out, ready for battle. It had dawned on him he couldn't exactly pitch the fit he wanted to with Corrina around, so when Arthur came out of the duplex alone and held up a warning finger, Gabriel was almost glad to see him.

"Oh, *don't* you raise your fucking finger at me. Where the hell have you been? Why haven't—?"

"Gabriel, don't."

The tone caught Gabriel by surprise. Arthur marched him around the line of cars, around the duplex, and through the snow behind the line of evergreens they intended to use as a discretion screen for when Gabriel came over to see Dale. Once they were hidden away, Arthur stopped walking and faced him. The look on his face cut away the last of Gabriel's anger, leaving him only with upset. "What's wrong? What happened? Is Dale okay?"

It took Arthur too long to answer. "No. But he will be. Here's the thing though, honey. I need you to trust me. Okay? You need to let him tell you what's wrong in his own time."

The hurt came rushing back. "But he told *you*?"

"Yes, baby. And I wish to all hell I didn't have to know." He shut his eyes, looking wrecked, tired. This was a side of Arthur Gabriel never saw. "It isn't my story to tell. It belongs to him, and it should be shared between the two of you, not you and me. Don't take that from him, please. Because you could get it out of me pretty damn easy, and then we'll all be sorry."

"Arthur." Gabriel slid arms around him, kissed his forehead, bent to kiss his lips. "I won't ask you anymore. I promise."

Arthur relaxed into his embrace. "He needs you tonight. But be gentle as a lamb with him. He's nervous to be with you because he's not thinking straight and has it in his head he'll screw things up, but I think you're the best medicine for him. I can't think of anyone in the world better for him right now than you."

Now Gabriel felt foolish for being jealous. And flattered for being Dale's best medicine. He kissed

Arthur again. "I'm sorry for all the texts. I was worried."

"Didn't see any of them. I was so focused on keeping my mother from making an ass of herself."

Gabriel laughed, then stopped. "Wait, she's with him now."

"I know. But I had to make the hard call." He squeezed Gabriel's hands. "He'll be fine. It'll be fine."

The longer they stood outside, the more terrified Gabriel grew of what he was about to find in Dale. "Okay."

They went in, then, and it was one of those moments when Corrina Anderson and her intrusive, overbearing ways were a gift. Because as she showed Gabriel the dish set she'd found at Salvation Army and the adorable love seat someone had donated and the DVD player she didn't need because she had Blu-ray now, unless Dale needed Blu-ray, but they weren't that expensive anymore at Walmart and anyway he had something to watch and wasn't it handy he knew the librarian with all the DVDs in the meantime—while she chattered on, Gabriel sought out Dale's gaze and tried to figure out, at least a little, what was going on.

Dale was clearly exhausted and wrung out, sad in this vague way, but honestly Gabriel couldn't tell much else. Not until he looked him in the eye, and then he simply seemed nervous and oddly guilty, though it made no sense at all. Gabriel wondered if maybe there had been another guy in Minnesota, but how it could have happened in one day he didn't know, and anyway, if they were polyamorous, was it cheating? He supposed it was possible—it was about not telling, cheating—but again, one day? In any event, he didn't think this was Dale guilty because he'd had an affair. More like perhaps he'd run into an awful ex.

Except nothing about Arthur's devastated expression explained anything either.

Arthur cleared his throat. "Mom, Dale drove all day yesterday, and he's dead on his feet. We need to let him get settled. Give him some space."

Corrina glanced at her watch. "Oh, you're right. But you'll call me, yes, Dale, if you need anything? I left my number on the fridge. You won't need to cook for a week, with what I left you in there. But if you do want to cook, there's plenty of things for that too. And some wine and beer."

"*Mom.*"

She sighed and held up her hands. "All right. I need to get going anyway. Big Tom and the kids are going to be home soon. I'll spread the word for you to be left alone tonight, Dale. But I'm sure you'll have plenty of visitors tomorrow, people wanting to stop by and wish you well." She patted Dale on the cheek. "Have a good evening, dear."

Then, finally, she left.

Arthur followed her to the door, shutting it behind her, drawing aside the curtain on the window to watch her get into her car. Once she pulled away, all his focus was on Dale. He walked up to him, grave faced but calm, scrutinizing him. "You doing all right?"

Dale nodded. "I'm all right." His voice sounded raw.

Arthur didn't touch him, but Gabriel had the sense somehow Arthur was stroking him all the same. "You're okay. Everything's fine." When Dale's gaze darted to Gabriel, Arthur's did too. "Is it cool that he's here?"

Gabriel's heart rose to his throat. The thought of being rejected hurt too much, and he rushed to remove himself before it could happen. He started for the door. "I'm sorry. I was just worried because no one was answering my texts. I can leave."

"No." This was Dale, and the sound of his voice made Gabriel stop. "I want you to stay, Gabriel. Please."

Gabriel melted inside. "Of course."

Arthur touched Dale's arm. "Do you need *me* to stay?"

Dale shook his head. "I'll be okay. Thanks."

"Fair enough." Arthur removed his handkerchief from his pocket and pressed it into Dale's hand, raising their palms flat together for a moment before releasing them, leaving the hanky with Dale. "In case you need somewhere to put things."

Dale smiled at him, a weary half-gesture. He hugged Arthur, a tight, lingering embrace. "Thank you," he whispered.

Arthur patted Dale's back, then went to Gabriel and embraced him too. A more intimate embrace, and Gabriel might have been imagining it, but he felt like Arthur was drawing something from him, asking him for strength. When Arthur pulled him down for a kiss, Gabriel tried to give him what he asked for, acknowledging something serious had happened that had worn Dale through and wrecked Arthur. When Arthur ended the kiss, he added another on Gabriel's cheek, the familiar brush of his beard sending a comforting thrill through Gabriel.

"I'll come by in the morning with a change of clothes. Text me if you need anything else from home." His lips quirked in a wry grin. "I promise to keep my ringer on this time."

He kissed Gabriel once more, and then he left, and it was Gabriel alone with Dale at last.

Funny how Gabriel had been so eager for this exact situation to happen, and now that he had it, he was so nervous he almost didn't know what to do. Dale was too, and at first they stood there awkwardly in front of one another. Finally Gabriel got over himself though and found his manners, his social sense. He glanced around the duplex. "Well, I suspect you'll want to put your own style on it, but it's a start, I suppose."

Dale looked around too. He seemed so exhausted. "It's all right."

Gabriel wandered around idly, taking it in. The decor was an odd mix of middle-age woman and middle-age woman's idea of what men—straight men—wanted in decor. He bit his lip, covering his mouth to stay his laugh as he spied the decorations above the bookshelf near the kitchen. "Oh dear. There's a plaque here that says *Man Cave*."

Dale came up beside him, and the nearness of him thrilled Gabriel, especially when Dale reached over his shoulder to take it down. "That is leaving the house immediately."

"We'll put it up in the repair shop. See how long until they notice it."

He'd hoped to make Dale laugh, but when he turned to look at him, Dale simply seemed weary again.

Gabriel took the sign from him, captured Dale's hands, and held them tight. He noticed Dale still held Arthur's handkerchief. "I don't know what's wrong, and you don't need to tell me. Can you let me know what will help you right now? Because I'll give you whatever you want, whatever you need."

Dale rested his forehead against Gabriel's and shut his eyes. "You. I need you."

Gabriel shut his eyes too, let go of Dale's hands, and slid his palms up Dale's chest. When he twitched a little, Gabriel slowed, gentled his touch, until his fingers tickled Dale's nape. "You have me."

Dale's arms went around Gabriel, drawing him closer. "I just want to hold you. I'm so tired. I feel like I could sleep for a year."

"I love being held by you. And Arthur will tell you

I'm a champion sleeper." His stomach rumbled, and he blushed and nuzzled Dale's cheek. "Could we heat up some of that food Corrina mentioned first? I haven't really eaten since breakfast."

Dale nodded, nuzzling him back. "Sure."

They went to the kitchen together, holding hands as they poked through the carefully labeled containers, choosing a tray of lasagna to put in the oven and nibbling on some vegetables and ranch while they waited for it to heat. Corrina had stocked the fridge with several different kinds of craft beer, but Dale opted for a soda, and Gabriel, after searching in vain for a box of herbal tea, filled a glass of water.

"I'll get you some when I get a chance to go to the grocery store," Dale promised.

They'd settled into the love seat to wait for their dinner, dragging over the ottoman from the over-stuffed chair and draping themselves with a crocheted afghan.

"Do you want to watch television?" Gabriel asked, feeding Dale a ranch-laced carrot.

Dale ate the carrot and shook his head. "I don't watch much TV."

Gabriel ran a foot along his leg and smiled at him. "Are you saying that just to get in good with the librarian? Because I don't have anything against other media, though of course I do have a small bias toward books."

"No, I've never really enjoyed the narrative. I prefer the containment of a film. Theater is my favorite, to be honest."

Gabriel popped a cherry tomato into Dale's mouth. "I don't think you have any idea how much you're turning me on right now. But I am going to try to get you to like *Black Books*. I'll bring the DVD collection over from the library."

Dale swallowed the tomato, leaned forward, and kissed Gabriel sweetly on the lips. "I booked us tickets for the theater for the weekend we're in Duluth. I found this really great place I think you'll love, and it might help us figure out the Logan project too. Got us a room in a hotel down the street as well, off the Lakewalk."

"Sounds utterly perfect." He stroked Dale's cheek, ruffling a thumb in his beard, making the decision to comment no further on whatever was bothering Dale. "Thank you for finding it for us." A rush of love swept Gabriel up, and he feared he shouldn't say the word, so he kissed Dale instead. "I missed you so much when you were gone, though it was only for a little while."

The shadow flickered over Dale's face once more, but this time he sloughed it off and some of the old Dale shone through. He cupped Gabriel's face, his tongue stealing almost shyly over Gabriel's lips. Gabriel parted immediately to let him in, but even then Dale was hesitant, entering him slowly. When he finally broke the kiss, Gabriel was breathless, desperate for more.

"I would give you anything." Gabriel whispered the

words, stroked Dale's face, neck, gazed into his bright blue eyes. "I love being with you." He took Dale's hand and placed it on his solar plexus, slipping his thumb inside his shirt between the buttons. "Take what you need from me tonight."

Dale regarded him with desire, with love. There was something else in his eyes too, though. The shadow. A shade of sorrow, of fear. His fingers kneaded against Gabriel's chest. "I would never hurt you. I would never, ever hurt you."

Gabriel frowned slightly, not sure where this had come from. "I would never think you would."

But Dale was insistent now. "I would *never hurt you.* If you let go to me, I would never hurt you."

Gabriel studied Dale carefully. *I know,* he wanted to say, but didn't. He thought of Arthur, of how upset he had been. It came to Gabriel then, a terrible revelation.

I wish all to hell I didn't have to know.

Someone had hurt Dale, terribly.

Gabriel put his hands over Dale's palm, the one held over his own heart, lifted it to his mouth, and kissed the center of it. "I would never hurt you either. I couldn't bear to, not on purpose. Not for one moment, not ever."

This time when Dale kissed him, all of his lover was present and accounted for. The full force of Dale pressed him into the side of the love seat, pulling his knees apart to fit their groins together and grind into him. Dale held Gabriel tight and bore down on him, until he broke away long enough to undo Gabriel's jeans and draw them and his briefs away.

Gabriel lay in the corner of the love seat, letting his legs fall open so Dale could see him, breathing hard as his lover stared at his body with naked want. Gabriel's cock filled from the eroticism of being so ogled, and it took all his discipline not to fidget, to wait for Dale to tell him what to do next.

Dale's gaze flickered to his. "Take off the rest."

Gabriel unbuttoned his shirt, fingers trembling in anticipation. When he'd peeled it away, he tugged the undershirt over his head, until he sat there, naked, silent, waiting, while Dale loomed over him, fully dressed, staring intently, his intentions unclear.

The moment was interrupted by the sounding of Gabriel's phone timer, announcing the lasagna was ready to eat. They blinked at one another, the moment unraveled.

Gabriel did his best to rescue it. He leaned over and fumbled with his phone, stopping the timer. "Turn off the oven—it'll heat a bit more, but it'll stay warm, until we're ready." *Then come back and finish this with me*, he wanted to add, but didn't quite have the courage.

Dale disappeared into the kitchen, and while he was gone, Gabriel did his best to screw his courage to the sticking place. When Dale came back, Gabriel gazed up at him, waiting to see what happened.

Dale had lost some of his fervor with the interruption, but the shadow had left his expression too. There was a quietness about him, a breathless simplicity, and Gabriel kept the silence, enjoying it as Dale sat on the ottoman with Gabriel's foot in his hand, caressing it idly, almost beseechingly.

"Tell me," Dale said at last. "Please." When Gabriel frowned at him, not understanding, Dale drew a deep breath and added, in a voice of one unearthing his own courage, "What to do. Tell me what to do. To you."

Gabriel didn't let himself blink, schooled his surprise. Pushed through it and focused on the need and ache in Dale's expression. Then he ran his other foot over Dale's leg and said in the bravest voice he could, "Kneel down and suck my cock."

He felt foolish, a fraud, because he was the most un-toppy man alive, and yet the second Dale did as Gabriel asked, all those thoughts fled, replaced by the white-hot pleasure of Dale's mouth. Gabriel cried out, melting into the couch, his legs flailing awkwardly until Dale hooked them one by one over his shoulders, thereby giving himself an even better angle by which to attack.

Except this was going to be over far too soon. Gabriel fought his orgasm as best he could, but soon he knew he had to redirect. "Stop," he rasped, and to his surprise, immediately Dale did. He didn't want him to *stop* stop, though, so he thought quickly. "Suck...my balls."

Dale fell to this task as well as he had the other, and Gabriel was as lost as he had been before, though not simply tormented, because he couldn't get to where he desired. His body ached for more, and his brain had finally registered that for once it actually had control of his sexual situation. "Touch me. Finger me." He grunted as Dale's index finger poked at him dry, and though that was dirty fun for a moment, it wasn't what he wanted.

"Lick me. Suck my hole." Gabriel's cheeks flamed at the dirty words, but he didn't stop. "Then finger it."

Dale did this too. Wordlessly, no complaint, and it was so good, so wicked and so filthy wonderful, Gabriel had to watch. Dale's dark blond head bobbing between his thighs, his slick tongue working inside him, then long, strong fingers pressing deep, spreading him. He gasped, cried out, blitzed himself on the riot of sensations until tears ran down his face.

"I need to come," he whispered at last.

"How do you want it?" Dale asked, his voice gruff with arousal.

Gabriel didn't know. What he wanted was for Dale to fuck him into the couch, but something told him it wasn't the best thing to ask for right now. He scrambled to imagine the next best thing. "Finger me and suck me off at the same time." He let dark need roll over him and added, "Rough. I want it rough."

He shivered as Dale laved a great deal of spit into his ass, then paused. "Do you need me to get actual lube?"

Gabriel wanted to say no, then made himself think

about how sore his ass would be in an hour. "Yes."

Dale disappeared, and Gabriel used the moment to collect himself. Dale was back quickly, but he didn't have lube with him. He had...a tub of shortening.

"All my stuff is still packed or at Marcus's." He swiped a liberal amount of the shortening with his fingers and knelt between Gabriel's legs again. "Too weird?"

Gabriel shook his head, but his belly fluttered as he felt the cool, slippery stuff enter him. "Oh God, it feels gross. Dirty as hell." He shut his eyes and rubbed his face into the back of the love seat. "Use more."

Dale took more from the canister and kissed the inside of Gabriel's thigh. "I love you."

Gabriel opened his mouth to return the words, but Dale pushed more shortening and two fingers into him, and he groaned instead, the sound becoming a high-pitched cry as Dale fucked him harder, separating his fingers and then taking Gabriel's cock into his mouth.

The shortening was absolutely pervy, thick and rude inside him, and every time Dale thrust Gabriel could hear it moving, a slick *swish-swish* that made him shiver and spread his legs wider. Dale shoved his fingers deep, twisting them, then adding a third as he hummed around Gabriel's cock. When Gabriel flailed too much on the sofa, Dale draped him over the ottoman, giving him a better angle to finger fuck him, until Gabriel dug his heels into Dale's back as he arched off the ottoman and fucked into Dale's throat.

Dale's fingers were still inside him as Gabriel drew him up to kiss him, putting his hand on Dale's to urge him to continue finger-fucking him until he couldn't handle it anymore. Then Gabriel drew Dale's fingers out and nuzzled his nose.

"Come for me," he whispered to Dale. "Pull your cock out and come on top of me."

For a minute he thought Dale wouldn't do it, but with one last kiss, Dale stood and unzipped his pants. Gabriel took one look at his long, beautiful cock and couldn't hold back. "Fuck my mouth first, just for a minute."

Gabriel sighed as Dale held his head carefully and guided his cock inside. He lay there, spent and happy, sucking as Dale fucked carefully into his throat, pulling out sometimes to rub the tip over his lips. When he could tell Dale was getting close, he pulled his mouth away. "Come on my chest. But touch me while you come. With your cock, your hand, your body, whatever you want."

He lay still until Dale's cock brushed his nipple, and then he jolted. When Dale's fingers touched the same spot, Gabriel arched toward him, inviting him to take more. He wanted a little pain, but Dale only gave him a caress, and Gabriel rode his decision, watching him pleasure himself, until he couldn't stand it any longer.

"More," he whispered.

Dale teased the peak, his other hand working himself faster, and as he came, spurting across Gabriel's chest, he pinched tight enough to give Gabriel the bite he wanted.

Dale knelt and kissed him when he finished, and he kissed the nipple too. "Did I hurt you?"

"Only the way I wanted you to." Gabriel grabbed his head and nipped his lip. "I love you too."

Dale kissed him hard, carnal enough that if they had been younger, they might have gone another round. As it was, they were not young, and both their stomachs were grumbling now. He stroked Gabriel's belly, beside the cooling spunk. "Would you like a towel, and then some lasagna?"

"Yes, please," Gabriel replied.

And that's exactly what they did.

ARTHUR WANTED A drink, or six.

If he were honest, he wanted Gabriel. It cut a little, to know he'd given him up, but not really. He didn't *need* Gabriel, he only wanted him in the same way he wanted his house and other comforting aspects of his life. Dale needed him. Arthur's mom had always chided him for being shitty about sharing. Well, here was his chance to shine.

Besides, Arthur had a fuck lot of people in his life who could comfort him, and one of them doubled as someone he'd promised to have a word with on Dale's behalf.

He found Marcus at his house, which was where all

his friends were, in fact, gathered in the kitchen. Frankie and Kyle, though mostly Frankie, were angry, and since Arthur hadn't knocked, only come in through the kitchen door, he was able to hear Gabriel's name and something about "walking right out without explaining anything." Arthur's shoulders grew heavy as he saw their hostile faces and realized he couldn't lay down his sword yet.

Except he discovered he'd already sheathed it somewhere between the duplex and here, and when they turned to him, he held up both hands. "I need to talk to Marcus. Please."

Frankie, who looked like he had had about enough of everything, folded his arms tighter in front of his chest and placed himself in front of his fiancé. "No. If you have something to say, you can say it to all of us. Because I'm pretty sure it has to do with why Gabriel ran out on Kyle and me, why Dale seemed so upset, and why you canceled on Paul. I'm tired of these secrets. We're all friends here. You can tell us what's going on."

Arthur cut a desperate gaze to Paul, begging him with his eyes. But this was a mistake, because now Kyle, who had been sitting quietly to the side, got angry too—at Paul. "Are you telling me you've known what this is about this whole time and you haven't said anything?"

Paul sputtered, glancing between Arthur and Marcus as Kyle backed him into the kitchen island. Arthur sank onto the bench by the door, letting his head fall forward into his hands. God, he didn't know the last time he'd felt this tired, this awful, this wrung out. For all his feeling disbursement show-and-tell with Dale, he wondered if he hadn't somehow absorbed some of the man's darkness. He sure as hell felt it.

"*Enough.*"

Marcus's voice wasn't loud, but it was low and sharp, and though the man didn't play at all, if he did, he'd be the biggest, baddest daddy in the county. He loomed as large as a grizzly over the chaos of the kitchen, silencing Frankie and Kyle, putting a hand on his fiancé's shoulder and then nodding at the door to the other room.

"I need a minute with Arthur. Then we'll join you. Wait for us in the living room."

Kyle and Paul shuffled out, Paul murmuring quietly the whole time, reassuring his fiancé. Frankie lingered a little, having some kind of silent exchange with Marcus, then he left too. Then it was only Marcus and Arthur.

Marcus crossed to Arthur and pulled up a chair, resting his elbows on his knees, patiently waiting. Then, finally, Arthur sagged into the coats behind him and let his mask fall off.

"What happened?" Marcus asked.

Arthur stared at Marcus's shoulder. "I lose track of what I'm allowed to say and what I can't. I think I'm going to break some confidences."

"I can be discreet. You want to tell me what you

need first, or tell the story?"

Arthur considered. "Am I right that Minnesota passed one of those laws about pictures, making it illegal to do stuff with private pictures you take of people?"

"You're talking about revenge porn laws? They're debating one right now. But there's question about whether or not it will stand up to a constitutional challenge." Marcus's lips thinned, disappearing into his beard. "Don't tell me...Dale."

"Oh, honey. You don't know the half of it." Arthur rolled his eyes to the ceiling. "The guy who took the pictures has been abusing him for years. Mostly mentally, but I think...I think also physically. I don't know all of it. I don't know if I want to know all of it, and I feel pretty shitty for saying so."

Marcus put a hand on Arthur's knee, a steadying, comforting pressure. "It's all right. But where is he? Is he okay?"

"Gabriel's with him. And yeah, he's fine. We spent the day on the lake, fishing and talking. I kind of did a scene with him to get the stuff out of him—not kink, just control. That's his thing. He..." He stopped, feeling as if he was spilling too many beans. "He's tender underneath. He's like you. Everybody thinks he's all tough, and he can be, but underneath he's gooey center, and you know how easily that bruises."

"I do." Marcus sighed. Dale heard so much sorrow in the sound. "I had no idea. I feel terrible."

"I think that's how abuse works. We never know, until we know. I had the training, so I smelled it. God, I never realized how little I wanted to use the knowledge until today. I'm glad I could, but..." He wiped at his eyes. "I'm going to get him to talk to the counselor lady who ran my course. Like I said, Gabriel's with him, and he's got us. But...I don't know what to do about the pictures the guy has. I was doing fine until I knew about that gun on the mantle. I gotta tell you, it's everything in me not to get in my fucking truck, drive to the Cities, and gut the fucker right now."

"You would get arrested." But Marcus's tone suggested he too was annoyed with the law keeping them from solving the problem with murder. And he was a lawyer.

"How is this okay? How is it okay for this guy to be able to threaten him this way and I can't go down there and feed him his puréed testicles?"

"Because justice isn't simple, and it isn't swift." Marcus leaned back. "What so far were you allowed to tell me, and what did you let slip?"

Arthur rewound the conversation. "I was allowed to tell you about the pictures, and the abuse generally. I think I actually mostly stuck to the letter, which is frankly a miracle. Probably wasn't supposed to tell you about the scene or that he likes giving up control or that he's all soft inside."

"So he's willing to talk with me? He'll let me represent him? Because I assume the threat is that the abuser will expose him to friends and coworkers."

"Yes. He wants your help. He's worried about his job, his reputation at his company and with his investors."

"Good. I have some contacts I want to reach out to right away to help me, but I already know how I want to approach this."

"I was hoping you would."

"We'll get him through this." Marcus moved his hand to Arthur's shoulder, squeezed. "How are *you* doing?"

Arthur gave up, let a few of the tears fall. "Pretty shitty, to be honest. Been fucking faking it and acting tough for everybody all goddamned day, and all I want to do is curl up in a corner and cry." He paused and added, "Or cut the guys balls into bits and fuck up his face, but you said I can't do that, so crying's all I've got, I guess."

"How about getting drunk on your favorite beer in my den while we watch the tape of the playoff game? That sound better than getting arrested for assault or crying?"

Arthur punched him weakly in the shoulder. "Obviously."

Marcus got him the beer—two—and led him to the den, past the others, who looked expectant until they saw his tears, then went stone silent. Arthur said nothing, only let himself be plunked in Marcus's leather recliner and arranged in front of the game, which he did want to see but had a hard time following. He had to keep wiping his fucking eyes.

The door to the den opened not long after, and Paul entered the room. Arthur tried to clean up his face, but Paul waved a hand at him, as if to say *Don't get up*, not *Don't bother hiding your tears*. "What's the score?" he asked as he sat, like he hadn't watched the game already. Twice.

"1-0." Arthur passed him the second beer and the opener. "Wild's up."

Paul accepted them both. "Excellent." He cracked the top, toasted Arthur, and settled in to watch.

DALE DIDN'T MEET with Marcus for about two weeks, though every time they saw each other at meetings for the Logan planning commission, all he could think about was the fact that Marcus knew his secret. Overall his transition to life in Logan was going well. He'd gone shopping for some more personal things in his house, ordered some furniture he preferred, and in general made the duplex his home. He'd rented office space downtown and had regular meetings with city council members and business leaders from Logan and sur-rounding communities. He had regular mini-dates at home with Gabriel—discreetly—and they still had their time together planned in Duluth, moved to later in May so he could take advantage of a meeting with a leader there at the center. He was a little too busy to get away as much as he'd like, but he was doing well enough.

He followed through with Arthur and went to see the counselor, which he didn't particularly enjoy, but it wasn't as awful as he'd feared it'd be either. She said much of the same things as Arthur had, though mostly she let Dale talk. He ended up talking a lot about his past well before he knew Ronny, about the days when he'd first moved to Minneapolis, which seemed odd, but she said whatever felt right for him was what was the right thing to talk about. Their first meeting was in person in her office just north of Duluth, but they arranged to meet by Skype weekly thereafter.

Dale still had to talk to his oldest friend in Logan about what had happened to him, to follow up on the plans Arthur had set in motion, but it took him some time to work up the courage. Finally, one day at the beginning of May he went to Marcus's office at his house, when Frankie wasn't home, and he told him the story, though he knew Marcus already knew most of it. It was getting easier each time he told it, and he was able, mostly, to simply repeat it and not get lost in the feelings. Though he did have to clutch Arthur's handkerchief the whole time.

When he was finished, he let out a breath and waited for Marcus's reaction.

Marcus sat in the wingback chair across from him, elbow resting on the arm, finger pressed to his beard. "I'm sorry you went through that, Dale. I'm sorry I never knew you were going through it to reach out and help you sooner."

This wasn't the reaction Dale had expected, and he blustered a bit. "I suppose I worked hard to not let people know. I didn't want you to find out, didn't think I needed helping." He thought about what he'd discussed with the therapist and added, carefully, "I didn't believe I deserved it."

"You do deserve it, and more." Marcus leaned his elbows onto his knees. "I've put in calls to some colleagues, and we have some options. If this law goes through the statehouse, which it looks like it will, you'll have the ability to pursue him if he makes the photos public, and I can send a letter to him on your behalf, making it clear your intent to press charges using this law if he follows through on his threat. But you need to know this plan isn't foolproof. It could goad him into acting another way. He could try to call your bluff or decide your misery is worth the exposure. This law also won't go into effect right away, so if he does something with the photos before that happens, we're in a legal grey zone. Now, we can play pretty dirty in the game, making sure his wife sees the letter, thereby letting her know he's playing around with men at work, but again, these are high stakes, and I don't know if you want to go there. Of course we always have the direct route. He admitted to you he drugged you and coerced you into sex, *and then* used the evidence of the encounter to blackmail you into additional encounters. That's assault. We can go to the police—"

"*No.*" Dale interrupted him before he could finish the thought. He was queasy just thinking about it. "I don't want to go to the police. I don't want to play games with his wife or his family. I want it to go away."

"This is what I thought." Marcus handed him a folder. "With your permission, I want to hire a private investigator to get us some background on this individual. In the event we should need to, I want to be able to move swiftly. Nothing illegal, simply a gathering of information and general intelligence. I don't want to put you through having to recount what I can learn easily enough, and I'm sure there's more he's hiding away. This will also make a handy packet to share with his employer should the opportune moment arise. Does that sound amenable to you?"

Dale opened the file to see the brochure for a Minneapolis-based private investigation service. "Yes, it sounds fine. So we do nothing for now? Ignore him?"

"No, not nothing. We monitor him and gather data. Other than this, no, we take no action. If this is what you want."

Dale considered this, then nodded. "Yes."

"Good." Marcus took the folder back, then leaned forward in his chair. "On a personal note, speaking as your friend and not as your attorney...I wanted to say that while I haven't gone through what you're going through, exactly..." He struggled a moment, vulnerable in a way Dale had never seen. "I know you're aware of what happened between Steve and me, and what everyone brings up is the betrayal, how it must have hurt, and so on. Which is all true. But what they never mention, and yet what hurt in its own, sometimes more potent way was the manner in which people looked at me." He lifted his gaze to Dale's, full of remembered pain. "'What's a big guy like you all cut up for?' Some of them came right out and said it. As if because I were a big man I couldn't bleed, couldn't feel. Couldn't be weak sometimes."

Dale moved his gaze to the floor, his whole body trembling.

Marcus put a hand on Dale's knee. "You get to be weak, Dale. Don't let this jerk or anyone else tell you differently. You have as much a right to be soft as you do to be strong. And sometimes you can say you're not only soft, you're not solid enough to carry things on your own. You have a friend in me, and in all of us. I'm glad you were able to talk to Arthur, that Gabriel could comfort you. All of us are here for you. Always. For all the strengths of men you need to be."

Dale caught Marcus's hand, squeezed it tight. "Thank you," he whispered.

"Anytime," Marcus replied.

Chapter Twelve

T HE FIRST TWO years of Logan's winter festivals were whipped up practically out of thin air, but now that they were trying to plan for a simple summer test run of a yearlong version of what they already had, no one could agree on anything. As May rolled on and June loomed around the corner, Logan's Christmas in July still struggled to fall into place. The funding was secure, between the investors and the grants, but in an odd way this became the problem. When it was Corrina and the library board running around with wild hairs and Gabriel trying to shore them up with the help of the others, they had a lot of wiggle room. But even with Dale on site now, appeasing the investors and satisfying the conditions of the grants and still attracting vendors *and* the actual attendees was something of a struggle. At least they had the corporate advertising department on their side, drawing up flyers and creating commercials for local and Twin Cities radio and television.

Gabriel didn't have much officially to do, but he had fallen into some kind of unofficial role as Dale's assistant, since they often used his travels to neighboring towns as excuses to sneak in some time together. Of course, the flip side was the more they got to know people in farther-flung towns, the more places they wrote off as options for getting away as a couple. Though as rural as their part of Minnesota was, they didn't exactly hold hands at the dinner table or kiss in the movie theater.

Duluth, however, was another story.

Gabriel had been looking forward to their theater weekend ever since Dale told him about it, and when he saw the Zeitgeist Center, he fell in love at once. The cafe had wonderful ambience and incredible food, which was all grown locally. The show Dale got tickets for was edgy and had them both talking animatedly at the bar for an hour once the curtain closed. Then they returned to the theater and laughed at an improv until the evening was officially over.

The social part of it anyway.

Dale had made them a reservation at Fitger's Inn, which Gabriel could tell from the lobby was a nice hotel, but they didn't have simply a nice room. It was one of their luxury penthouse suites. Gabriel wandered the elegant space, secretly thrilled at the opulence, though he felt he shouldn't be. "A regular room would have been more than fine."

"I wanted you to have the best." Dale caught Gabriel's face in his hands and kissed him slowly, sweetly. "I wanted this weekend to be perfect with you."

They had graduated well beyond making out in the backs of cars like teenagers, but there was something to be said for initiating sex they knew wouldn't be interrupted by a knock from a neighbor with a Bundt cake, meaning Gabriel had to hastily hide in the bedroom closet and Dale had to get dressed in less than thirty seconds or pretend he was just about to get into the shower. People had to be gossiping about the number of showers he took and the odd times of day when they happened.

Tonight, however, not only was no one interrupting them with a knock on the door, they had no need to rush, no need to do anything but what they wanted. Dale was quite sweet, which melted Gabriel to his toes, especially when he led him to the balcony, dipped him low, and kissed him like they were in a movie.

"I thought I'd take advantage of being able to do that in full view of a whole town for a change," Dale teased, but Gabriel knew a stab of guilt.

"I'm sorry." He traced Dale's lips, aching but also feeling so in love with him in that moment, swept up in the romance. "I'm sorry we have to stay a secret."

"It's all right." Dale threaded his hands around Gabriel's back and nuzzled his nose. "I mean, do I wish we lived in a perfect world where we didn't have to be so subversive about our relationship? Yes. But it's not the world I want. It's you."

"You have me." The night was so crisp and cool, the lights of the harbor twinkling around the perfect blackness of Lake Superior, the wind rustling Dale's hair and Gabriel's curls. Gabriel stroked Dale's face, his mustache, his lips, his beard. "You have me."

Dale kissed him, slow and sweet at first, then deeper, moving his hands over Gabriel's body. They stumbled into the room by silent agreement, where they stripped each other naked and rolled around the bed, fighting to lay claim to skin. Gabriel shifted his arm at the same time Dale dove for his stomach, which resulted in Dale's teeth grazing his biceps and Gabriel crying out with a soft gasp.

"Sorry," Dale murmured.

Gabriel caught his hair, massaging his scalp. "No. I wasn't expecting it, but..." He dragged Dale's head gently toward his chest. "Perhaps in a more discreet area..."

With a chuckle, Dale nipped at Gabriel's sternum, making Gabriel arch and gasp again, tugging on Dale's hair.

This new game went on for some time, until Gabriel couldn't take it any longer. "Fuck me, please," he rasped, and Dale did.

He lubed him gently, opening him, but Gabriel was impatient and drew him inside so that when he thrust, Gabriel shuddered and cried out from the pleasure-pain. "You all right?" Dale asked, but Gabriel simply made an inarticulate noise and urged him on. Harder.

Faster.

Dale pulled out and shot over him, jerking Gabriel off in time to his own final thrusts, encouraging him loudly to come, *Come on, baby, come on, baby*. Gabriel did, and then Dale followed him, collapsing on top of him until they were a tangle of bodies, of limbs, glued together by drying semen.

They cleaned up and went to bed, but in the morning Gabriel woke Dale with a blowjob, and after a whispered request, Dale finished in his throat, with his head cradled by a pile of pillows as Dale fucked deep into it. Dale insisted on getting Gabriel off after, returning the favor of the blowjob and fingering him with the tub of special lube he'd stowed away in his suitcase. They'd stopped using shortening, but with the help of Arthur and his never-ending research on all things kink, Gabriel had become addicted to Boy Butter, a lube which was basically a commercial version of the same thing, same consistency, same content. Not safe for toys or condoms, but perfectly fine for getting fingered.

"I can't believe you brought that." Gabriel winced and shivered in pleasure as Dale anchored him against the headboard and worked two, then three fingers into him.

"It's kind of our calling card," Dale murmured into his neck. He spread Gabriel's knees wider, pressing deeper. "Besides, you love it. You love how it makes you feel. You love how embarrassed it makes you."

Gabriel blushed, but he leaned into Dale, whimpering as he twisted his fingers. "I do," he whispered.

"I love that about you so much," Dale whispered back, and gave Gabriel more of what he wanted—slowly, lovingly kissing him all the while.

They made out in the shower, languidly, then had breakfast in the room, and after more kissing on the bed, had sex one more time before their appointment to meet the owners and managers at Zeitgeist who had agreed to explain how their programs worked.

Gabriel was impressed with the depth of the programming, which incorporated agencies all over the city, including getting food from the cooperative to food deserts and bringing employees from lower income areas in via bus to work at the center, chiefly with the food they would then take home to their communities. There were so many great ideas, but the problem was many of them wouldn't translate to Logan, and Dale brought that point up before Gabriel could.

"What I'm hoping for," he said, "is that we can find a way to lift the spirit of your program and work to find a fit for our project." He indicated a list of programs the manager had in front of her. "Can you walk me through these, tell me how you got there, what motivated you, what you struggled with, what you learned? I want to hear all of it."

The manager was all too happy to tell him, and for hours, Gabriel sat beside Dale, listening with him, sometimes taking notes, sometimes asking questions, but mostly watching Dale work, realizing how incredibly good he was at his job. He got the Zeitgeist people to tell him what he needed to know, but he also synthesized the information. Gabriel began to see the answers they were missing, even some of the questions they needed for the next phase, just by sitting beside him and paying attention.

When they left the meeting, after Dale and Gabriel had shaken everyone's hands and promised to be in touch, they went outside to walk back to their hotel, and as soon as they were clear of the door, Gabriel pulled Dale into the corner of a building, drew his face to his, and kissed him hard on the lips.

Dale pulled away, stunned, smiling. "What was that for?"

Gabriel stared up at him in wonder, still touching his face. "You don't know, do you?" He traced Dale's mouth, his heart full. "Are you aware everyone in Logan calls you Santa Claus? Not only because you're turning us into Christmas Town. It's because everywhere you go, you bring magic. You have this uncanny ability to know what someone wants, and you give it to them, usually before they ask. I think I just saw how you do it. You listen. You know how to ask the right questions, but you *listen*, and then you do what no one else does. You follow through. Because you figured out the missing pieces, didn't you? You're going to knock the Christmas in July festival out of the park, and you'll make it feed the Winter Wonderland festival, and you'll have us turning into Logan, Minnesota, Christmas Town before we know what happened."

Dale looked a little abashed, but he covered it with a wink. "Well, you're going to help."

They held hands as they went down the Lakewalk, the wind and lake spray and sun making the moment somehow more perfect than it already was. Except one thought haunted Gabriel, and eventually he voiced it. "Dale, this might be a dumb, possibly a rude question, but I need to ask it, so if it *is* rude, I apologize in advance."

Dale raised an eyebrow and turned to face him, smiling with a *this ought to be good* smile. "Okay. Hit me."

Gabriel tried to find the best way to phrase it, then simply blushed and forged on. "When I dated Arthur, when I fell in love with him, my idea of happily ever after with Arthur was marrying him." He bit his lip. "Sometimes I don't know what I'm supposed to wish for my happily ever after with you. Am I not supposed to? What do *you* wish for?"

Dale laughed, his chest rumbling, his eyes twinkling. "What a charming, monogamous-centric question. It's not rude, just…"

"Stupid?"

"I prefer *undereducated*. The short answer is, there are a lot of ways to view a happily ever after, and marriage doesn't have to be one of them." Dale nipped at his nose, still smiling. "But who said you can't marry me too?" When Gabriel gasped, Dale threw his head back, his laugh so rich and deep it sent a thrill through Gabriel. "Look at you. You're worried about being a bigamist, aren't you?"

"Well…yes!"

"You can only have one legal marriage, and Arthur gets that one. But you can hold someone's hand in the woods and declare loyalty to them and call it whatever word you like, and you don't need any government involved to do that."

The thought made Gabriel's head spin. "But I can only live with one of you at a time."

"You're splitting yourself pretty evenly with us right now, in your own way, and look how well we're doing. My point is, you can shape your world however you want."

Gabriel thought about that world, and his mouth watered. This seemed a good time to tell him. "Speaking of the world I want. I discussed it with Arthur, and I think, once the Christmas in July festival is over, I want to find a way to come out to Logan."

Dale's eyes widened. "Wow. Really?"

Gabriel slipped hands around his neck. "Not until you're ready too. But I needed to tell you I was. Ready, I mean. I wanted you to know you were important to me. That I don't hide you by choice. I'm always trying to find a way to…well, to get the world to catch up faster, so we can live in it the way we should."

Dale kissed him, stroking his face, drawing him closer. Then he pulled away far enough to whisper,

"Let's go to the room."

"Let's," Gabriel agreed.

GABRIEL AND DALE returned from their date weekend flushed and euphoric. Dale didn't linger long when he dropped Gabriel off, but he couldn't stop smiling, and he glowed so much Arthur figured if it were night, he wouldn't need to use his headlights. Gabriel was much the same, blushing and grinning and touching his hair and glasses, leaning into Arthur and smiling like he was trying to break his face as he watched Dale backing up to drive away.

Arthur bided his time with his arm around Gabriel's waist, but he was grinning too, because he'd been to this rodeo, and he knew what was coming. If Gabriel's joy was the metric he measured by, *boy* was he about to have a hell of a time.

When Dale's car disappeared around the corner, Gabriel took Arthur's hand in his, dragging him to the house. They were barely inside before Gabriel attacked Arthur, kissing him as if he were drowning and Arthur had the only air in the universe, fighting at his clothes with a desperation that Gabriel never had, not unless he'd just come back from a date with Dale.

Arthur returned Gabriel's kiss, but he also locked the front door—his mother had a knack for shit timing—and slowed his fiancé's clawing and steered him to the couch. "Easy, baby. I'm not going anywhere."

Gabriel transferred his lovemaking to Arthur's neck, sucking and nibbling between his words. "Arthur...it was so amazing. I had the best time. It was perfect."

Arthur ran a hand along Gabriel's spine. "I can tell." He let Gabriel squirm a little longer, moving languidly against his fervor, then kneaded his hip and whispered in his ear. "Do you need rope, honey?"

His lover's whimper and nod sent a rush of desire through Arthur, and he indulged in a long, drugging kiss, briefly joining Gabriel's mindless intensity. Then he released him with a loving caress. "Get undressed and kneel for me."

Arthur went upstairs to get his rope, but he also changed his clothes, because he knew it would give Gabriel a thrill. He put on his chaps and a mesh jock, his suspenders, and since he was feeling fancy, his cap. Then he grabbed his supplies of rope, lube, some random plugs—he brought it all because he could tell Gabriel was going to give him a *really* good time.

Indeed, Gabriel waited for him as instructed, wearing nothing but his glasses, kneeling with his hands behind his back, cock half-erect and bobbing, his gaze hot and eager as he watched Arthur come down the stairs. Arthur took a moment to admire the love bites and marks Dale had left on his man, considering where he'd like to add a few of his own. When Gabriel got a good look at Arthur's gear and visibly became more aroused, Arthur wanted to growl in satisfaction. Instead he set his tools and toys aside and stroked Gabriel's cheek.

"I love how you come from time with him and all you want to do is be with me."

Gabriel shut his eyes and leaned into Arthur's touch. "It's like something snaps when I come home to you. I realize how it's all possible because you pushed us here, because you do so much of the work to keep us healthy. I'm so grateful and full of love. All I want to do is dissolve into you, try to find a way to show you how glad I am to have you as my partner."

Arthur bent to kiss him, a lingering meeting of lips. "Then let me give you the playtime I know you're craving."

He made a great display of showing Gabriel the rope, letting him see the length, running it over his skin, sliding a bit of it over his lips too, giving him the full, sensual experience. Then he set the rope aside and told him about the tie as he inspected Gabriel for bruises or weak spots. "We're going to do a modified elbow tie. Nice and tight." He touched Gabriel's ass, ran his finger down his crack. "Then I'm going to plug you, tease you, spank you." He nuzzled Gabriel's hair, burying his face in the curls. "Then fuck you, and when I'm finished, make you come in my mouth."

"That's intense."

"You need intense."

Gabriel leaned into him, turned his head, and brushed a kiss against his neck. "Yes."

Everything went, essentially, as Arthur told Gabriel it would. They had done a great deal of ropework in their time together, and he'd made it a priority in his kink education as soon as he'd learned how much his lover liked it. He always took it slow, because Gabriel loved the *act* of being bound as much as he loved sitting helpless to Arthur's whims. He loved the move of the hemp over his skin, loved the subtle burn of the fiber, loved the pressure and the tug as Arthur wrapped him. Arthur, for his part, got off on the idea that Gabriel trusted him so completely to let him tie him up in such a complicated way, then tease and dominate him.

That last part of the playing was *his* favorite, and once Gabriel was bound and drifting in his subspace, Arthur knelt behind him, stroking the front of his body, rope and skin, as he lubed Gabriel to prepare him for the toy.

"Are you going to take this for me?" He sucked on Gabriel's earlobe, teasing it with his teeth as he showed him the plug. It wasn't small, and that's why he'd chosen it, to make Gabriel uncomfortable.

Gabriel, though, was lost to his ropes and still high from his weekend with Dale. "Yes."

Arthur did growl then, moving the plug to his other hand so he could slip it inside of Gabriel. "You're so hot, sweetheart, when you're like this." He pushed the toy inside, going hard as Gabriel gasped but didn't fight it, shifting his knees wider and slackening his muscles to let it in. "You're softer with two men, baby." He eased the plug the rest of the way inside, then carefully arranged him over the ottoman. He'd meant to play with him more, but he couldn't wait. This was the side effect of Dale and Gabriel being together too: Arthur also got swept up in the passion. He never wanted to fuck Gabriel more than when Dale had spent an evening or weekend doing the same.

He spanked Gabriel with his bare hand, light taps that turned him red and drove the plug in deeper, but nothing that would do more than make it tender to sit for the rest of the day, nothing more than what the fucking Arthur intended to give him would do. Which was what Arthur did next, removing the plug and plunging into Gabriel, reveling in the heat and comfort of his body until he spent himself—something that didn't take long at all, as feverish as the scene had made him.

When he finished, he propped Gabriel, dazed, dreamy, happily lost in his desire, in the corner of the couch, and then Arthur parted his thighs and took his cock in his mouth. Long and slow, lovingly licking and sucking the flesh until Gabriel whimpered and cried, arching and twisting against his rope. When he came, he screamed, a high-pitched, slightly surprised but joyful yelp of victory. And then he collapsed, breathing heavily, onto the cushions.

Arthur kissed his way up to Gabriel's mouth, fitting their bodies together on the narrow space. "Ready for some water, honey?"

Gabriel smiled, nuzzling Arthur's nose. "Not yet. I want to stay here, like this. That was amazing."

Arthur had to agree. He ran a lazy hand down Gabriel's shoulder, pausing to caress the hemp. "You enjoy this tie."

"I do."

"Do you want me to show Dale how to use rope? He can start with a simple one."

Gabriel shook his head. "No. I want it to be our thing."

God, but that made Arthur's chest puff out. He kissed Gabriel's forehead, shut his eyes, and soaked in the moment.

Eventually, though, he knew he had to get Gabriel out of the tie, because he was falling asleep, plus Arthur had another job to do. He nudged Gabriel to a sitting position, cut him out of the rope to save time, and checked him again to make sure he hadn't gotten hurt. He insisted Gabriel drink some water and eat some crackers, left him some more and a few grapes on the coffee table along with the water. Then he covered his lover with a blanket. Gabriel was asleep before Arthur was up the stairs.

He changed his clothes, got himself some water and a snack, grabbed a different bag from his bedroom closet, swiped his phone, sent a text, and went outside.

The duck blind wasn't far from the house, but he took his time, because it was a nice day, and he wanted to enjoy it. Plus he needed the time to clear his head, to shift the buzz from the intense, beautiful sex with Gabriel to what he was about to do now, which was also beautiful but wasn't about sex.

Dale waited for Arthur outside the blind, pacing slightly nervously, but he smiled when he saw Arthur, came over and hugged him. "Hey there. You guys have a good reunion?"

Arthur grinned. "Oh yeah."

Dale rubbed the back of his hair. "Is this okay, us having our playtime right after? I realized as I was waiting it was kind of odd."

"Baby, there's nothing about the way the three of us operate that's standard issue. But it's all good. Happy to be with you." He patted Dale on the back. "So. What do you need today?"

As usual, Dale tensed when asked what he needed, but this was what he, his therapist, and Arthur had decided was the best course forward for him for now. To start his one-on-one play sessions by stating what he wanted. To teach him he was consciously handing over control, that it was his to give away to start with. He frowned and shifted uncomfortably, kicking at some sticks on the ground before he could give his answer. "What I want is complicated."

Arthur tucked his hands behind his back. "I can work with complicated. Tell me more. What is it, and how is it completed?"

"I want it heavy. I want something raw and rough that will ring with me for a long time. I want pain, and I want...I want a little shame. But at the same time I'm still..." He flattened his lips and turned his head away.

Arthur gave him a moment to be frustrated, to experience his feelings. "It's going to take time to disengage from abuse. Your mind will process it in its own way. But that doesn't mean we can't find a path through it. We're going to have to go slow with you and talk through your scenes a lot."

Dale went red-faced. "That takes the fun out of it."

"Not necessarily. You forget, this is all my job, to balance your needs and keep it pleasurable for you." He walked a slow circle around Dale. "Let's focus on the goals you set. Pain and shame through heavy play. Sounds like a party to me. What kind of shame, baby? You want me to mock you, or do you want to feel shameful inside yourself?"

Dale hugged himself nervously. "Inside me."

"Good to know. Details are important, Dale. What's shameful for you? What's your favorite shame? I know you like being opened up." He stroked Dale's arm as he passed, trailing a hand over his ass. "You want that? You want me to open you up? Tell you how you look when you display yourself?"

Dale shut his eyes, took a breath. Nodded. "Yes. Please."

Arthur stopped behind him, stroking his ass rhythmically. "What about pain? I brought your favorite paddle."

Dale stilled, then leaned into Arthur's touch. "The

rubber-coated one?"

"Mmm-hmm." Arthur shifted his strokes to Dale's crack, running up and down the seam. The man had already begun to slip under him. "You have anywhere you need to sit the rest of today?"

Dale's legs quavered. "Just have to drive home."

"This is why you need a cabin out here, honey. So I can do you and you can hobble home, red ass wiggling as you go, and then you lie on your belly on your bed the rest of the day, listening to the birds outside and thinking about how sore I made your backside, how good paddling feels on you." His voice rumbled low. "Goddamn, boy, but you take a whipping like nobody I know. You gonna do that for me today? Gonna show me your spread hole and enjoy how dirty that makes you feel, then let me spank it until it's so raw it's on fire, until you're high from pain?"

Dale was half drunk now simply from talking about it. "Yes. Yes, that's what I want."

"Then get out of your clothes and kneel in front of your stump."

Dale hurried to comply. Arthur watched him, appreciating the view but mostly thinking, not for the first time, he was going to have to figure out a way to explain to the boys the next time they went hunting why this stump had been smoothed down on one side and two knee-sized prints worn in front of it. Arthur had cushions in the blind, and he'd get one to place between Dale and the stump before he began whaling on him, but Dale liked to start with his knees in the dirt and his palms on the rough wood, the grass tickling his cock.

Arthur let him hover there a bit, fetching an oft-used stick from inside the blind and tapping it inside his thighs to encourage them wider apart. "Goddamn but I can't wait for duck season, until you and me and the boys are all sitting here drinking beer, waiting for birds, and all you can think about is how often you hump this stump. How's that for some shame, sweetheart? That rev your engine?"

Dale smiled, but it was a loose, slippery grin, and he bent farther over the stump, sticking his ass out more. "Yeah."

Arthur nudged him again with the stick, not hurting him, but letting him feel the edge of it, teasing it around his hole without actually using it in him, because hell, that would be cruel. He allowed himself a moment's thrill, loving that somehow he'd fallen into this arrangement with Dale, so proud that Dale trusted him, that Gabriel did too. Arthur didn't view what he did with Dale as sexual per se, at least, the sex was more a tool for the play he and Dale enjoyed. Dale was the only BDSM partner outside of Gabriel where they went this far. He'd paddled his share of bare asses and helped wrangle half-naked men in puppy play wearing little more than a thong and a tail, but this was different. Because he was about to touch Dale. Not fuck him, not get him off, but touch him. It definitely ran against the line.

But as he'd told Gabriel, they made their own rules.

Gabriel enjoyed his greasy Boy Butter, but when Arthur worked Dale, he used Gun Oil, because Dale was all about the sensation. Arthur worked him slowly, letting him feel it, giving him lots of talk the whole time. "Look at you, out here in the woods, naked, getting done. Getting spread. Getting nice and loose. You undo so sweet, baby, you know that? Three fingers in you slick as you please. Anybody ever fist you?"

Dale shut his eyes, nodded. "Long time ago," he replied gruffly.

"You like it?"

"It was okay."

Arthur wasn't surprised. Gabriel loved getting stuffed, but Dale was more about the show. When he was feeling better, Arthur wanted to take him to a leather weekend. Dale would love being done for a room. But not yet. He wasn't ready for that.

"Let me see what you've got for me."

Dale complied, hunching his big body over the chunk of wood, sliding his knees wide in the dirt and sticking his ass up. His dick was hard, but Arthur could tell the man needed more. Like Gabriel, the weekend had pushed him into overdrive. Normally Arthur could leave Dale like this, play with his hole, maybe plug him, and that would be enough, but not today.

Well, lucky for Dale his Dom came prepared.

Arthur sidled to the other side of the stump, his

bag slung idly over his shoulder. "So, I had a thought. A new direction we could take your play, since you love displaying for me so much, and since you want it to be about shaming yourself. I ordered you something, and it came the other day." He stroked Dale's face. "Do you want to see it? Decide if you want me to use it on you?"

Dale looked up at him, needy, submissive, but peaceful. "Yes."

Arthur winked and unzipped the bag. "It's little. I don't think you'll be into the extreme ones. Because for you it's the thought that counts. The idea that this would be in you. That if anyone would know, if you thought about it too much, your whole body would be hot with shame."

Dale's gaze was hungry as Arthur reached into the duffel, waiting, curious, eager. He tracked as Arthur withdrew something long, hidden in his hand and against his wrist until he turned it over and displayed it on his palm.

When Dale's breath hitched, Arthur grinned.

"Anal speculum. Medical grade. Perfectly safe. No rough edges. You can inspect it yourself if you like. But it'll feel cool and blunt in there. You'll know it's in you. It'll give you the pressure you love. I can leave it in while I do your warm-up paddles too, or while I take a short walk away from you. Leave it inside you. Let you sit there with it hanging. Feeling all the shame for letting me do it, for enjoying it. For coming out here for the sole purpose of me sticking this inside you. For begging me to." He crouched in front of Dale and ran the metal edge of the speculum down the sides of his face. "What do you say? Want to beg me?"

Dale swallowed hard. "Please," he whispered.

Arthur tapped his nose. "Please what. Be specific. Really specific. I want to hear the shame in your voice, Mr. Davidson. I want to hear how filthy your desires are."

Dale shut his eyes, took a deep breath. "I want you to use it on me. I want you to open me with it. I'm begging you to spread my ass here in the woods, sir, with that speculum." He opened his eyes, his gaze meeting Arthur's, beseeching. "Then please, sir, fuck my mouth while it's in me. Then paddle me with the rubber paddle until I can't stand, until I'm weeping from it. Until I'm sobbing. I want you to wreck me with it. I want it in my teeth, I want it so bad."

Arthur was the one unsteady now, and he had to take a minute to recover himself. He put a hand on Dale's hair. "Baby, I thought we were going slow."

Dale leaned into Arthur's stomach, nuzzled his groin. "It's okay. It makes me feel better, to do scenes with you. Taking it back. I know you're safe."

Arthur's heart swelled with pride...and with love. He bent and kissed Dale's forehead. "You will tell me if you need to slow down or stop."

Dale kissed the zipper of his jeans. "Of course."

Arthur held his head close a moment, savoring the connection. Then he stepped back, twirling the speculum on his finger. "Let's go."

Chapter Thirteen

IN EARLY JUNE, Gabriel and Arthur took a day to travel to Minneapolis with Dale.

He needed to meet with his team, but he was nervous about running into Ronny, so with the help of some brainstorming by Marcus and the others, some subterfuge was laid out. The meeting would take place at a local park as a picnic, and Gabriel and Arthur would have a simultaneous meeting with Spenser and Tomás and their family for their long-overdue planned discussion about what it was like to be foster parents.

Marcus had come along as well. Gabriel would have preferred it to be the three of them, but he acknowledged Arthur needed a keeper and that he could not be it. Marcus's role was to keep Arthur from throat-punching Ronny in case he *did* appear. He also doubled as Logan's representative in the team meeting, and so it was that they all spent a lovely Saturday driving down in Marcus's SUV, chatting about the upcoming festival, which was finally in full planning swing. They talked about other things too—about the disappointing Stanley Cup Finals, about the latest chapter of *American Gods,* which Marcus had begun reading too. Dale insisted they should all take a group vacation to House on the Rock before the STARZ broadcast began, and when he heard none of them had been to the Wisconsin tourist site, he threw his hands up in disbelief and *insisted* they organize a getaway as soon as possible.

The park where they met their respective parties was a lovely place, the pavilion for Dale's meeting not far from the shelter Spenser had reserved for their less-formal gathering. The Jimenez crew was already there when they arrived, the kids playing on equipment, Renata supervising. Duon wasn't present, nor was José. Apparently they were both working.

"It's so good to see you again." Spenser hugged Gabriel and Arthur hello, and Tomás followed suit. They'd already laid out a spread of food, homemade tortillas and fruit and salsa, meat and beans, but also sandwich meat and bread. Arthur and Gabriel had brought chips and soda and a pan of scotcheroos, which they added to the bounty.

Gabriel had been in regular email correspondence with Spenser since they'd met at the festival, but it was wonderful to speak to him and Tomás in person. They caught each other up about what was going on in their lives—for the most part—and then they delved into the real reason they'd gotten together.

"I know you've only been foster parents for a little while, and that you can't talk about specific children." Gabriel noticed the children playing on the jungle gym, two of whom were standing slightly to the side, not joining in quite the same way as Tomás's nieces and nephew. "But you do have children outside your relatives now, correct?"

Spenser nodded. "We've had a non-relative placement, yes. We can answer questions about the experience in general, but you're correct, we can't give any specific examples of children in our care."

Arthur slathered butter on a tortilla and rolled it into a slim cigar before nibbling absently on it. "What's the most difficult part, would you say? What's the thing there's no way we can prepare for?"

Tomás and Spenser glanced at each other and raised their eyebrows. Eventually Tomás spoke. "Good question. I think…I think I'd say there's no way you can be ready. I think that's any parenting. You're going to want to make everything perfect for them, but you can't. Most of your job is trying to align the world for them and then having to watch them hurt as they navigate it, trying to decide how long and how much you let them bleed. But with kids who weren't born to you, who started out someone else's children—and with foster children, that's the thing, the whole idea is DHS wants them to go home—it's more complicated. You sit there and think, 'Well damn, if I could have had them when they were six, or whatever…' you start imagining stuff, is what I'm saying. You rewrite history. But you can't do that. History is what it is. What you actually have is right now, the road in front of you. And that's hard. So you do a lot of learning to make do what with you have and what they can handle."

Spenser smiled and took his husband's hand on top of the table. "You learn a lot about yourself as a foster parent. You get humble fast. And you learn how to bleed efficiently."

Gabriel swallowed a long drink of soda. Goodness, that was intense.

Spenser, as if sensing his nerves, shifted the conversation. "I know you two wanted to focus on LGBT teens. That's so wonderful. It's the most underserved population."

Arthur waved his tortilla, punctuating his thoughts. "I had a question about that too, actually. Do you know, is it going to be trickier for us, since we're so rural? How far will they move kids? I mean, just by the numbers, there aren't many LGBT youth in our county full stop, let alone youth who need foster care."

Tomás regarded him thoughtfully. "You know, that's a good question."

"I know the answer there, sort of." Spenser got out his phone and thumbed around on a website. "Okay, I don't know it as well as I thought. It's complicated. LGBT youth are crazy overrepresented in the homeless population. But a lot of it is because they run away from foster care or from home. I don't know how or if they would assign you LGBT youth specifically. They tell us they can't officially say they do that, though they know it's a priority for us. But we also said we want to take whatever youth has the most need, especially youth who need to stay in Hispanic households. Which is how we ended up with the placement we have. So…there may be a way to work it. It's going to come down to your workers."

"Speaking of." Tomás gave them a long look. "Get ready for a mixed bag. They mean well, almost all of them. But they're overworked and underpaid, and sometimes boy does it show. Keep copies of everything. Get ready for them to tell you they never received the thing you mailed twice, that kind of thing. You're going to need a lot of patience, both with the kids and the system itself."

"But it's worth it," Spenser said. "In so many ways."

They chatted another hour, until the kids got antsy, and Gabriel and Arthur sent them away, insisting the meeting was nearly done and not to worry about it—which was the truth. Ten minutes after they packed up and left, Marcus and Dale came over, reporting the meeting had been Ronny free and entirely productive. They piled in Marcus's car and drove back to Logan.

Gabriel was quiet on the way home, though, and he noticed Arthur was too, engaging somewhat with the boys in the front seat, but mostly contemplating something silently out the window.

"That was certainly a lot to think about," Gabriel ventured, to see if Arthur would elaborate, but he only agreed it certainly was. And they didn't bring up the foster parenting situation again for the rest of the week.

Gabriel had some thoughts, some things he wanted to discuss. But first, he needed to do some homework.

He did a great deal of online reading, followed up with some emails to Spenser, which led to an email introduction to someone else, and more research, and soon Gabriel was well down the rabbit hole and feeling, though a little sad, also calmer. He sat with his discovery a few days, letting himself digest it. Then, one beautiful summer night as they sat in their chairs, holding hands, drinking beer and wine and watching the lake, he broached the subject with Arthur.

"Arthur," he began carefully, "I want to talk to you about the foster parent thing."

He knew he was right when he saw Arthur's shoulders tense. "Okay. But we can't do much until we finish the remodel."

Maybe that was the way to start the conversation. Gabriel swung their hands gently. "Have you noticed, hon, we keep putting *off* the remodel?"

More tension. "It's a huge job. It's going to take so much time, so much work. And money. You don't even know."

"I'm sure all of that is true. I think there's something else, though." Gabriel stroked Arthur's hand with his thumb. "I think we might be putting it off because though we want to be parents, love the idea of children, we're not ready to do it. In fact, we might not ever be ready for it."

Arthur put his beer aside. "You think that's what I'm doing? That this is what I think?"

"I think it's what we both think." Gabriel turned sideways in his chair, curling his legs against the wooden slats. "Don't get me wrong. I'm torn. I want them still, but…Arthur, I love our life right now. I love that we're sitting here on the lake, just the two of us. I love that you keep talking about how you wish Dale had a cabin on our land. What *if* he did? What if you two could have your play sessions in your mutual backyard? What if when it was my night with him and I forgot my toothbrush, I could wander over here, or if you wanted to bug us, you could knock on the door?"

Arthur's tension had eased somewhat. "What is it you're saying, exactly?"

"I'm saying that what I want is to be with the both of you the way we are now. I like what we're doing. I don't need more. When I said I wanted kids, I felt I was empty still, as if there was something I needed to fill. And I still want to work with children—I have a whole other idea I want to tell you about. But first I wanted to tell you I'm happy with what we are now. If you're not, if you need children, if that's important to you, we will make it work, the same way you've made this thing with Dale work for me. But I have this feeling we've both been putting it off because it was a dream we shared which has moved on, somehow, or changed."

Arthur's shoulders sagged. "It has changed for me. But I didn't want to say anything because I knew it was important for you. And I felt guilty. I figured it was nerves." He laced his fingers with Gabriel's. "This sounds…weird, but I'm really into this thing with me and Dale. I feel so protective of him. Not as if he's my kid, God no. But it's…I don't know, the same space inside me? I get what you mean. There was emptiness, and I thought, well, kids, that must be it. And maybe that would have worked. I think it would have been fine. I think it would be fine, if we did it." He frowned. "I feel like we should do it, because there are kids who need us."

"Hold that thought." Gabriel scooted his chair to face Arthur's and took both his hands. "I have some ideas, initial ones, about how we can maybe incorporate helping youth into Christmas Town. Not underage youth—that's the switch we have to make. No tow-headed little boys or girls, no little boots by the door. Not unless later we decide we want to do this after all. Which we could still do. But if LGBT youth are our focus—as Spenser said to me, eighteen year olds are still youth, though they're adults in the eyes of the law. They age out of the system and have nowhere to go. What if they could come work here? What if the youth who didn't want to live in a city could work in Logan? Gay-friendly Logan? And we could help them." He smiled. "They could room with us too, if we wanted. Maybe we do a smaller remodel, for only a few guests at a time. Adult guests. *Young* adult guests."

Arthur's gaze was alight with interest…but sorrow too. "It sounds great. Exciting. But…you kind of tugged at my heart with the little boots by the door."

Tears in his eyes, Gabriel drew Arthur's fist to his lips. "How about we start with the young adults…and you meet me at the lake in a few years, and we see how hard the little boots by the door are tugging at your heart then?"

Arthur smiled. "It's a deal."

Then he drew Gabriel onto his lap, wrapped him in his arms, and kissed him on the mouth.

As SUMMER GOT into full swing and so did the windup to the festival preparations, Gabriel and Dale descended into the full-on swoon stage of falling in love, and Arthur assumed every day was the day they would get found out, because they were getting all kinds of sloppy. He complained to Paul when they were alone in the shop as a release valve.

"I mean, I get they're drunk on the new relationship and all, but Jesus H. Christ, they need to pay attention." He set a screwdriver on the workbench and picked up a ratchet. "Anyway, I was never that bad."

Paul glanced up from his work at him. "You were."

Arthur glared. "I wasn't. *You* were. And so was

Marcus. But I wasn't."

He waited for Paul to argue back or at least roll his eyes at him, but he didn't, he only continued to work on the lawn mower engine he had taken apart. "Your mom called while you were out, by the way."

Arthur frowned. "I wonder why she didn't call my cell." He fished it out of his pants and saw that, in fact, she had. "You okay if I call her now?"

"It's fine. I'm going to stay late, wait for Kyle. It's his first day on the new shift. We're going to celebrate with a late dinner at the cafe after."

"All right." Arthur aimed his phone at him as he headed for his office. "I'll be out tomorrow morning to do more work on your place."

Once he'd shut his door, he plunked into his chair, put his feet on his desk, and dialed his mother.

"Arthur," she said, and from her tone, he knew.

She knew.

He straightened, his heart picking up a few beats. "Hey, Mom. Paul said you called me?"

"Yes." Oh, fuck. Yeah, she knew. She hadn't only heard, she'd seen. "I have something I need to discuss with you. It's important."

"Sure. Do you want me to come to the house?"

"No, the children are here, and I need to speak to you alone. I was hoping I could catch you at the shop after closing. Have you turned the sign over yet?"

Arthur winced. God, the list of shit he owed Paul was longer than both his legs now. "Yeah. Come on over whenever. I'll wait here for you."

He hung up and went into the main body of the shop, heart beating faster again. "Paul." He'd meant to tell Paul he had to go, but he couldn't. "Paul—my mom's coming here. To talk to me. She knows."

Paul put his tools down and came over to him. "Shit. You're sure?"

"Pretty." He ran a hand through his hair. "What do I do? What the fuck do I do?"

"I think you have to tell her the truth, right?"

Obviously, yes, but… "Do I bring them over? Tell her myself?" He was struck by a brilliant idea. "Will you stay and tell her with me?"

Paul held up both hands. "Oh hell, no."

"Come on, you can back me up, explain when I don't make sense…"

"No. This is your mom. She wants to talk to you. Not me." Paul swiped his keys from the counter but didn't go. "Tell her the truth. Explain what happened. She knows you have sex. She knows you're kinky, whether you think she does or not. She probably knows more than you give her credit for. Maybe she even knows what polyamory is."

"Gabriel didn't."

"Your mom was a hippie. Tell her it's free love." He patted Arthur on the shoulder. "It'll be fine."

Like hell it would. Arthur's stomach was in knots and she hadn't shown up yet. "You're buying the beer tomorrow, so it's clear."

Paul saluted without turning around, and then he was gone.

Arthur had five minutes to pace, to consider texting Gabriel and Dale, to delete several tries unsent, then pace some more, before his mother walked in. Then it was too late. He was doing this on his own whether he wanted to or not.

Fuck.

She smiled at him, a weary, worried gesture. "Hi, sweetheart. How are you doing?"

"I'm fine." He fidgeted and rubbed at his beard, deciding the way he wanted to play this was to cut her off at the pass. Because he hated this already, and the thing he decided he didn't want to hear was his mother tell him, with concern, that she knew Gabriel was cheating on him. "Before you say anything, Mom, I know what you came here to tell me, and you're wrong."

She pursed her lips. "Arthur—"

He held up a hand. "No. Listen to me. Mom, it's not what you think. It's not cheating. It's like free love in the seventies, okay? Gabriel is not cheating on me."

Her eyes went wide, her mouth fell open, and Arthur's stomach flipped over three times as he realized he had made a terrible, terrible mistake.

"Oh shit." He covered his mouth with his hand and turned away, but there was nowhere in the world to go to get away from what he had just done.

She hadn't known. This had been about something

else. He had outed his fiancé to his mother.

To the biggest gossip in Logan.

She followed him wherever he turned, her eyes and mouth going wider every second, until finally she recovered enough to speak. "You…you're saying…Gabriel.…*Gabriel*? Is cheating on you?"

Arthur seized on this, his only lifeline. "*No*." He aimed a finger at her. "No. He has a boyfriend. It's entirely different."

Oh, shit, he'd fucked up more.

"*He has a boyfriend?*" She sucked in air, a great noisy gasp, and now she was pointing too. "Dale—it's Dale. The rumors *are* true then. They *are* a little too friendly. Of course, the rumors also say you're sleeping with Frankie—"

Arthur recoiled. "*Frankie*? What the hell? I mean, I love the guy, but give me some fucking credit, *Frankie*? If I were going to poach one of my friends, I'd go for Kyle. Except he wouldn't have me, and Paul would never forgive me."

"And yet *your* fiancé has a boyfriend and it doesn't bother you at all?"

Okay. More territory he could handle. "No, it doesn't. It happens, Mom. People can love more than one person at once. It's called polyamory, and—"

She waved an annoyed hand at him. "I know what it is. I just… Well, I didn't think you were."

"Well, I'm not. But I'm annoyed to hear you'd be disappointed in me if I was."

She frowned at him. "But you said…"

"I said *Gabriel* was. I'm not. I don't mind that he is. It really isn't complicated." And honestly, it wasn't. He was beginning to get annoyed with everyone else for making it that way.

She sat down on a stool, looking dizzy. "Did you know he was polyamorous when you proposed to him?"

"Mom, *he* didn't know."

She blinked at him, more lost than ever.

So Arthur pulled up another stool and did as Paul had advised. He told her the truth. An edited version, but the truth. How they'd invited Dale to have a bit of fun with them, but things had changed, and quickly. He explained how miserable the both of them had been, denying their feelings, and how wrecked Gabriel had been trying to avoid what he'd discovered about himself. At that point he'd had to get his mother tissues.

"The poor dear. I'd wondered why he was so quiet this winter. I had no idea. And there you were, all alone, trying to help him. And you did. By…giving him to another man. My goodness, Arthur. How bighearted you are."

Arthur didn't need a tissue, but he did feel a bit like he was eight years old and getting praised for the rare good grade. "I want Gabriel happy, Mom. I love him. This is what happy is for him. And this is the thing: we're happy. Not to get TMI, but the sex is better. But it's more than sex. Do you have any idea how hard it is to work on these relationships, especially when we have to keep quiet about them? We have to keep our metaphorical houses clean at all times, basically. You can't get sloppy. If I get jealous of Gabriel and Dale, and right now with them being all new and shiny that happens, I have to tell them about it. And then we work on it. We can't get passive aggressive. We have to get real. And they have to talk to each other even more, because they can't do couple stuff in public. It's intense and insane sometimes, but it's so good, Mom. He's not my boyfriend, but if those two broke up, I'd be heartbroken. I would miss his relationship inside our relationship."

She took his head in her hands and kissed his brow. "I can't say this is what I would have chosen for you, sweetheart. But so little of your life is what I would have planned for you, and you've done such a wonderful job with everything else. I wouldn't stand in the way of this for anything."

"Well, at some point other people will find out, and they probably will."

She considered this. "Some people won't care for it, true. And you're right. It's going to come out eventually. But there was a time when the gay and lesbian couples were the ones whispered about, not accepted in the aisle at church. And believe you me, if anyone tries to keep you or Gabriel or Dale out of church, they'll hear about it from me." She sighed. "Though you've just undone what I came to argue with you about."

Arthur raised his eyebrows. "Church?"

"Getting married in one. I don't like this idea of Frankie and Kyle's of you getting married in some tent on the Parks farm. It's not right. I understand it's your wedding and you have a right to do what you want. I can get behind the triple wedding, however unconventional, but when Frankie told me you weren't getting married in a church and Dale was getting certified to officiate—" She gasped and covered her mouth. "*Arthur*, that's practically a scandal."

He grinned. "Yeah, we thought so."

She swatted his arm. "Don't think I'm not done arguing with you about this."

He loved, in fact, that he knew she was not.

Chapter Fourteen

D ALE WASN'T QUITE prepared for the reality of
Corrina Anderson being in on the secret of his
and Gabriel's relationship.

He didn't mind when he heard Arthur had acci-
dentally outed them to her, and he didn't understand
Gabriel's hysteria, not until the next day when she
showed up at his office with a coffee cake, an iced
coffee, and a big hug and kiss on his cheek. "You're a
wonderful man," she said, then made him promise to
let her know if there was anything he ever needed,
because she had ways, and she could do just about
anything, given enough time.

He told her he was good, thank you, and went on
with his day.

But she began stopping by a lot, and whenever the
two of them were alone, she would wink conspiratorial-
ly and ask him how things were going with, *you know*.
He also discovered untold number of brochures for
romantic Minnesota getaways in his mailbox, often

with items circled and a note saying *G would really like this!* Mostly he found it all amusing, until he began getting emails, to his *work email*, with all kinds of tips and information about how to best manage your polyamorous relationship.

"Arthur, your mother is a menace," he said as he came through the cabin door that night, which happened to be the evening of what they jokingly called their Family Weekend. Once a month, or as close to that as they could manage, they closed themselves in for a day or sometimes a little longer and ate, laughed, had Gabriel read to them, and had wild crazy monkey sex.

But first they always cleared the air, and today, boy did Dale have some air to clear.

He put the bread he'd made and the kale salad he'd finally gotten Arthur to admit he liked in the fridge, then leaned against the counter, trying not to let his frustration get the better of him as he vented. "She can't email me stuff like that at my work email. The IT people in Minneapolis aren't exactly going through every single thing, but it's not *my* email, and it could get me in trouble, or at least get people asking me awkward questions." He threw up his hands. "I tried to explain that to her, and she just winked at me, as if it explained everything. What the hell was *that* about?"

Gabriel folded his arms over his chest and gave Arthur a *see, I told you* look.

Arthur sighed and tipped his head back. "I know. I

can't say I'm sorry and make what I did go away. I'll talk to her. You're not going to like this, Dale, but you might need to give her a private email to send stuff to. Because I hate to tell you, she's going to send it anyway. It's who she is. It's how she shows love. Heaven help you when she finds out you're not close to your family."

Gabriel made a *humpf* noise, but then he glanced between Dale and Arthur, beautifully hungry. "Wait. Does this mean Dale gets invited to Thanksgiving?"

"Oh, hell yes. He'll get one of Thomas's turkey decorations and everything." Arthur hooked his finger in Gabriel's belt loop and grinned as he drew him down for a kiss. "Am I out of the doghouse yet?"

Gabriel nuzzled his nose. "Hmm. No. But you can come into the yard."

"Good. Because if I had to stay in much longer, I was going to install some carpet and put in cable."

Arthur took hold of Gabriel's hips, lazily stroking them, and when Gabriel canted subconsciously into him, Dale's libido kicked in, hoping this was one of the Family Weekends where they started with dessert.

But instead of deepening the kiss and inviting him over, Arthur murmured something in Gabriel's ear, Gabriel nodded, and they pulled apart. Their hands joined for a moment though, and that clasp lingered as Arthur went out the front door. Then Gabriel approached Dale with a slightly nervous, shy smile.

"There's something I wanted to show you." He

gestured to Arthur's construction corner, where the blueprints and other papers were rustling in the breeze under an open window. In fact, there were some new papers on the top, Dale noticed, and Gabriel picked one up and spread it over the table.

Dale's hip bumped Gabriel's companionably as he scrutinized it. He squinted, then left long enough to get his glasses from his bag and leaned in, taking care to position himself against Gabriel once more because he enjoyed the contact. "These are your renovation blueprints, but they're not the same. You've changed them. You've scaled back. Way back." He stood, turning to Gabriel in confusion. "Why? I don't understand. You said you were going to be foster parents, and with this setup, you could only take in one or two kids, tops."

"That's what I need to talk to you about."

Gabriel took his hand and sat at the table, and Dale did the same, his heart beating a little faster in worry because he couldn't figure out what was going on, and it couldn't be good. He squeezed Gabriel's hand. "Did something happen?"

"In a way." Gabriel laced their fingers together, swayed their hands back and forth, and kept his gaze on them as he spoke, but his voice was gentle, his eyes smiling. "Arthur and I had a long talk about it. We've decided right now we don't want to be foster parents. We haven't written it off for sure, but we know it's a high possibility that we've moved on from that vision of our future."

Dale squeezed his hand tight. "But, Gabriel—that was your dream, both of you. You were so excited, so proud when you told me about it. What changed?" He had a sinking feeling, and he went cold inside. "It was me, wasn't it? They said no because of me."

"They haven't said anything, because we haven't applied." Gabriel brought his other hand to the table and stroked Dale's wrist sadly. "But if we did, yes, it would be a complicating factor in a significant way. We'd either have to lie and become incredibly discreet and risk getting in a great deal of trouble for hiding our relationship, or we'd need to disclose it, which we could certainly do, but they might limit our placements because of it or possibly deny us a license entirely. And we're already at risk because Arthur is visible in the leather community, which they would find in their background search of us. It's not an automatic disqualification, but suddenly we have a lot of strikes against us, depending on who our licensing worker is. There are a lot of ways for us to fail, in short, and after a lot of soul-searching, we've decided it's not something we want to go through. Especially since what we want for ourselves has changed too."

Dale was crestfallen, and it wasn't his dream. "But this isn't right. You would be so good with kids, both of you."

"We still want to work with youth, and I have some ideas for that. Spenser and Tomás put us in contact with a shelter in the Cities, and I want you to meet the people there. I want to see if we can work out something with youth and the Logan project, maybe a summer program to get them up here for the festival as workers or as performers for the arts series. Maybe some of them end up moving here, if we can find some way to have a network here. And maybe Arthur and I have a host home program for some of those kids, for the summer or for a while. Or maybe we don't."

"But you wanted kids." Dale couldn't let it go. "You wanted a family."

Gabriel's smile wasn't shy anymore, and it lit things up inside Dale. "Well, this brings me to the other thing I need to talk to you about. I said you complicated things, and it's true. Because the thing is, when we'd talked about wanting kids before we met you, we were talking about a hole in our lives, a sense that something was missing. We wanted to fill that gap, and we both liked kids, so it seemed to be the logical solution. And probably there's a timeline of my life where we adopt a pile of teenagers and have to get clever about keeping our kink behind closed doors, and that's all there is to it. But that's not the timeline I got. I'm in the one where you flirted with me over a bag of chestnuts, Arthur thought we should have a three-way, and I found out my heart was more complex and beautiful than I knew."

Dale's own heart swelled. "I don't know what you're saying."

"I'm saying I found the family I was searching for.

We both did, in different ways. In you." He wrapped both hands around Dale's. "I want you in my life, Dale, as much as I want Arthur in it. If you look through those blueprints, you'll find another set for your cabin, at the edge of the property, overlooking the lake. So you can be close to us. So I can be with both of you, so you can come be with us when you want to be with your family. Because we are both your family, in different ways. I want to marry Arthur in the legal ceremony this Christmas. But I want another one for you and me, in the woods, like you said, not about the government or the law or anyone but about us. I want to marry you too."

Dale could barely breathe. This couldn't be happening. It couldn't be his life, couldn't be... He clasped their joined hands with his free one, tears in his eyes. "You really want that?"

"I want it so much I ache." Gabriel drew their hands to his mouth and kissed Dale's knuckles. "Do you want it too? Will you say yes?"

Dale's breath came out in a huff, a breathless laugh. The *yes* would have burst out of him, but his therapist's voice whispered in his ear, and he forced himself to slow, to draft an addendum before he spoke. "Yes. *Yes, I absolutely want to marry you.* My yes needs to come with a promise, though, that I tell you something." He hated the shadow that fell over him, over the moment, but he reminded himself this was the reason to share the story with Gabriel, so the shadow didn't stay with him. "I don't want to do it tonight. But tomorrow, I need to. It's…important."

His stomach knotted, worrying what Gabriel might think. Gabriel, though, didn't seem upset. If anything, he was almost hopeful, possibly relieved. "Is this about what you couldn't tell me when you came home from Minneapolis early?"

"Yes." The feelings crept up on Dale like smoke, but he imagined himself blowing them away, the fog retreating.

"I'm happy to hear your story whenever you want to tell me." Gabriel squeezed his hand. "I'm happier to hear you say yes."

Dale let go with one hand so he could pull Gabriel's face forward for a kiss. "*Yes,* I will marry you. I'll say it as many times as you want to hear it."

Gabriel kissed him again, but before their celebration kisses could get too carried away, he drew Dale to his feet and led him out the back door and down the steps to the yard, where Arthur stood gazing out at the lake. Gabriel led Dale up to him, beaming. Arthur turned as they approached, grinning. "Well?"

"He said yes." Gabriel pulled Dale tight to his side.

Arthur laughed and clapped them both on the shoulders before kissing them each on the cheek. "Well there you go, honey, getting yourself two husbands. At once. Go back and tell that to your thirteen-year-old self." He rubbed Dale's arm, turning serious. "When we figure out how to break this to Marcus, we'll have him make us legal documents to give you some protections. Powers of attorney, put you in the will, and so on. We can talk later about if we want to get creepy and do the thing where Gabriel adopts you so you're legally related and have visitation rights in the hospital and all that, but basically, what you need to know right now is we're going to find a way to include you in every aspect we can."

Dale kissed Arthur on the mouth. "Thank you."

Arthur cupped his chin and slipped him a little tongue, sending a shot of arousal through Dale's system. "I think it's time we have our family meeting. And it's such a lovely summer day. Let's have it outside." He ran a finger down Dale's T-shirt, sliding under the hem to tease under his waistband. "Get naked, baby." He turned to Gabriel, capturing his mouth and kissing him deep as he tweaked his nipple before moving away. "Same goes for you. Strip, both of you, and kneel facing each other on the blanket while I get ready."

Dale wasted no time peeling off his shirt and pushing his jeans and briefs to his ankles, keeping his gaze on Gabriel as he followed suit. He felt a hot rush of need as his beloved's body was revealed to him, but he felt a swell of gratitude too. Something deep and unnamable came over Dale as he replayed Gabriel's proposal in his mind, as Arthur's welcome settled into his psyche. Yes, he had the cloud of the conversation with Gabriel ahead of him, the confession of Ronny's assault, but it felt like a hop over a stream in the face of all this.

Gabriel and Arthur loved him. Not simply as a playmate. They cared for him. They wanted to make him part of their family. They had carved a place for him, because they could not bear to imagine life without him.

Dale's emotions were raw, a pulpy bed inside him as he knelt before Gabriel, lifting his hands to meet his palms, leaning in to kiss him, brush his nose, feel his nipples, his chest, his belly, his semi-erect cock, Gabriel's thighs against Dale's own. Gabriel smiled into Dale's mouth, teasing his lips with soft kisses, licking at the edges of his mustache, lacing their fingers tighter, shifting his body so their nipples kept nudging one another.

Arthur's chuckle wrapped around them as he approached and ruffled each of their heads. "Funny how you two read my mind."

He crouched beside them, gently prying them slightly apart, sliding a hand up Gabriel's belly to his nipple. Gabriel gasped, and Dale looked down to see Arthur had attached a clamp to Gabriel's nipple, one with about six inches of chain and a second clamp on the other end. He had a matching chain in his hand, which Dale assumed was for him. He was thinking it wasn't quite enough link to make it between a pair of nipples when Arthur brought the clamp to Dale's nipple instead.

For a moment Dale had a hot flash of panic. Arthur had played with his nipples plenty since that day in the file room, but the sharp flash of pain of the clamp was too much. It took Dale back to that day, to the feeling of being trapped and helpless while Ronny did things to him he didn't want and couldn't stop. The sense of darkness came over him in waves, but the wind whipped up, sent Arthur's scent to him, reminding him he was not in Minneapolis, this was not Ronny, and he could change things now.

"Yellow," he whispered.

Arthur removed the clamp immediately and put a hand on Dale's shoulder. "Talk to me. Tell me what just happened."

He realized he was caught, because he still hadn't told Gabriel about Ronny. He shut his eyes, took a deep breath, opened them. "Flashback. Too similar of a feeling, for a moment. I needed to get out of my head. I'm better now."

Gabriel touched Dale's face, worried. "What's going on? What are you flashing back to?"

Dale turned his face to kiss Gabriel's hand. "This is what...I'll tell you...tomorrow. Right now..." He straightened, pushed the darkness down, found his center. "I want to try again." He lifted his chin. "He doesn't get this."

Arthur stroked his shoulder and ran a hand to his nape. "Good boy. But we're going to go slow. All right?"

They did go slow, and it was more difficult than

Dale liked. He hated how it made him panic to have Arthur put the clips on him, how the tight pinch brought both arousal and fear. But instead of Ronny behind him, pinning him and laughing, it was Arthur, soothing him, kissing his shoulders and telling him how strong and beautiful he was. Arthur, who had given him so many good, kinky, sacred scenes. Who had, inch by inch, helped Dale rewrite so many shadows.

He was going to reclaim this one too. Ronny didn't get to keep a fucking thing.

"I'm going to switch up my plans." Arthur kept touching Dale, almost petting him. "You watch me while I play with Gabriel for a bit. You'll feel it too, because every time he gets flustered he'll tug on you. But you control it, baby. If it's too much, lean forward with him and it'll stop. You can play with him too. I'll ask you to give him some little pulls, and you can decide if you do it by teasing you both or using your hand to tug on him alone. The thing I want you to focus on though, Dale, is that I am making you take control here. That's the power over you I'm exercising. I have you naked in my clamps, sliding under my hands, and you know you'll do whatever I ask you to do, whatever I tell you. What I'm telling you to do is take control of this. You drive your pleasure with the clamps. When you feel like you're ready, when you've chased some of those shadows out of your head and want to give me the reins again, I'll come around and play with you too."

Dale did his best. He focused on the panic, on riding it out, of turning it around. He tried to use some of the tactics the counselor had taught him, of acknowledging the pain without pretending it wasn't there, making it part of his pattern but not letting it overpower him. It was part of him, but it wasn't who he was.

There was something magical about being connected to Gabriel, though, of watching Arthur kiss and nuzzle him from behind, binding his arms in a tie, and making Gabriel arch enough to pull the chains, giving them both a jolt of sensation. The first time it happened, Dale wasn't sure how he felt about it, but the second time he rode it out. The third time he shut his eyes and tried joining in, leaning and heightening the sensation, thrilling at the way it made Gabriel gasp, how it sent a sharp ricochet through his core. For a long time they toyed with this, moving back and forth, Dale getting better and better at managing the sensations, until it truly didn't bother him any longer.

"I'm ready," he told Arthur at last.

Arthur knelt behind him, kissing the back of his neck as he caressed his ass, then slipped a cool, lubed finger inside him. The wind blew around them, the sun filtering through the trees, the lake glistening in the distance. It was a beautiful afternoon, shaping up to be a perfect evening. Dale thought of the cabin he would have here someday soon, of having as many evenings like these as he wanted. His heart burst open, flooding him with love.

Gabriel leaned forward, kissing him languidly as Arthur worked deeper inside him.

They made out leisurely as Arthur fingered him, Dale easing his thighs open as Arthur slipped beads inside him, a long, thick set that left him full and ready. Arthur nipped at his shoulder, then wiped his hands and came around to Gabriel again.

He had used regular lube on Dale, but he produced the now-infamous can of Boy Butter for Gabriel, passing it in front of his face so he became flustered and protested, insisting Arthur shouldn't use it. "Arthur, don't. Please."

Arthur chuckled darkly. "Use the right word, if you don't want me to use it."

The exchange made Dale shiver, because it had been so casual, not done for Dale's benefit—that was simply how they were. Gabriel liked to play at lack of consent, but it was just that, play. Arthur did this every time, Dale realized, reminded him all he had to do to get his control back was claim it. And so as Gabriel protested, wincing and turning red as Arthur had him spread his knees wider and accept thicker and thicker chunks of lube, telling him *no, stop* the entire time— what he was really saying was, "Yes, please, make me do this, let me pretend I don't want it." And Arthur was having fun making him.

This was how the game was supposed to go. This was the way consent was meant to be played.

Gabriel leaned into Dale, whimpering, breathing

heavily into his neck, tears of embarrassment in his eyes. "Oh my God, Arthur, it's too much. I'm about to say it."

Arthur kissed the base of Gabriel's spine. "You need quite a bit, sweetheart, for what I have planned for you. If you can trust me, you'll be glad for this." He nodded at Dale. "Hold him."

Dale wrapped arms around Gabriel, going erect as he watched Arthur fuck first three, then four fingers into Gabriel. Gabriel gasped and tensed, but didn't call a stop, and in fact Dale could feel his erection bobbing against his.

"There you go, baby." Arthur kept finger-fucking him, harder and harder. "Stretch your knees wider. There you go. Need to loosen you way up. In a minute here Dale's gonna take over for me. Stuff as much into him as you can, honey. Because once I get undressed, we're gonna lay on this blanket, and Gabriel, you're gonna have a whole lot more than fingers in you."

Gabriel tried to lift his head, but he could only shiver and groan. "Arthur..."

Dale traced his fingers down to join Arthur's, mesmerized because he knew where this was going. He shifted, lowering his shoulder so he could push two fingers into Gabriel too, groaning as the movement tugged on the chain. He didn't stop. In fact, he pushed deeper.

"You look so sweet, honey, all these fingers going into you." Arthur used one hand to pull Gabriel's cheeks wider. "Think how nice you'll look with two cocks."

Gabriel cried out, a moan between arousal and agony. "Arthur, it feels so dirty. It's too much, and it's too thick."

"Do you want me to take it out? Or do you like it? Do you like how dirty you are right now, baby? Both of us fingering you, all that stuff in you, squishing around? Can you hear it? God, you're so dirty, Gabriel. Such a dirty, dirty boy."

Gabriel tensed, cried out, and set his teeth on Dale's shoulder.

Dale shifted his shoulder again and fucked deeper.

When Arthur pulled out, Dale lifted his head and waited for instruction. Arthur guided them to the blanket, laying them side by side, hiking Gabriel's leg over Dale's thigh. "Kiss him," he told Dale. "Fuck his mouth."

Dale did, losing himself in Gabriel while Arthur led his hand to Gabriel's hole once more, using his fingers to open him up, but before long he guided Dale's cock there instead, and Dale pushed inside, driving home, hot and slick. The Boy Butter was a little much, and it was in fact incredibly dirty. He loved it. He loved the sound, loved the way it made Gabriel whimper, loved the way he knew Gabriel was secretly both loving it and hating it.

When he felt Arthur's cock nudging beside his, he slowed his strokes, waiting for direction. He broke the kiss too, letting Gabriel have his mouth so he could cry out.

"Oh God." Gabriel tipped his head back into Arthur, who had wrapped his arm around Gabriel's body as he fucked slowly inside him. He screwed his eyes shut tight, his stomach going taut as Arthur continued to stretch him. Dale groaned too. It was more than dirty now. It was tight and wicked, Arthur's cock alongside his.

Arthur kissed Gabriel's ear, breathing heavily into it. "You all right?" Gabriel made a high-pitched whine, but he nodded. Arthur kissed his ear again, this time with tongue. "You liking all that dirty lube now?"

Gabriel had tears leaking down his cheeks. "It's so much." His voice was barely a whisper.

Dale worried for him now. "Is it *too* much?"

Gabriel shook his head emphatically, his curls bouncing. "It's just so intense." He took several breaths, keeping his eyes closed. "You're both inside me. Both."

Arthur kissed his cheek. "Both your husbands, baby." He winked at Dale and made a subtle *come here* motion.

Dale leaned forward, kissed Gabriel's mouth, but then he slid to the side and kissed Arthur too. They became a confused mass of mouths, beards brushing, mouths seeking, noses bumping, breaths mingling.

"Going to start fucking you now," Arthur said, and began to move.

They all groaned, Dale and Arthur a low rumble of want, Gabriel a higher gasp of intense pain-laced pleasure as he was stretched further yet. Dale began to move as well, alternating strokes at first, but then joining Arthur, fucking into Gabriel in time, Dale sealing his mouth over Gabriel's and swallowing his screams while Arthur growled and bit against his neck.

Arthur came first, a rough explosion into Gabriel, and Dale followed soon after. The beads inside him heightened his orgasm, making him shudder. When they pulled out of Gabriel, Arthur came around behind Dale, putting his arms around him, massaging the skin around his nipple clamps.

"You did a good job." He reached over to stroke a fucked-out Gabriel too, who smiled up at him and weakly touched his hand. Arthur took hold of both Dale's clamps. "I'm going to release these now, and then I'm going to give you your reward for doing such a good job. Are you ready?"

Dale nodded. "I am."

He hissed when the clamps came off, pain hitting him as blood rushed back. He waited for the panic, but it didn't come—not this time. He knew there would be other times it came, out of nowhere probably. But he would deal with it, as he had now.

Arthur massaged the nipples lightly, getting their feeling back. "Good job. Very good job. Now get on your knees for me, sweetheart. Bend over, face down by Gabriel, knees apart, ass in the air."

Dale did as he was told. He felt quiet, calm, and good, especially when Gabriel ran fingers through his hair. When Arthur touched his ass, first with his hand, then with something flat and cool, he didn't flinch, only waited to see what would happen to him.

"You did such a good job," Arthur told him. "You managed your panic so well, and you got the better of a bad moment. I'm going to take the beads out of you in the way I'd planned, but first I'm giving you a treat. You earned this. I want you to know that I know what you want. You pay attention to what other people want—I pay attention to you. I know what Gabriel wants, and I know what you do too. This is your reward, honey. This is all for you. All you need to do is stay just as you are."

"Yes, sir," Dale replied, and felt himself give over, relax.

Arthur said, "Gabriel, I'm going to help you sit up, and I want you to come over here and watch this."

Dale was aware of movement on the blanket, of Arthur helping bound Gabriel get to the other side and sit against a stump, positioned where he had a line of sight of Dale's upturned ass but wasn't directly behind him, with some space for Arthur to move there.

Arthur ran his hands over the globes of Dale's ass. "Look at this, honey. Do you see how nice he's spread?" Gabriel made an approving, sated noise. Arthur touched the ring end of the beads protruding out of Dale. "He's stuffed full of beads. Big fat ones.

The whole time he fucked you, they were banging his prostate. Look how lovely he is, displayed like this. How submissive he is." He petted Dale's globes, parted them. "Soak in this view, Gabriel. He likes you seeing this, you know. He loves you to see him like this, all vulnerable. That's the thing with him. He loves to be displayed. In fact, let's do him up a bit better."

Something cold clicked on Dale's ankle, and Arthur nudged Dale's other knee wider, and then wider, until he strained to comply—and then something snapped over his other ankle as well. His knees, his feet, were spread apart, and he couldn't bring them together. He could feel the wind on his ass, could feel his hole stretched open more, his balls hanging, his spent dick dangling. They could see it all. They were looking at him, as Arthur said, displayed for them.

A sense of calm settled over him, and he tried to spread his knees wider, to give them more.

Arthur chuckled and patted his ass, then leaned over to kiss it. "So pretty. It's going to be even prettier once I paddle it.

Dale whimpered and tipped his ass higher, eagerness making his body hot.

Arthur ran the rubber paddle over his ass, down the crack, wedging it against his hole. "Are you ready for this, honey? I'm going to turn your ass red. I'm giving you as many as you want. This is your present, so tell me when we're done."

Dale got on his hands, bracing for impact. "Yes,

sir."

Arthur gave him a few warming taps, to let him know the feel. Dale whimpered, ready for the real sting. Finally Arthur said, "Ready?" And when Dale nodded, they began.

He had a fleeting moment with these too, remembering spankings Ronny had given him in his office, but he pushed this aside, reminding himself that was then, not now, and Ronny did not get to claim his pleasure. He dug his fingers into the blanket, gathering the edges until he'd bunched it far enough he could claw the dirt, until he breathed through the blows and tossed his head back to ride out the pain, to *ride* the pain, to make it his. He let it take him into the places where he didn't have to think, *couldn't* think, could only feel the bite of the pain, the buzz and the ride of it. Until all he knew was the sting of the paddle and the quietness inside him, the stillness he found at the heart of himself.

I have a family.

I have a perfect family, for me.

The pain began to be too much, making him shake, and Dale had to call an end. "Stop," he said, and Arthur did immediately. He brought out lotion, soothing Dale's skin and rubbing him down. But then he disappeared, and after a rustle, Gabriel appeared before Dale, aroused, dark-eyed, beautiful, with his glasses back on.

"Fuck his mouth, Gabriel," Arthur ordered. "I'm

going to take care of this ass."

Dale opened for Gabriel, shutting his eyes as he let his lover fuck his throat, moaning as Arthur pulled, with a viciousness he loved, the balls from his hole. But he moaned again as he felt Arthur slide inside him, rolling into him, fucking into the fiery skin of his well-paddled ass.

They fucked him at both ends, filling his body, the same as they had done to his heart.

Arthur unstrapped him from the bar when they finished, and they collapsed on the blanket, touching and kissing and napping until the mosquitos came out and thought to make a meal of their flesh. They meandered into the cabin, smiling and laughing and nuzzling each other.

"I'll get the grill started," Arthur said, tugging a new shirt onto his body.

Gabriel took a shower and afterward joined Dale on the couch, head in his lover's lap, curls still wet. "I'd set the table, but I'm so tired."

Dale was too, his ass burning, but he loved it. "I'll do it." He kissed Gabriel's nose and got up. "You lie here."

They ate together, then settled in the living room and listened while Gabriel read another chapter aloud from *American Gods*. They fell into bed together, the three of them, and Dale woke early to take a walk along the lake, letting himself soak in the wonder of the moment. He felt amazing. He was so happy right now, happier than he could remember being in his life. He was ready to tell Gabriel about Ronny. He didn't even feel the shadow of it anymore. He felt as if he could handle anything, that everything would turn out all right.

When he got back to the house, he was surprised to see Marcus's car there, and Paul's—and Corrina's. Puzzled, he hurried up the steps, wondering what was going on, worried something had happened. As he came into the house and they all turned to look at him, misery on their faces, his blood ran cold.

He saw the envelope on the table, a flyer of some kind peeking underneath. He saw the corner of a picture. The sight pierced his heart, right through all the good feelings Family Weekend had made.

No. Please, no. Please, no.

Marcus came to him, grave, his expression marshaled where everyone else had emotion rioting over their faces. "It came out of nowhere. It was a bolder move than I ever would have guessed. Has Ronny been in contact with you? Any threats?"

Dale shook his head slowly. He felt as if he were underwater.

"I put in a call to Cassidy, the PI. They're on their way now. They said they've got a few angles we might be able to work, and of course we have the legal option. But we have the damage control to do here now. Because it wasn't only me who got this. It was the mayor, and Corrina, and everyone on the project."

The pain in Dale's heart became so sharp he could barely breathe. "Let me see it."

Marcus hesitated, then stepped away to fetch the flyer from the table. Dale dared a glance at the others, and as he saw their faces—Corrina's shock and concern, Gabriel's confusion, Frankie and Kyle's wide eyes, Arthur's pain—his happiness shattered like lake ice in spring and hung suspended in the air, hanging above his head as he took the paper from Marcus.

It wasn't simply a photo. It was the Logan project flyer, the Christmas in July ad frame, but instead of Dale's headshot below the carefully selected village shot, it was a full-color image of Dale naked on his knees, shot from the perspective of the person receiving the blowjob. Dale's ass protruded, red with Ronny's handprints. His face was centered in the frame, mouth full of Ronny's cock.

He was wearing a Santa hat.

The suspended shards of Dale's happiness melted and rained to the ground, mingling with his tears as they slid down his cheeks.

Chapter Fifteen

ARTHUR WAS GOING to kill him. He was going to find this Ronny bastard, drag him somewhere quiet, and he was going to kill him.

He knew it with a certainty he'd never known anything in his life. It filled him with a crazy kind of calm, that knowledge, even though behind the calm was a wall of white-hot rage. It was the only way out of this, he reasoned. This asshole was clearly going to keep coming. Who knew how many photos he had? Who knew where else he'd sent them? There would be more.

Watching Dale stare at the flyer had been like watching him get shot. Arthur was never letting that happen again.

He glanced around the room, at his family and friends talking over each other, crying, comforting each other. Looked at Dale, so still and motionless on the far side of the room. He memorized their faces. His gaze lingered on his mother, and he ached. It fell on Gabriel, and he burned, acid on his heart.

Dale and Gabriel will have each other, he reminded himself. *That's one of the perks. It'll be okay. Go on. You can make this all right.*

Trembling, floating on a cloud, he crossed to Gabriel and kissed him on the cheek.

Gabriel clung to him. "What's happening? What is that? Who sent it? Why?"

The rage threatened to boil over, but Arthur forced it to mellow. "I'll take care of it." He kissed him one last time, embraced him, buried his face in his hair, and drank in his scent.

Then he let him go, grabbed his keys, and headed for his truck.

He got as far as his hand on the door before Marcus and Paul came out of the house. "Where the hell are you going?" Paul called.

"I'm going to take care of it." Arthur climbed into the truck and started the engine.

"*Arthur!*" Marcus shouted, but Arthur ignored him and locked the door, focusing on his task. His hands shook, though. He should have hugged them too. And his mom.

Marcus banged on Arthur's window, hard enough he thought it might break. "Arthur Adam Anderson, get out of that truck right goddamned now!"

Arthur put it into gear.

But when he tried to accelerate, he couldn't, because Paul was standing in front of the vehicle.

Arthur laid on the horn. "Get the hell out of my

way."

Paul leaned on the hood and braced himself. "Not a fucking chance."

Grumbling, Arthur put the truck in reverse—but as soon as he glanced in the mirror, he saw Marcus was standing behind him.

He rolled down the window. "*Let me go.* I'm the only one who can do this. You have to let me do this."

"We are not letting you drive to Minneapolis to beat up a man and get yourself arrested."

Arthur set his teeth. "I'm not going to beat him up. *I'm going to kill him.*"

Paul glared. "Oh, yeah. Never mind then. Sure, we'll let you go."

Arthur gunned the engine a few times, honked the horn some more, then got out, swearing. He searched the random mess of cars, trying to decide who had left their keys inside.

Marcus came up behind him, pinned his arms behind his back, and frog-marched him toward the shed. When he struggled, Paul took up the other side and locked him into place. They shut the door behind them once they were inside, and Marcus and Paul blocked the way out, meaning all Arthur could do was stand there and sputter in front of them—and with nowhere else to go, all the rage he'd been so carefully controlling came screaming out at them.

"Who the fuck do you think you are, keeping me in here?"

"Your friends," Paul said.

"*Fuck you.*" Arthur pointed in the general direction of the Twin Cities. "He's just sitting there. Laughing. Knowing he hurt Dale. Knowing he can do it again. If I'd gone to take care of him before, he couldn't have done this now. He's *fucking scum.* He needs to be taken out. I can do it. You know I can. You've seen me fight. I could *break his neck.* I could be fast. I want to be slow, but I'll be fast, I promise. I'll make it so he doesn't hurt Dale like this or anyone else ever."

"Listen to me." Marcus didn't touch him, and he still blocked the door, but he crowded Arthur, getting into his space. "The PI is coming. We're going to use the law to do this. There's a lot we can do, and we're going to do it."

"You told me yourself it's slippery. It might not stick. He's a fucking player, he's counting on this. He thinks he's above all this, that no one will stoop to his level. *I will.* I'll fucking give this shit back to him. I'll make him eat it. I swear to fucking God."

Paul put a hand on him. "You have to calm down."

Arthur shook him off, and somehow the motion drew the first of his tears too. "*He hurt Dale.* He was doing so well, he worked so hard, and *this asshole* gutted him. I'm gonna fucking return the favor."

Marcus was so goddamned calm. "We're going to help him. All of us. You too. And not by getting yourself convicted of murder. He needs you. You're his friend. Gabriel needs you too."

"Gabriel has Dale. It's fine."

Marcus dogged him. "Gabriel needs more than friends. He needs you, his lover. His husband."

Paul shook his head at Arthur, a silent warning. Which was the worst thing to do, because right now every *no* was *yes* to Arthur. And so for the second time, to the second worst person, he spilled his lover's secret.

He turned to Marcus, thinking he'd bowl him down with this one and get away. "Gabriel and Dale aren't just friends. They're lovers too."

Marcus blinked at him. "What?"

"*Arthur, stop,*" Paul pleaded.

Arthur didn't stop. "They've been together since February. They're all serious now, doing a commitment ceremony and everything. They were going to do a marriage thing, not legal, just meaningful to them, at the same time as our legal marriage. Except now they can get regular married. I can do this for them. That's what I can do, Marcus." He was supposed to wait for Marcus to be flustered and upset about infidelity, but he couldn't stop. "I have to protect them. He's not my lover, but he's mine. I don't know how to describe it. I don't feel like I have to. He's *mine*, and this is what I can do for him. I can set him free. *Let me do this.*" The tears started up again, and he clenched his fists, beating them on Marcus's chest. "*Let me do this.*"

Marcus caught his hands, his face full of sorrow. "I won't."

Arthur shouted, fought, his rage pouring out of

him now, but Marcus held him fast, Paul stepped away from the door to help out, to keep Arthur from getting away. Eventually the rage was gone, and there was nothing left but Arthur's sadness and his pain.

"I couldn't protect him," he whispered. "It was all I wanted. Just to keep him safe. I would have done anything. He's worked so hard, he's come *so far, you don't even know.* And I couldn't do enough. You can do all the legal shit you want, and he's still going to hurt."

"You can kill all the people you want, and that won't change it either. You can't take away his pain," Marcus said.

Paul stroked Arthur's hair tenderly. "Or yours."

Arthur gave up then, sagging against them, weeping like he'd never wept before, letting it all out until he was spent.

Marcus and Paul held him until he was finished.

"We're going to fix this," Marcus said. "I promise you. We will take care of him. And you."

"We need to get inside and start on that," Paul pointed out.

On the way past the truck, Arthur grabbed his keys and handed them to Marcus. "Keep them. Don't let me have them back until you're sure I'm...sane."

Marcus smiled and pocketed the keys. "Can do. Let's go see what fixing we can muster up." He put a heavy hand on Arthur's shoulder. "On the way, however, you're going to explain to me what you mean, Gabriel is marrying you *and* marrying Dale."

THERE WAS SO much happening, and Gabriel barely understood what was going on. Worse, he was sure everyone in the room knew more than he did about the disturbing prank someone had sent about Dale, and four hours after the revelation, no one had bothered yet to clue him in. Which meant this also had to do with whatever Dale had been about to tell him but hadn't.

How in the world that story had something to do with the flyer, Gabriel couldn't imagine. He did his best not to be upset that somehow whatever it was everyone else already knew. It ate at his brain, imagining what story could be acceptable to keep from him alone but share with everyone else. He tried not to think about it, but he might as well try not to think about a black bear wandering around his library.

They had reconvened to Marcus and Frankie's house, where a private investigator Marcus had hired met them with a fat file of information. Dale had been whisked away upstairs with Arthur and a counselor friend of his who had come up from Duluth, and though Arthur had come back downstairs, Dale and the counselor had yet to reappear.

When Arthur pulled him aside, Gabriel dug his fingers into his side, ready for Arthur to say he still couldn't tell him anything, but that wasn't what happened. Arthur took him to the kitchen, held his hand, and told him everything.

"Dale was involved with someone who abused him.

For a long time. Sometimes their contact was consensual, sometimes it was questionable, and several times it was outright abuse, but the guy did a good job of making Dale think it was fine. Most of the abuse was mental. There are two incidents in particular, though, upsetting him acutely right now. One happened the Christmas before last, and it involved photos and video. The other happened the day he went to get his things, which is when he found out the photos existed and the guy was holding them as blackmail over his head. He's been wanting to tell you about it, but he's still working through getting rid of his sense of shame of having been abused at all, and it's hardest around you, because he doesn't want you to see him that way."

Gabriel had barely breathed through everything Arthur said, but it was here he crumbled. "But I would never…" He gave up trying to speak and wept.

Arthur wiped away his tears. "I know, baby. I know. But it's not so simple. I think, ironically enough, he was about to tell you when they showed up with the stupid flyer. He'd put so much behind him. That was what his yellow was about during playtime, by the way. His flashback. He worked through it, and he was so proud. I was proud of him too." He flattened his lips. "It's as if the guy knew. But I suppose that's how assholes like him roll. They have a sense of when their victims gain ground, and they know when and how to pull them back."

"Why did he do this? Why send such a horrible

thing?"

"To shame him. To make Dale feel he doesn't belong here, so he comes back to Minneapolis broken and alone. Then the abuser would wait a bit and approach him again. Make Dale his toy once more."

Gabriel wanted to throw up. Then commit murder. He gripped the edge of the counter behind him. "I want to kill him. I want to go to Minneapolis and tear the Twin Cities apart until I find him and kill him."

"Oh, honey." Arthur's laugh was low and edgy, and Gabriel saw how his fiancé was shaking. "I already tried to do that. I walked out of the house to go to Minneapolis, and Marcus and Paul followed me. They blocked my truck, then dragged me into the shed until I calmed down. Growled at me until I remembered I had to stay out of prison because you and Dale need me."

This gave Gabriel a whole new level of terror. "Oh, Arthur—you would have broken my heart."

"I know. I'm sorry. And I have another apology to make to you too, because in the middle of it I kind of outed you and Dale to Marcus. So that's two strikes on me for keeping your secret. To the two people we'd decided we really shouldn't tell."

Gabriel stared at him, blinking. Then he sighed, laugh-cried, and drew Arthur to him. "You're lucky I love you so much."

Arthur hugged him back. "I know." He drew away and nodded at the door to the other rooms. "Okay. Should we go see about how we fix this?"

They found the others in the living room, listening to Cassidy, the private investigator, who was explaining what they'd discovered during the investigation. Cassidy was young, in their mid-twenties, and they dressed with a hip, urban edginess that would have made them stand out anywhere in Logan, but on top of that Cassidy had a fluid mixture of gender expression: a clearly male set of hips, but also a bright blue bra beneath a black halter top outlining a modest pair of breasts. They had blunt-edged acrylic nails set on unabashedly masculine hands on arms boasting ample hair, and stubble on their chin beneath deep plum lipstick and a full face. Their hair, however, was a bleached neutral buzz, close cut along all the sides except for a spiked crop of bright green at the crown.

"He's a full-on creeper." Cassidy had a Tootsie Pop in their hand, and they tucked it into their cheek, speaking around it as they shuffled through their notes. "Dale's not the only victim on his leash by half. I've got two other guys and three women at the office alone, and two guys at his gym. But the lead I'm pressing on now is I heard a rumor he goes after the babysitters. The thing is, he's smart, and he covers his tracks. I pulled in favors today from a few other friends in the field, and if one of them can get anything on him with a minor, we might have more legs."

"Or even the sum total of all these together." Marcus tapped the files in front of him with the eraser of a pencil, running his eyes over everything, as if he were looking for the Holy Grail. "It's got to be done right. I don't want him to slip away."

Frankie sat on the couch, listening, but at this he shook his head. "I can't believe you're showing us all this, telling us all this, and acting like it won't be enough to call him out? The man should be *in jail.*"

"Prison," Marcus corrected. "And no, it might not be enough. Not at all. You remember the Stanford rape in California? The Steubenville High School case in Ohio? I could stand here all day and rattle them off, most of them you haven't heard of. They don't go well. And those are women. Not gay men. Not gay men with photographic evidence that could easily be twisted into whatever the hell a lawyer wanted to turn it into."

Gabriel stiffened. "That's not fair."

Marcus was patient, grim. "No, it's not. Because the system isn't fair, much as I wish it were. It's made up of people, and people are biased, and they have screwed-up ideas about consent and blame and what men in power should be allowed to get away with. So that's why I hired Cassidy. They're young, yes, but they're the best."

Cassidy pulled the sucker out with a loud *pop* and a grin. "Thanks, boss."

Marcus nodded gruffly at them and continued to address Gabriel. "We need all the ammunition we can get. And we need to consider that the best way to get him might not be through the law. It might be through his job. It might be through his marriage. It might be through his connections." He picked up one of the folders on the coffee table. "These were sent through work—that's a huge violation right there. But understandably, Dale won't want them seen by the CEO or his staff. Ronny's father-in-law is a city councilman in Eden Prairie. I don't know how much leverage that gives us, but that's an angle." He selected another file. "This is my favorite so far. Ronny's investments are all tied up with the business owned by a godfather of a friend of mine. It wouldn't beggar him, but it would shock the hell out of him, because he wouldn't see it coming."

Kyle crossed his arms over his chest. "What about the new revenge porn law? Why can't you use that?"

Marcus's expression was black. "Oh, we could. He'd be charged not only with the misdemeanor but a felony, because I'd argue he intended to harass. He'd be looking at five years, and I'd do everything I could to make sure he got them all. Except the law doesn't go into effect until August 1. So this is moot. What we have is what's in front of us. Nothing more."

They were quiet for a moment, taking it in.

"Did he send anything to Dale's work?" Arthur asked.

Cassidy shook their head. "It was only Logan. I imagine that's phase two, though."

Corrina had been quiet in the back of the room, but she came forward now. She looked rattled but resolute, tipping her chin up as she addressed them. "I think you should tell his employer. I think you should tell them this." She gestured to the mess of folders. "All the information. Get him fired, if you can. Then get his name out there, to everyone who might hire him. Do the same thing to him as the pictures, but with his story. Because that's the thing he's trying to use over Dale. He's counting on him being too ashamed to say anything. So take away the shame. Turn it back on him. Ruin him with what he was trying to use to ruin Dale."

They glanced at one another, the idea rolling around the room. "It might work," Cassidy said at last.

"It would work."

Dale stood in the doorway with the counselor. She held back as he came into the room. He seemed exhausted, but more stable than Gabriel would have thought. Resigned, somewhat, but he wasn't wrecked in the way Gabriel had feared. He stood beside Gabriel, took his hand, and stared at the sea of files.

"I think Corrina is right. That's the thing he'll never see coming, the only thing he can't counter. The only thing he can do after that is post the pictures online, and then he only has another month and some change before the law goes into effect."

Gabriel stroked Dale's hand. He realized he was doing it in front of everyone, but he didn't care. He'd explain it later. "Would it cost you your job?"

"Well…I'm already breaking away, aren't I? I think that's why he sent it here. I want to work with Logan, to make running Christmas Town my full-time job, not turn it loose and move on to a new project. So he can't do much to me there. I burned that bridge myself, in his eyes. I didn't mean to close off my connection to Kivino, so this is a risk, but I don't want him holding it over my head. So it's better if I tell them about it, not him. That way if he sends around a flyer, he's the stalker asshole." He let out a breath. "And I'm the victim."

"Survivor," the counselor said from the doorway.

He smiled a sideways, melancholy gesture. "Survivor," he corrected.

Cassidy and Marcus exchanged a look. "It's not a bad plan," Cassidy said. "A bit nuclear, but yes, the scorched earth cuts Ronny off. It might even cost him his job, *and* it might get his other victims to come forward. You could put the word out, Marcus, that you were willing to talk to them, help them out. I don't know what you could do, but that might spook him. He might get sloppy. Or maybe we nail him."

"What do we do in the meantime, here in Logan?" Paul asked. "How do we help Dale here?"

Now Corrina's eyes were lit with a kind of fire. She didn't smile, but her whole being licked with dark pleasure. "You leave Logan to me." She reached for her purse, then went around the room, hugging and kissing all of them, her gaggle of boys. She also gave Cassidy a quick peck on the cheek, pausing to give them a moment's consideration.

"Mom," Arthur warned. "They don't need a date."

Cassidy blinked, then laughed. "Well I wouldn't *mind* one. But do you really think you could find me one up here?"

Everyone else in the room groaned or laughed, and Corrina patted Cassidy on the arm. "We'll talk later. You'll be at the festival, yes? Marcus, make sure he comes to the festival."

"*They*, Mom," Arthur corrected. "They use they pronouns."

Corrina frowned for a moment, processing this, then nodded. "All right. Marcus, make sure *they* come." She slung her purse onto her shoulder, then went back to give Dale an extra hug. "Don't worry. I know just what to do."

She left, and they watched her go. The counselor spoke a few last words to Dale, then followed her out.

"What in the world is she going to do?" Cassidy asked when Corrina was gone.

Arthur shook his head. "No idea. But it will either magically make things okay against all odds or bring the whole fucking thing down around our ears. Either way, there's no stopping her now."

Dale still had hold of Gabriel's hand. He turned to Gabriel, addressing him alone. "I need to speak to you for a minute. Privately."

"Of course."

They went into the den and shut the door. Gabriel sat on an ottoman, and Dale sat on a chair before him. They held hands, staring at them, twining their fingers together.

"Arthur told you?" Dale said at last.

"Yes." Gabriel stroked Dale's hand. "I'm so sorry that happened to you."

Dale stroked back, a sad echo. "I'm sorry I didn't get to tell you the story myself like I wanted. And I'm sorry you had to see the pictures. This isn't the way I wanted you to view me."

"I don't mind the pictures. I wouldn't have minded that you took them at all, except I hate how someone coerced you into taking them, how they used them to hurt you. I hate that someone hurt you. I wish I could take it away."

"That's the thing, actually. I spent the last hour with Marla, my counselor, talking through all this, but what I kept coming back to was how you guys were all down here reacting to it as if it had happened to you, not me. And I realized it did happen to you. Because you care about me."

"Of course we do. I do, and Arthur does, but we all do. All of Logan does."

"I know, but..." Dale squeezed. "Hear me out. When I saw the flyer, all I could think of was how perfectly he hurt me. You told me Logan saw me as Santa, and I never told you, but I love that. I want to be Logan's Santa forever. I love the way they look up to me. The way you all cherish me and value me. I saw the flyer, the photo, and I was so sure he'd taken it away. The thing I wanted the most, yanked out of my hands, and he didn't even have to show up. He didn't have to be here, and he knew." He smiled at their joined hands. "Except it didn't work. I don't know if Corrina can fix all of Logan yet, but I already know Ronny couldn't get at the most important parts. He couldn't get at Corrina, at Marcus or the others, at Arthur. At you. Because when you saw that picture, you didn't turn me away like he wanted. You pulled me closer. You bled with me."

Gabriel let go of Dale's hands and caught his face, kissing him sweetly. "We always will."

They lingered there a moment, resting in each other, but soon they both wanted to rejoin the others, so they went to the living room. Cassidy had left for Minneapolis to get ready for Project Scorched Earth as soon as Marcus told them to pull the trigger, but the others were milling about, talking softly.

Arthur came over to them as soon as they emerged. "Everything all right?"

Dale still had Gabriel's hand. He didn't seem interested in letting go. "I think so."

Gabriel looked around the room, saw everyone's eyes on them. Saw them notice Dale's hand in his. Gabriel maneuvered himself so he could be in the middle between Dale and Arthur, and held his other lover's hand as well. "I think it's time we shared the rest of our secrets."

Everyone was standing, but Gabriel led the three of them to the couch, and they sat, still holding on to each other. The others, on cue, took seats, Paul and Kyle sitting in the love seat, Marcus and Frankie tucked into the big leather recliner. They glanced at one another, then at Gabriel and Dale and Arthur.

"Do you have something to tell us?" Frankie prompted.

His tone told Gabriel they already knew. He wondered how long their secret had been out. But it didn't matter, because whatever they thought, wherever and whenever they'd heard anything, it hadn't come from them. And so, for the next hour, the three of them told their story.

They took turns, Gabriel starting, then Dale, then Arthur, weaving the tale of how they had discovered their relationship, their own feelings, how it had grown, how they had managed it, where they were taking it now. Gabriel listened to Arthur speak passionately about how he felt about not only his relationship with Gabriel but how much he believed in Gabriel's relationship with Dale. Gabriel realized too how strong their own relationship had become, Dale and Arthur— and the three of them, whatever it was.

It was theirs. It didn't need to be anything else, didn't need any other name.

Dale had recovered a great deal of his strength and energy during the conversation too, and he brought the tale to a close. "I hadn't thought about belonging to Logan. I'd always wanted a permanent relationship—or a few of them—but I'd struggled, and I'd given up. And no, Ronny didn't help. But what I've had with

Gabriel, and my friendship with Arthur and with all of you, has rewritten everything for me. In an odd way, what should have been Ronny's devastating blow has only shown me that while my walls can still be shaken and rattled, even damaged, my foundation is strong." He squeezed Gabriel's hand. "That's you. That's all of you."

The others had listened quietly, and after they finished, Marcus smiled, held out his hand, and said, "Welcome to the family."

Gabriel glanced at Arthur. "You're not upset?" he asked Marcus. "Because of what happened to you, with your boyfriend before Frankie?"

Marcus frowned at him, confused, then gave Arthur an exasperated glare. "You think I don't know the difference between infidelity and polyamory?"

Arthur looked sheepish. "I wasn't sure you did, no. But now it's you and my mother both who've surprised me."

"That's Logan," Frankie said, leaning onto Marcus's shoulder. "It has its ups and its downs, but at the end of the day, it stands by its own."

Dale let out a heavy sigh. "Let's hope they decide I'm one of them, then."

"Oh, I think they will." Kyle smiled slyly. "And if they don't, Corrina will help. And so will we."

Chapter Sixteen

TAKING DOWN RONNY was an endless, soul-sucking process that Dale wouldn't wish on anyone. Not even Ronny.

Cassidy kept digging up dirt, their file getting fatter and fatter. They delayed Project Scorched Earth indefinitely as Cassidy became increasingly convinced they could achieve their objective without revealing Dale's situation to his employer. Whether or not Ronny knew they were on to him, he remained quiet. No more flyers appeared, but every day Dale worried another shoe would drop, and every time he had to face someone from Logan he couldn't stop wondering if they'd seen the flyer and what they thought of him.

Dale avoided going into town as much as possible. He'd tried to go to his office, but every time he started toward Main Street, he'd broken into a cold sweat, and he couldn't take it. Marla had told him to go with it, to not push himself but to not back down either. His friends had worked with him too, helping him get groceries, bringing him his mail, because he'd basically moved in on Arthur and Gabriel's couch, though he was able to stay at his place occasionally by the first week in July.

At the advice of his counselor, Dale joined a support group for assault survivors, and hearing their stories of dealing with the justice system, the police, the hospitals, made him acutely aware how much worse his horrors could have been. All the other members of his group were women, which he'd expected, but that bothered him as well. He knew there was no shame in being a male survivor, but it was difficult to shake the feeling.

After the third meeting, though, when he'd finally shared a few details of his own story, a woman came up to him afterwards. Her name was Christina, and she took Dale to a quiet coffee shop and told him her story. It wasn't the same as his, exactly. But the more she spoke, the more he understood why she'd pulled him aside.

"My abuser and I were together a long time. She was my first girlfriend, my first partner of any kind. She didn't want me to have any other relationships. She kept me from connecting with other people. When I started to think I might not be gay but bisexual, she shamed me for those thoughts, and that's when she began to physically abuse me too."

Dale didn't want to touch Christina uninvited, but he laid a hand near hers, his heart aching for her. He hated that this had happened to her, hated even more that he could tell she had more wounds to share. "I'm sorry."

She put her hand over his briefly and smiled. "It went on a long time, and it was worse because so much of my family had rejected me simply for being queer. My aunt saw me one day after Tanya had hurt me pretty badly and helped get me out of the situation, but she ended up damaging me more, blaming my being lesbian for the assault."

"Oh my *God.*" Dale struggled to contain his outrage on her behalf. He failed. "Christina, I'm *so sorry.* What a nightmare for you. You should never have had to endure that."

"You're exactly right, I shouldn't have. It took me a long time to understand, though, and Marla was a big part of that. Coming to our group has been good for me too. It was rough at first. I knew I was different than the others, and it bothered me. Which was why I wanted to reach out to you. I know I'm not a man who was assaulted. But I am queer. I understand what it's like to feel as if you're carrying an extra boulder while you try to navigate this painful road, that you're a wounded unicorn. I wanted you to know I'm willing to walk with you."

Dale stared at Christina, unable to speak for the emotions clogging his heart. She was about his age, mid-thirties he'd guess. Curly blonde hair pulled back in a red headband. Pretty smile. Lovely girl. Confident.

Happy. Put together. She *looked* like a survivor. No sign of victim on her. Whatever scars she had she'd turned into strengths. Now here she was, offering to share her strengths with Dale simply because he was gay and so was she.

Because he was a survivor too.

He hadn't planned to talk. He opened his mouth to say thank you, and the finest grains of his story, his feelings, his fears, his hopes, his everything, came pouring out instead.

"My friends are trying to take him down. My abuser." Dale's fingers fidgeted on his coffee cup, climbing it and tracing the rim endlessly. "I didn't want to prosecute. I didn't want the publicity of a trial. I don't believe anyone would do anything to him. My friend is a lawyer, and I know he'd try his best to help me, but I'm a man. I didn't go in after and let them collect a rape kit. And we were in a relationship, even though it was a bad one. I don't trust the system would take care of me. I'm afraid they'd mock me because I'm a man." The pain bloomed in him, and a few tears fell. "I don't want to go through a trial, but I hate that I don't believe they would listen to me."

"I know. It's not fair. They don't believe women either, but yes, they're not fair to men who are assaulted. We are horrible to assault survivors in this culture. The culture itself feeds the enablers. It's not your fault. You didn't do this. You get to feel upset that the law is prioritizing your abuser over you, that there's such a poor path for you."

"But then I think about him being still out there, and I think, what if he attacks someone else? Then it's my fault, isn't it?"

"*No.*" Christina put her hand over Dale's, looking him right in the eye. "You are not responsible for him. It isn't your job to fix him. Your job is to take care of you and the people who love you."

Dale squeezed her hand and shut his eyes. "They hired a PI. They're trying to get my abuser fired, maybe financially ruin him—I don't understand all of it. I'm glad they're doing it. But sometimes I feel like I should be doing something. Shouldn't I be taking him down? Isn't that how I will find my resolution, if I do it?"

"Well…maybe you want to take it to Marla. But speaking for myself…I can't go to Tanya and have some kind of retribution. I don't have evidence anymore of the abuse, just my hearsay, so I don't know how I could have her charged. I don't want to, either. I don't want the circus of a hearing. There are people who go that route, and it's important for them. Sometimes it works. Sometimes it's awful. But sometimes it's a combination of awful and cultural earthquake. Look at the Stanford survivor and the letter she wrote to her rapist, and the aftershocks it's created. She chose to do that. Only she and her family know what that meant to her, but her letter meant a lot to me. I advise you to read it. The point is, though, you get to find your own way to respond to your abuser. It doesn't have to be a letter read in court. It doesn't have to be something he sees or feels. It can be how you live your life. For me it's that I pushed aside my shyness and approached you, trusting my instinct that you needed help."

Dale gave her a watery smile. "Thank you. I did."

"See, that's worth it to me. It's not something they're going to put on the evening news, and I'm not glad I was assaulted and abused, but I'm glad I could take my experience and use it to help you. You get to use your experience too, Dale. You don't have to clap back, though. If your friends can take him down, wonderful. But if they can't, you can destroy him by not letting him under your skin anymore. That's what he wants. He doesn't want your body, or even your brain. He wants your will. He wants you broken because he gets off on that. You see him coming now, though, and you have armor. You have backup. You have so much that he can never take. Sometimes the greatest victory over an abuser is not looking at them. It all depends on *you*. On what *you* need."

He shook his head. "I suck at saying what I need. You have no idea."

"I know. Me too. But you'll get better. I'll help you, anytime you want me to."

He laced his fingers through hers and let out a shaky breath. "Thank you."

He met up with Christina often, usually in Duluth, but she also came to the first LGBT potluck Frankie and Kyle hosted at the Logan library. It was Dale's first official public outing since the flyer, and he was so nervous he shook, but he managed as it was Sunday when the library was closed and Arthur and Gabriel slipped him in through the back door.

The event was small, but fun. Most of the couples were older, though a few younger people showed up, some nineteen year olds from Pine Valley who identified as asexual and non-binary, and they pointed out the potluck group name didn't include them. After some debate, the LGBT potluck was renamed the Rainbow Potluck, with the subheading that it was for queer-identifying individuals and their allies. Kyle and the younger members argued for a long time over whether or not they should use LGBTQQIAAP+ instead of using the term queer to sum everything up, and Dale smiled, mentally making a note to add the acronym in addition to the term queer.

Nothing quite like queer politics to make him feel right at home. To have it happen in Logan was so perfect he couldn't stop smiling, even when Marcus had to separate people before they came to blows.

As the day of the Christmas in July festival came closer, Dale should have been happy. It should have been a joyous occasion, because they'd all worked so hard for this moment, and intellectually he knew things were actually not so bad, but still the idea of facing everyone, the whole town, knowing they all knew his shame, was more than Dale wanted to do. Everyone kept assuring him things would be okay, that he had nothing to fear. The mayor and city council and committee members had been shocked by the flyer they'd received in their mailboxes, but Corrina had a golden tongue, and she had turned them to his side, to the point that the mayor himself had come out to Arthur's house and shaken Dale's hand not three days after the flyers had arrived, telling him grave-faced that he was sorry he'd been put through such a thing, that everyone had their private moments and they should be expected to be regarded as such.

Some people used Dale's disgrace to their advantage, such as the Concerned Citizens for Logan. The mayor, Corrina, Marcus, and all Dale's friends countered their gossip as best they could, but for a long time there was little Dale could do to deflect the whispers that he was some kind of deviant. They had photographic evidence, after all.

Then two weeks before the festival, the *Minneapolis Star Tribune* made its way to Logan, revealing Cassidy's investigation.

Because Dale had asked to be kept out of it, he heard about the story when the papers landed, and he read it along with the rest of Logan. Apparently not long after they'd left Logan, Cassidy's search had morphed into a police investigation for child pornography. It seemed Ronny took photos of everyone. Even the babysitters, and one of them had hacked his phone and mailed herself a photo. She hadn't known what to do with it, though.

Cassidy was all too happy to show her. Then they'd hacked into Ronny's computer and found the rest of his files. The man had volumes of videos and photos of adults, but he also had quite an impressive stack of teenagers. He was being charged with twenty-three counts of possession of child pornography, but in several instances they were able to also charge him with assault of a minor. Several of the adult victims had come forward as well. The bottom line was, the man would be going to jail for the rest of his life, without question. All because of Marcus and Cassidy.

Corrina had a whole stack of that edition of the *Star Tribune* distributed around Logan and the entire county. She also made sure everyone understood the *horrid flyer* the Concerned Citizens were touting was made by the same monster, that this man had hurt Dale as well, and did they really want to be associated with that? Was this the kind of behavior they were celebrating? Did Logan want to stand with an abuser, or with Dale?

Dale knew the tide had turned. Ronny had been arrested, the case was air-tight, and it was over. At the same time, Dale still wasn't ready to face people. He didn't want to see their pity. Didn't want to see the little old ladies recoil in disgust or pat him on the arm. He wasn't sure he wanted them to act like nothing happened, either. He didn't know what he wanted, except that he wanted the fucking flyers to never have happened.

He had to go to the Christmas in July festival, because he was at the center of it. He was still Logan's Santa, for better or for worse. He was entering the festival grounds with Gabriel and Arthur in the "sleigh," which was actually a carriage with decorative runners at the base. He had to meet the Zeitgeist people who had come to see him, as well as the investors from his company, the council members, the local mayors, and so on.

Marla came to help him through it, and so did everyone, even Corrina. Oddly enough, Corrina was his favorite. She kept feeding him and fussing with his Santa outfit, which was a little too warm despite being made of cotton, though it was quite fetching. "We went with Santa-esque," she said. "Just the red jacket and hat. You're too pretty to hide under all that beard. Also, it's too hot. We have a hired Santa in the air-conditioned trailer for that."

He caught his reflection in the mirror and had a flicker of unease. "This isn't...too much like the flyer?"

She squared her jaw. "It's nothing like the flyer. Don't you think about that anymore. No one else is."

He glared at her.

She sighed. "All right. They are. But not what you think. I'll tell you this. You're not making it any better, hiding. Get out there. Enjoy the festival you worked so hard for. Don't let him take this from you."

Those were, as always, the magic words. He glanced at himself in the mirror and drew a steadying breath. "All right. Let's go."

Gabriel and Arthur came down the stairs, Gabriel in a fetching elf outfit and Arthur in some kind of Swedish alternative Santa outfit. Corrina kept calling him a *tomte*, but honestly he looked like a gnome to Dale. Arthur was being a good sport about it, whatever his costume was supposed to be. He was holding hands with Gabriel, and as the two of them approached Dale, Gabriel took his hand as well.

Arthur waggled his eyebrows. "Looking fine, Santa. Ready to do this thing?"

Dale wasn't. But he went anyway.

The festival was held in the square, but they entered from the north side of town, boarding their sleigh from Marcus and Frankie's house. Marcus and Frankie were already gone, as were the others, waiting in the square, but Arthur's father was there to help them get into the carriage.

"Knock 'em dead," Big Tom told Dale with a wink.

"I'll do my best," Dale replied.

Arthur deftly handled the reins and led them through the streets toward the festival. "They have the streets clear for us. We're the end of the parade, right before the actual Santa comes out, though he's going to basically be driven out of a garage straight to the air-conditioned workshop." Arthur tugged at his robe. "We're going to get sweaty enough. I know they made these out of the thinnest stuff they could, but it's still eighty degrees out and sunny."

The parade wasn't long, mostly local businesses

tossing out candy from floats. There were booths and activities on the square and in the storefronts all along the route, some in makeshift huts or under pop-up tents. But everything was beautifully decorated for Christmas, just like Dale had planned, and as they drove through the streets, he was pleased with how the festival had turned out. There were a lot of people—locals, but also three charter buses from the Cities. He saw the festival stage as they rounded the corner to the square, saw the dancers in place. Saw the Jimenez family, Ed and Laurie too, and a bunch of young people with them, laughing and having a good time.

It all looked perfect. The photos were going to be great. Next year's event would be twice as big from the promo alone.

He waved the whole time through the parade, and everyone waved back, sometimes people calling out to him, or to Gabriel—lots of children shouting excitedly for Mr. Higgins—or to Arthur. But as they entered the square, something changed. A susurrus went through the crowd, a rumbling of applause, and then as they passed the grandstand, the announcer spied them and grinned.

"And here we are, ladies and gentlemen—in the sleigh driven by Arthur Anderson and assisted by Gabriel Higgins, please give a round of applause to the man who made all this possible, the reason this festival has happened at all, Logan's very own Santa and newest native son, Dale Davidson!"

The entirety of the square stood as one, cheering like he was a football hero, not a real estate and utility developer. It was a beautiful moment, it moved Dale's heart, and it was enough to wash away the last bits of sludge from Ronny's swipe, at least the parts keeping him from being able to function in society.

And then they all began waving flags.

It took him a second to see what they had in their hands, and he couldn't sort it out until Gabriel and Arthur each held one up too, looking slightly sheepish but mostly devilish. It was a small red flag on a stick, a kind of homemade iron-on thing, and in the center of it was a photo of Dale's headshot.

Dale's headshot with a Santa hat sloppily photoshopped on. And underneath it was printed, in a terribly tacky font, *We love Logan's Santa.*

It was ugly as hell. He loved it more than anything, and he couldn't stop smiling. "Corrina?"

Arthur grinned over his shoulder. "Who else?"

Dale laughed, took Gabriel's flag, and waved it high to the crowd, to another round of cheers.

Chapter Seventeen

December 17, 2016

THE GREAT WHITE tent beside the Parks family field was full of wedding guests, and six official bridegrooms and their officiant were about to gather together in the center of the tent and begin the ceremony. But right now all seven of them and Arthur's parents stood in a small barn at the other end of the farm, one which had been decorated for another ceremony, a much more private one.

Gabriel had wanted to get them into the woods like Dale wanted, but in typical Logan fashion, a blizzard had ruined their plans. There was so much snow they would have stood in powder up to their necks and been popsicles before they got through half their planned ceremony. Kyle had come up with the compromise of the barn, and unsurprisingly, Dale said the woods weren't the important part. The words and being together to make their promises were.

Now it was time, at last, for both.

"We've gathered here tonight," Arthur said, "to witness these two men, these friends of ours, announce their lifetime commitment to one another. In a moment we'll hear them say their vows, but first I'd like everyone here to share a few words for the couple and present their gifts."

Marcus stepped forward and handed them a scarlet zinnia. "You are both loyal and loving to each other and everyone you meet. May that spirit stay with you through your union and spread to everyone you encounter together."

Frankie smiled as he offered a yellow tulip. "You make me happy. I love having you both in my life. I look forward to more adventures we'll have together."

Paul's gift was a sprig of lily of the valley. "Your devotion to each other warms my heart every time I see it. May you inspire others the way you do me everywhere you go in life."

Kyle presented them with a bluebell and a bright smile. "You two remind me to treasure what I have, to look for blessings in unexpected places. I love having you both in my life." He kissed them both on the cheeks.

Corrina and Big Tom came up together, hugging them, Corrina weeping. They presented them with a daisy, and for once the indomitable Corrina was mostly speechless, simply saying, "I love you boys so much," over and over and over until she retreated to her place.

Then it was Arthur's turn.

He didn't have any flowers, only a small bag. He waggled his eyebrows as he opened it, letting them see the contents: roasted, perfectly split chestnuts. He grinned and took both their hands, clutching the flowers and the bag of nuts with them.

"I'm so happy for you both. I'm happy for all of us. In a few minutes it's going to be Dale's turn to officiate, and I get to melt into a puddle of goo. But right now...right now all I can say is I couldn't be happier to see you two doing this." He let go of Gabriel's hands and took up Dale's alone. "I love having you in my life. I love protecting you, working with you. I love sharing Gabriel with you. I love fishing with you, watching hockey with you, cooking with you, hunting with you. I love everything about you in my life." He drew Dale to him and kissed him gently on the lips.

Then he turned to Gabriel—and Gabriel started to cry.

Arthur did too, but he also laughed, getting out his handkerchief to wipe his tears, then Gabriel's. "Slow down, baby, let me at least get the mushy words out." He took Gabriel's hands and squeezed them tight. "Oh, honey. Who would have thought, huh? I knew two years ago I wanted to have this day with you. But even a year ago, I had no idea I was going to have such a *special* day. Such a wonderful life with you, and with Dale too." He touched Gabriel's face, his thumb caressing each tear as it fell. "You take six husbands, sweetheart, and I will welcome them all. My love for you isn't measured by how you limit your life for me. I will never keep you from following your heart. I will always want to see you love as far and wide as your spirit wants to take you."

Gabriel wiped at his face with his fingers. "I think six is a bit much," he whispered.

Arthur winked, dislodging some of his own tears. "You've got a pretty amazing capacity to love. I wouldn't put it past you."

He kissed Gabriel, long and lingering. Then he took a step back, and it was time for Dale and Gabriel to give their vows.

They'd decided not to write their own, but to choose favorite verses for each other. Gabriel chose Percy Bysshe Shelley—"*true love in this differs from gold and clay, that to divide is not to take away.*" Dale chose a passage from Edna St. Vincent Millay. "*It doesn't matter with whom you fall in love, nor how often, nor how sweetly. All that has nothing to do with what we are to each other, nothing at all to do with you and me.*" They spoke a little too, of how they felt, in their own words, not written down, because they had agreed not to prepare.

"I'm so happy to have found you," Dale said to him. "I look forward to every day with you. And I agree with Arthur. I love sharing you with him. I love living in Logan with you, love finding ways to make it better with you. I don't care how we're together or what we call it or how the world views us. I'd like Logan to accept us, but I'm okay with it working toward us on its own terms." His eyes twinkled as he smiled. "I'm okay with staying out of the gossip for a while longer."

He kissed Gabriel's knuckles, his sign that he was finished.

Gabriel took a deep breath, trying to decide how he wanted to follow that up. He looked around at his friends, his family, at Arthur, and then he knew. He smiled at Dale.

"When I came to Logan, I was alone for a long time. I didn't think I would ever find a happy ending. I was dragged"—he glanced meaningfully at Corrina—"kicking and screaming into my chance. Then a miracle happened. Last winter, I couldn't open a chestnut. Neither could my fiancé. And then here came this handsome man, who not only opened the nut…he opened my heart yet again. I'm not going to lie. That was terrifying. But it's turned out to be more than okay. It's wonderful. It wasn't just a chance at an adventure. It was my heart knocking on its own door, inviting me to be open to my whole self. You led me there." He squeezed Dale's hand, then looked around the barn, his eyes full of tears. "And then you all came along with me."

Sniffling, he kissed Dale's knuckles too.

Arthur put his hands on top of theirs. "May this union flourish, may it be strong."

Marcus rested his hand on Arthur's and repeated the same vow, and then Frankie, Paul, Kyle, Corrina, and Big Tom did the same. Then they released their hands, Gabriel and Dale put rings on each other's fingers, and Gabriel had his first husband.

They all hugged each other, kissing cheeks, everyone offering congratulations, until Corrina pointed out there were three other weddings that had to be done before the night was over, and they had to get to it. And so they hurried down the lane to the big tent, took their places, and began the second part of the show.

It was a very different kind of ceremony, this wedding. For starters, there were five hundred people there, crammed inside the tent, alongside space heaters, cameras, lights, and all the other business that went with formal weddings. It was cold, yes, and everyone had blankets, but definitely everyone was thinking, *Why did you have a wedding in December outside, you fools?* and also, *Would you please hurry this up?*

They did not, however, hurry it up. Corrina had wanted a lot of pomp and circumstance for this one, and so pomp and circumstance there was. It was decorated for Christmas, of course, the room full of lights and evergreen boughs, smelling of earth and forest and crisp winter air. In a way, this was Dale's forest, and he was the Santa in the center of it all. He was even wearing a red tie and cummerbund, with a sprig of holly pinned to his lapel, and in the trip from the barn to the tent, he'd managed to get snow on his beard.

There were no less than twenty children as their attendants, cousins or nieces or nephews of one groom or another, and they made an adorable parade around the center ring of the tent. Kyle's sister Linda Kay came down the aisle on the arm of a handsome young man, and she wore a lovely bridal gown, complete with veil, and she blushed and waved as if this were her wedding. Then the three sets of grooms had to enter, and because Corrina thought it would be cute, they entered by the order in which they had gotten engaged, which meant Arthur and Gabriel went in second.

But before they did, Arthur made them pause, and he held up his handkerchief to Dale's lips, collected a kiss, and put it in his pocket.

It felt like a circus, Gabriel thought as he went down the aisle arm in arm with Arthur. In part this was because the ceremony was held in the round, with one narrow path in and out. The three couples stood flanking each other, Arthur and Gabriel in the middle. Once Kyle and Paul were in place, Dale came down the aisle to officiate.

It wasn't that Gabriel didn't enjoy this ceremony. This was his legal marriage, his marriage to Arthur, the one he'd waited two years and in so many aspects his whole life for, one he shared with all his friends. But as he read through the slightly cheesy vows Corrina had prepared for him and Arthur, he couldn't help thinking the private affair in the barn would always be the one he regarded as the real ceremony, not only for him and Dale but for all three of them. Because he hadn't felt he'd just married Dale. He felt he'd been married, period. To Dale, to Arthur. To the part of himself that had sat up and said, "All right, I belong to people now, it's official."

He suspected both his husbands felt the same way too.

As the ceremony wound to an end, Dale's voice boomed over the tent. "You may all kiss your new husbands," he said, and the crowd went wild. But as they cheered, the three of them, Dale, Arthur, and Gabriel, looked at one another, smiling as they shared a secret.

Arthur pressed the handkerchief with Dale's kiss briefly on Gabriel's lips, right into his smile. As the crowd *oohed* and *ahhed*, as a disco ball fractured light like snow across the tent's ceiling, Arthur placed his lips to Gabriel's as well, sealing both their unions as their friends and family cheered them on to the next adventure.

About the Author

Heidi Cullinan has always enjoyed a good love story, provided it has a happy ending. Proud to be from the first Midwestern state with full marriage equality, Heidi is a vocal advocate for LGBT rights. She writes positive-outcome romances for LGBT characters struggling against insurmountable odds because she believes there's no such thing as too much happy ever after. When Heidi isn't writing, she enjoys cooking, reading, playing with her cats, and watching television with her family. Find out more about Heidi at heidicullinan.com.

Did you enjoy this book?

If you did, please consider leaving a review online or recommending it to a friend. There's absolutely nothing that helps an author more than a reader's enthusiasm. Your word of mouth is greatly appreciated and helps me sell more books, which helps me write more books.

If you want to tell me personally how you feel about the story, you can reach me at heidi@heidicullinan.com or find me online. I look forward to connecting with you!

Want to make sure you never miss any of my books? Sign up for the release-announcement-only newsletter.

www.heidicullinan.com/newssignup

Looking for more than the standard author newsletter? Do you want the inside scoop on my upcoming releases, advance notice of what I'm working on next, chances to win my favorite books? Do you want to be the first one to get my works in advance reader format? Consider joining my Patreon. You can learn more about it here.

www.patreon.com/heidicullinan

Did you know several of the characters in this book exist in other books?

Santa Baby is actually book four in the Minnesota Christmas series. You can read about how the rest of the Logan gang found their happily ever afters in each of their books, including how Arthur and Gabriel met.

MINNESOTA CHRISTMAS SERIES
Let It Snow (Marcus and Frankie)
Sleigh Ride (Arthur and Gabriel)
Winter Wonderland (Paul and Kyle)

Ed and Laurie, the dancing instructors, and their friends Tomás and Spenser, appear in the Dancing Series.

THE DANCING SERIES
Dance With Me (Ed and Laurie) *also available in French*
Enjoy the Dance (Tomás and Spenser)
Burn the Floor (coming soon)

Other Books by Heidi Cullinan

LOVE LESSONS SERIES
Love Lessons (also available in German)
Fever Pitch (also available in German)
Lonely Hearts (also available in German)
Short Stay
Rebel Heart (coming 2017)

THE ROOSEVELT SERIES
Carry the Ocean
Shelter the Sea (coming 2017)
Unleash the Earth (coming soon)

CLOCKWORK LOVE SERIES
Clockwork Heart
Clockwork Pirate (coming soon)
Clockwork Princess (coming soon)

SPECIAL DELIVERY SERIES
Special Delivery (also available in German)
Double Blind (also available in German)
Tough Love

TUCKER SPRINGS SERIES
Second Hand (written with Marie Sexton)
(available in French)
Dirty Laundry (available in French)
(more titles in this series by other authors)

SINGLE TITLES

Nowhere Ranch (available in Italian)

The Devil Will Do

Hero

Miles and the Magic Flute

Family Man (written with Marie Sexton)

A Private Gentleman

NONFICTION

Your A Game: Winning Promo for Genre Fiction

(written with Damon Suede)

Many titles are also available in audio and more are in production. Check the listings wherever you purchase audiobooks to see which titles are available.

CPSIA information can be obtained
at www.ICGtesting.com
Printed in the USA
BVOW08s0819091216
470317BV00001B/10/P